The Anglophile

The Anglophile

by

Egan O'Neill

JULIAN MESSNER, INC.
New York, N.Y.

PUBLISHED BY JULIAN MESSNER, INC.
8 WEST 40 STREET, NEW YORK 18

PUBLISHED SIMULTANEOUSLY IN CANADA
BY THE COPP CLARK PUBLISHING CO. LIMITED

PRINTED IN THE UNITED STATES OF AMERICA
LIBRARY OF CONGRESS CATALOG CARD NO. 57–6257

All the people in this story are fictitious. The historical background is authentic.

"Each of the assailants would take up a child and use it as a buckler of defence to keep from being shot or brained. After they had killed all in the church they went into the vaults underneath, where all the choicest of women had hid themselves. One of these, a most handsome virgin, arrayed in costly and gorgeous apparel, knelt down to Wood, with tears and prayers begging for her life; and being stricken with a profound pity, he did take her under his arm for protection . . . but a soldier, perceiving his intention, ran the sword through her, whereupon Mr. Wood, seeing her gasping, took away her money, jewels, etc., and flung her down over the breastworks . . ."

—From a contemporary account of the action at Drogheda, during the Cromwellian expedition to suppress the Irish Catholics, September 1649

The Anglophile

ne

I

From the first the game had gone wrong—for Poole. It seemed to him that the other man knew every card in his hand; the preceding hour's play had been unlucky, but not so disastrous as this. It was small comfort to him that the little crowd of onlookers clustered about the table exuded silent sympathy; he was aware that it was sympathy engendered less by their friendship for him than by their dislike of his opponent.

He shrugged and laid down his cards. "Yours, sir. I have no fortune today."

"So it appears," said his partner with a little smile. "Shall we end it? I plead an appointment; otherwise I should take more of your money, captain." His smile broadened into a laugh, and Poole forced himself to join it. "Mere luck," said the other man gently, "mere luck. Another day you might fleece me." He scattered his own cards carelessly on top of Poole's and rose.

"Luck," echoed Fothergill behind Poole's chair. "Anyone may win or lose at piquet." On other occasions every man present had

[9]

heard him hold forth on scientific play, maintaining that skill was the only luck, but now there was a general murmur of agreement.

The winner beckoned a club-servant. "My cloak, Benson, and a chair. I make it twenty-eight guineas, captain." In silence Poole produced coins to add to those on the table. The servant came back and held the other's cloak. The men made all the conventional deprecatory remarks—bad luck, Poole, fortune against you, take him proper another time, eh? But eight eyes, as if absently, watched the fifth man as he leisurely fastened the frogs of his cloak, straightened the fall of lace at throat and wrists, accepted his tricorne from the servant. There was in those eyes a secret dislike and a secret envy that every man would have denied. The fifth man knew it was there, and in his eyes was secret amusement. Their dislike was unimportant; their envy pleased him.

Poole thought, I could have him down in thirty seconds, likely he can't use his hands at all, no man in a real fight. Fothergill thought, Damned upstart. Vail thought, I wonder if there is anything in that gossip; oh, God, of course not, this jackanapes, but women——! Masterson thought, There is something about these people: don't lose my temper easy as a rule, but these people—this smiling smooth devil! I'd like to stand up to him, man to man, just once. And in all four minds moved the unbidden, unwelcome envy.

"Servant, gentlemen." He gave them a careless bow and turned; they watched him out of the club-parlor. Only when the door shut behind him did Poole allow himself to swear.

"Bad luck," said Masterson. "Cool player, that one."

"I wouldn't care to take him on," said Fothergill, and Vail gave him a twisted smile.

"But you wouldn't so compliment him to his face, would you, James?"

Fothergill laughed and reached for his snuffbox. "Not unless the stakes were low."

"Charm," spoke a fifth voice, coming into the circle. "Charm. A dangerous quality, gentlemen." Old Andrews, creaking up from his chair by the hearth. "Who is that young man, Captain Poole? I have not seen him here before—I should have remembered."

"Yes. Only lately accepted for membership," returned Poole shortly. He reshuffled the pack and slapped it down on the table ready for play. "Under the auspices of Sir Julian Courtenay."

"McDermott," said Vail, "Dennis McDermott is the name."

"Ah," nodded Andrews. "But there is the explanation. He is Anglophile Irish, then. There you have it." He laid one bony old hand on Poole's shoulder. "He did not win from you, captain; you lost to him. He is a trickster, that I see."

"Any man with eyes would."

"And I should judge a famous charmer of women," pursued Andrews. Vail turned suddenly away and took up a decanter from the neighboring table. "A handsome man, a man to attract women only by his appearance."

"He's never waited for 'em to run to him," said Fothergill dryly. "Even with all the soldiery stationed in Dublin, he has a famous —or infamous—reputation as a womanizer."

"Of course. Charm," repeated Andrews. "Do not blame him, gentlemen—it is all your fault." He smiled gently at their stares. "He is Anglophile—but his forebears? A conquered race. Conquered peoples must cultivate charm and agreeableness; it is the only defense left to them. But I am a philosopher." He took the second chair and reached for the cards. "Who will join me—Captain?"

"No, I thank you. I have had enough for the day."

"Vail?"

"If you obtain a fresh pack," said Vail rather violently, setting down his wineglass. "Doubtless our friend has left these well marked."

[11]

Masterson looked up alertly. "Crooked play?"

"Or the muck of the cow-yard he came from."

"Where does he come from?" asked Fothergill. "Don't think I ever heard."

"Nor anyone else. Gentry Irish." Vail shrugged. "We all know what that means—or does not mean. I am more interested in where he will go."

Poole smiled. "I wouldn't place too much credence in common gossip." His tone was smooth, interpreting Vail's words as he had not intended them. Fothergill coughed; Masterson looked embarrassed. The last man to suspect the truth was always the husband. Celia Vail had held McDermott for near three months now, rumor had it, and that was a long time for him to stay by one mistress; any day she would be looking about for a new lover.

"Damn the man!" said Masterson. "Must we pay him the compliment of gossiping about him? Let him go. I will play you, Mr. Andrews." He took Poole's chair.

"Good, sir. That is a penetrating remark. McDermott, you said? A handsome man, yes, but it is much more. Any one of you gentlemen may be stronger, wealthier, and if we except poor James here, more intelligent. But charm!—what is it? The indefinable quality. Do not swear if I add that you would part with half your possessions to have his charm." But they did swear, and denied it. Andrews laughed.

"Damned upstart," said Fothergill. "Making out he's gentry. A lawyer, I ask you! What Courtenay was thinking of——"

"Let be, James, let be. Nought to do for it now." Masterson was impatient. He began to deal the cards; Vail refilled his glass, and his hand shook on the decanter.

Celia Vail was also thinking about McDermott. She smoothed the long brown curl lying over her shoulder and said, "Will you not take more tea, Lady Courtenay?"

"Thank you, my dear—only half a cup—thank you. Such a charming young man, is he not? Sir Julian and I have been pleased to do what we can for him. Such a sad life! Brought up in France, you know; his father's fortune quite dissipated by a villainous lawyer. No substance at all, but he has such determination, such pride—will accept nothing from his friends, which is but to his credit, do you not agree?" There was no malice in Alice Courtenay; if she had heard any of the gossip linking Celia's name with McDermott's, she had dismissed it as beneath consideration. Old fool, thought Celia; he is after your husband's money, have you no eyes to see it? Oh, he said tonight, but he will not come: I know it. He will not come, and tomorrow I will have an artful little note of excuse. He has had enough of me: very well, damn him and let him go! Why must I labor it? "And you, Mistress Anne? Another cake, perhaps?"

"Oh—thank you, Mrs. Vail." The girl started as if recalled from thought.

"How do you enjoy your visit to Ireland? You have not been here above two or three months, have you?"

"Just three months. Very much, of course." It was a conventional reply. Looking at Mistress Anne Deering, Celia felt a pang. So young she was, my God, so young, if but passably pretty. And why must she sit here being polite to these two simpering nonentities while the day dragged on toward midnight? She would wait, and wait, there by the private door, and he would not come, she knew. With effort she schooled her expression.

Lady Courtenay was patting the girl's hand. "Of course, my dear. It accomplishes my fondest wish—since your poor father's death you have been so alone. With Dennis you will be safe."

Celia went cold. Courtenay was proposing a marriage, then. The talk was that this girl was substantially endowed. Celia studied her with detached appraisal. Perhaps twenty or a little more, good figure, chestnut hair, fine skin, passable features: a silly little English miss, but Dennis would bed with a witch for sufficient profit. He had always said he would bring himself to marry an heiress one day.

She made herself smile. "That is understandable, Lady Courtenay. Our Dublin gentlemen must be a refreshing change to Mistress Anne from those in London, who I hear judge marriageable females solely by their fortunes—or lack of fortune."

Anne Deering met her eyes. "Oh, I never pay attention to common gossip, Mrs. Vail," and the last words were emphasized. Celia was oddly pleased. So the kitten had claws.

"That is charitable, Mistress Anne. You are sure you will take no more tea?"

"Thank you, yes."

Celia felt the covered silver pot as she filled the outstretched cup, and was glad the tea was half cold. Near four o'clock by the French gilt clock on the mantel. Reynold would be home soon. All those hours to be lived until midnight—please make him come, just once more, and I will let him make love to me, and then I will tell him, so coolly, so casually, that we are finished . . . tired of you, Dennis, we have enjoyed one another but these affairs do not last forever . . . he must come, I must be the one to end it if I am to keep any pride. This girl, this damnable girl.

The clock chimed and she started. "Nerves, my dear?" exclaimed Lady Courtenay.

"It cannot be a guilty conscience," said Anne Deering.

[14]

"Four o'clock," said FitzHugh, replacing the watch in his pocket. "Is he coming at all?"

"He will be here," said Calhoun. Very few men had ever seen Liam Calhoun outwardly angry, but there was a note in his deep voice not usual with him, and his eyes smoldered. "And before McDermott arrives, Kelleher, I would advise that if you have a word or more to say against him, you would best say it to his face. Let us bring this into the light and discuss it like reasonable men."

"I did not mean——"

"What were you meaning then?" snapped Burke. Kelleher slapped his glass down on the table.

"Oh, the devil!" he exclaimed in English.

"Enough!" said FitzHugh. "Let us also keep to a reasonable tongue." The other five men gathered about the little room in the rear of Burke's shop watched him as he rose to pace the floor. "It is as reasonable that I accuse you of treachery because you speak English as to accuse McDermott because——"

"I did not accuse him," said Kelleher sullenly, reverting to the Gaelic. "I said only——"

"We heard you," said Calhoun.

Burke looked up as a bell sounded. "That is very likely McDermott now." He went out to the dim narrow passage leading to the front premises. A heavy door hung with a curtain let him into the shop, a fairly large square room giving on the street. Two or three chairs, a plain table, a Turkey carpet completed its furnishings, for Burke's was no common jewel shop where trinkets were sold over the counter: at Burke's one bought the finest gems, with leisured conversation, over good wine. His assistant-apprentice, Slade, was waiting upon a gentleman seated at the table. McDermott stood in the center of the room, idly admiring the large painting hung on the opposite wall. As he advanced to greet him, Burke felt the same admiration he would have, as a judge of art, for anything so beautifully executed. By the accident of birth McDermott was a handsome man; if he had been ugly as sin he would still be charming. As it was, he had made of himself the perfect model of an English gentleman. He wore his own black hair tied back with a queue-ribbon that matched his dark-blue satin breeches and coat; against the black hair and the rich dark gleam of the satin his skin was startlingly fair, his eyes very blue; and if the blue shadow of a strong beard stained his jaw, that was no fault of the barbering. His classic features were accented by the sharp arch of his brows. The lace at his throat fell in the most gracious of cascades; his waistcoat was fashionable without being foppish, an austere affair of maroon embroidered with gold, reaching only slightly below his thighs. Nothing could be more correct than the plain black hose, the buckled shoes with heels not above an inch high, the black velvet tricorne innocent of ornament; yet, as with his good looks, if he had been dressed in rags he might still contrive to wear them with an air. Burke bowed to him gravely.

"Good day, Mr. McDermott."

"A good day to you, Burke." At least half the secret of that charm, the jeweler thought, was in his voice: a deep smooth voice that was as much black velvet as the stuff of that tricorne he held in his long white hands. "Have you aught to show me as yet? You spoke of a new shipment——"

"Yes, indeed, sir, I have several good stones to offer you. If you will step into my private room?" He held the curtain back deferentially, and McDermott preceded him into the passage. The customer had glanced up only briefly. Burke followed on McDermott's heels and took him by the arm. "A word before you enter," he added softly. "Kelleher is making trouble."

"That he has a talent for doing," returned McDermott also in the Gaelic.

"The rest of us are aware he is a fool."

McDermott looked at him in the dark passage. He was not a tall man; Burke, only a little more than average height, topped him by a good half-head; but he had the faculty of making larger men feel bulky and awkward. "Do you tell me," he murmured. He opened the door. The mellow light of half-a-dozen candles centered on the deal table, a brown bottle, a wine decanter, glasses, several documents spread away from spilled liquor. Five men looked up; four voices spoke greeting.

"We thought you would fail us," remarked the old priest Michael Devin.

"I was engaged in relieving a British officer of a little money. Would you have me spare him to spare you thirty minutes' wait? Liam—Patrick—Nealy," he nodded at them, taking the chair next to Kelleher. "Well, Thomas, why so downcast?"

"I was but saying," retorted Kelleher, "that you seem to take your responsibility lightly, to be so late meeting us."

There was a murmur of protest. McDermott looked around the group, smiling; at Liam Calhoun, immense, black-bearded, watchful; at John Burke, neat and nondescript; at Patrick Fitz-Hugh, ruddy and big-bellied; at Owen Nealy the horse dealer, little, brisk, shrewd; at Father Devin, stout, bald, phlegmatic; last at Kelleher the minstrel, all bony angles and red hair, his little harp across his knees. "You are quick to criticize, Thomas," he said softly. "But then you have never quite trusted me, have you?"

"I never said that, McDermott," muttered Kelleher after hesitation.

Burke made a diversion, fetching a clean glass. "My manners, Dennis—wine or *uisgebaugh?*"

"I will keep to wine, my thanks." McDermott brought out his pipe case and began to fill the long-stemmed clay pipe. "Before

[17]

we get on to the business of the meeting I have a piece of bad news, picked up while I kept you waiting." He struck fire and lit the pipe. "As I say, I was playing an officer at Durfee's. It seems we have attracted notice from His Majesty's government, by what Poole said. It happens now and then, you know. The Minister of Colonial Affairs is disturbed over the situation, and the Prime Minister—after, one supposes, consultation with His Majesty King George—has appointed a special military investigator to inquire into the state of affairs here. With specific regard to our sphere of activity." He contemplated his pipe, smiling.

"Who will," grunted Burke, "arrive in great pomp accompanied by a score of assistants, spend the next six months asking questions of all the officials, and prepare a solemn document detailing his findings—copied in triplicate, to be filed away and forgotten."

"I rather think not," said McDermott. "The special investigator is one Major Sir Harry Quintain. Do you know the name? Well, no more did I—until Poole told me a little about him."

"I know it," said FitzHugh slowly. "I am acquainted with a man in Belfast who served under Quintain in the war with Spain. Quintain is a soldier, but has also acted as diplomatic agent."

"Exactly. Poole said the man evidently has a reputation for quiet and secret work. He said Quintain"—McDermott shot a sardonic glance at the priest—"is like God, in that he works in secret ways. Whatever investigation the man undertakes may not be an open one."

"Need we cross rivers before reaching them?" Kelleher's eyes were still angry. "I grant the information is useful, but to keep six high agents waiting an hour while you finish a game of cards——"

"If you forgive it," said the priest, "I think more harm than good comes of such talk. We and all men like us are in this work together as brothers, patriots, and servants of the church. We cannot allow personal emotion to interfere with duty. Any man who has proved trustworthy to reach a place in this council cannot be seriously suspected of any veniality. Also——"

"I am not an idealist," said McDermott. "I would suspect my own mother on sufficient grounds."

The priest looked at McDermott. "I deplore your severance from faith, McDermott, but I know you for a patriot—and an idealist, though you deny it."

"Thank you, Father." McDermott's tone was ironic. Kelleher stared at him.

"Personal emotion! Very well, I say it—I mislike you, McDermott, and have misliked you from the time you work with us!" Calhoun rose angrily to speak and the priest raised an admonishing hand, but he heeded neither. "If I must speak an opinion, you are a man will do anything for gold and might well turn Judas! I——"

McDermott took the pipe out of his mouth and pointed it at Kelleher commandingly. "Thou ill-gotten spawn of a southron," he said pleasantly, using the formal address needful for impressive swearing in the Gaelic, "I would mislike you also if you were not a musician—and a good one. As a musician you are valuable, but as an agent less so. Need I remind you that this is a dangerous business we engage in? You six men at this table and a dozen—two—thirty men in this country, you are trusted with important work. But I am the man who does your fetching and carrying—your postboy, your groom, your body servant. You cannot expose yourselves to the men who aid us, but I do; that is my work, to be your contact. Each of you is known in his true guise to perhaps a hundred men—I am known to a thousand scattered in many places. If we speak of betrayal, I have a thousand times' better chance to be betrayed than any of you will ever have. Thus far I am lucky. Tomorrow, or next month, or next year, my luck will run out. I will go to the docks, or to a midnight meeting in an alley, or the house of an acquaintance, and find them waiting to take me, and I will be hanged. If it was in my mind to betray, I would have done that before now and retired on the proceeds." No trace of anger was in his tone, only cutting contempt. And then the little smile returned to his mouth. "I will go to hell when I am hanged," he said to the musician, "but not to the seventh circle, Thomas, among the traitors. More like to the—was it the third circle?—with the adulterers."

Calhoun sat down with a hard laugh and reached for the bottle of whisky. "That I would not doubt, Dennis."

"Let us get on with the business," said Burke quietly.

Two

I

Thank God he had come, and she could salvage her pride. "Dennis."

"My love?"

"I think this must be our last meeting." She moved a little away from his lips on her shoulder. "We have enjoyed one another—you make a pleasant lover—but these affairs do not last forever."

"True. So you find you are tired of me?" There was amusement in his whisper; he knew it was a lie. She made herself lie still as the lips moved across her breast, up her throat. "Well, perhaps we have had the best of each other—I can take my dismissal with good grace." He was not even pretending concern.

With blind desire to pierce his armor she said, "How would you have rid yourself of me if I did not dismiss you? It comes to my attention you are at last considering marriage—awkward to pay court and sustain a mistress at once!" And then she bit her lip.

"Not at all—you have some odd notions. Have you only just

heard that? It is common talk that Sir Julian is planning to foster a rich marriage for his beloved protégé." A whispered laugh. "I have already sent a formal letter to her guardian."

"So she is rich enough that you accept her?" She shrugged him away, strove to sit up; he pulled her back, and the familiar half-revulsion, half-pleasure caught her at the touch of his body, the mat of chest-hair against her. An animal—dear heaven, what a fool, seduced by a tuppenny charmer.

"I think so. I really think so. And so soon as you knew that, you decided to be generous—and keep your female pride—and dismiss me before I make occasion to leave you. Dear Celia!" Of course he had not missed that point.

"You assume too much." She tried to make her voice cool. "I had decided that before I heard any mention of Mistress Deering. As you say, we have had the best of each other."

"Admirable!" he said against her cheek. "One would think you had experienced twenty lovers instead of only one." She remembered how he had once said to her, "It is obvious you have never played Vail false before—you are ignorant of any but the most sanctified conjugal embraces! Well, I trust I have improved your education." Now she thought sickly how well he had done that, and wondered how she would go on without him.

"Let me go, Dennis. We need not labor the point—I have decided to dismiss you." She sat up, found the candle on the bedside table. In the growing little splash of light he turned on his back, arms under his head, and smiled up at her.

"What do you think of Mistress Anne?"

She shrugged. "She will do very well as a wife for a fortune hunter. It is nought to do with me."

"She is pretty—for an heiress, is she not? I was surprised. Sir Julian is quite besotted about me, you know. I have taken some trouble to ingratiate myself with him. This scheme has been in his mind for a year, since the girl's father died. Such broad hints, such portentous winks! I was prepared to find her a scrawny long-toothed frump, I assure you."

"She is well enough," repeated Celia, and then with impulsive spite, "if one likes that simpering innocent style! A little provincial, of course——" She checked herself. Fatal to let him know how she felt!

"Mind your tongue," he said in a different tone, suddenly, angrily. "What does a woman like you know of——" And in turn, she thought, he caught back further words. After a moment he laughed. "Oh, as you say," he said easily.

Celia looked at him, instantly dismissing the incredible suspicion that the girl meant more to him than the money . . . Dennis! It was the fortune he was in love with. She asked in a strained tone, "Is it indeed a large fortune?"

"Sir Julian has virtues, but discretion is not among them. Upwards of ten thousand a year. Worth a little of my freedom!"

"Obviously. Well, I wish you all success in it." She made her smile friendly. "And now, if you please, it is late. You must go, Dennis."

"Oh, it is not so late." He put up a hand.

"No! Since we decide to end it, please, do you find your clothes and leave me. I am tired."

"But there is no need we part so abruptly. I'll have one more meeting with you, and bring you a small gift in return for your generosity. Meanwhile——"

"No! Let me go——" She knew why he said that. To prove his mastery over her: to cheat her pride: to solace his vanity. He would wring an appointment from her and then fail to keep it, only to show that he cared not a snap of the fingers for her. Gift! He would bring her no gift but heartache, and whose fault was that? She knew him for what he was.

"Your voice, my love. We must not disturb your good husband's rest! Tomorrow night? No, I have an engagement. Thursday?"

"No," and her whisper was breathless. "I am to attend an affair at the Lord Lieutenant's—this important visitor to Dublin, a formal reception with half Dublin present. And in any event I will not——"

"Of course," he said absently, while one hand continued to stroke her. "The reception for Sir Harry Quintain—I have a card also. I cannot imagine why, unless Sir Julian asked—— Well, Friday then. The same time——"

"No! I have said I will not. And I must ask that you will not flirt with me at that affair on Thursday, with all Dublin society watching."

"I shall not. I shall be paying solemn court to Mistress Anne Deering."

"You will have small chance," flashed Celia maliciously. "Mistress Deering is an old acquaintance with this Sir Harry and told me she looks forward to a long chat with him of mutual friends."

McDermott sat bolt upright. "Sir Harry Quintain?"

"The same. I had never heard of the man, but he appears to have high connections. Mistress Anne spoke of him today when she took tea here. The Quintain estate adjoins her late father's in Somerset and Sir Harry's sisters are her friends. Very likely——"

"I see." He lay back slowly. "Well, no matter. I understand he is on a diplomatic visit—he will have little time for gossiping with females. Friday, I said."

"No! This is the last time." She made a move to leave the bed; he pulled her back.

"So you have quite made up your mind." The amusement was in his tone again. "You are hard on me, Celia—take pity. When have I visited you and left after pleasuring you once only?"

"Let me go——" She dared not make any noise; she struggled with him briefly. She would not—he should not—take her pride, prove the lie. His hand slid warmly down her body and she pressed her legs together. He was laughing, and then kissing her with deliberate brutal pressure; she could not withstand him; for a moment her body went slack, and his hand was intimate, knowing. He let himself down on her. Despite herself she was answering to him; her body arched to his. He broke the kiss violently and let her go. Cold air on her as he rose; he was laughing again.

"Well, if you will not, you will not—I never try to force a lady. So be it. Farewell and good fortune." He was beginning to dress. She lay still and hated him. To prove it like that, show her lie for what it was, shabby, desperate—and then deny it, showing his own indifference.

"Damn you, Dennis," she whispered, "go away—go away from me."

"The moment I am decently clothed, my dear. Be sure I am grateful for your generosity. I am making a sacrifice too, accepting the bridle of matrimony."

"Do not speak too soon. Her guardian may object to giving her into the care of a colonial—an Irishman—of no family or wealth— a first-generation gentleman so-called." For one moment she thought he was going to strike her; his eyes held black rage. Then he smiled.

"Be careful, Celia. You a man, I should call you out for that."

"Pretending to be a gentleman—your first instinct to knock me about like any farmer boy with his doxy!" He could always be reached with this sort of attack, she had found. "You—thinking to wed an English lady!"

"And damn you," he said cordially, shrugging into his coat, "for a trull. Only one difference between gentlewomen and whores, Celia—the whores are honest. I give you farewell, but no good fortune. And one word—if you will be casting about for some other to solace yourself, you would best do something to remedy your looks, you know. What charms you have are somewhat faded—thirty-five is not twenty." He was still laughing in a whisper as the door closed softly after him.

[25]

He had forgotten her completely when he was ten steps from the house. Women were never important, always there to be had, and he had known a good many more enjoyable than Celia Vail. The only importances to him were money and the job, and he was thinking of both now.

Poole had said of Quintain, "Yes, a soldier—he was at Culloden." Culloden, yet one more victory for the murderers, and the Stuarts broken and the Highlands broken at last. Four years since Culloden in April of 1745. Any man who had been in that fight was a soldier. "But he's more than a uniform-horse, according to Colonel Gore. Spy organizer in the low countries, diplomatic agent in Spain, Lord knows what else besides. Military secret why he's bein' sent to Dublin, but like any military secret, every other man knows it—the smuggling, sir, the smuggling! Wager you a thousand to one the officials from the Chancellor down are busy hatin' Quintain's innards—implication bein' they're not doin' their own jobs. But that's the truth." Questions in the King's Privy Council, what of all this lawlessness within the Irish colony? —and a special commission, with no private interests, appointed to investigate. The colonial authorities would resent Quintain and grudge him aid. All the same——

Poole had said, "Appears to be quite a fella, Sir Harry. Colonel knew him in the Guards—damn' all, devil take the hindmost in a fight, he says, but no fool—shrewd. Good man for any job."

And so Anne Deering knew Sir Harry well. Useful? McDermott thought about that, choosing his direction automatically, keeping to the center of the footpath, one hand on the knife under his coat—Dublin after dark was a warren of cutthroats. A chance to be close to the man, study him for the way his mind would work. No. Oversubtle and unnecessary. He was too fond of tortuous intrigue. Life was cheap, and a potential danger as easily removed as a proved one.

He knew Dublin and was unsurprised when he heard a stealthy rush of feet behind him. He whirled, the knife out, and gained a moment for speech by slashing at the burly nightmen attacking him. He spoke in Gaelic, quickly. "Hold, whoreson! Do you take me for Sassenach?" There were three of them, all larger than he. It was only a second's respite the familiar tongue gained him.

"No—worse, Judas!" He swayed away from the upraised club, caught a hairy wrist in his left hand, and struck with the knife. A panted curse and warm wetness on his hand.

"You will be confessing another murder to Father Devin in the morning," he said; and the men fell back as if he had aimed a pistol. McDermott laughed, resettling his coat. "What magic in the name of a priest! The nightmen are growing soft, to refrain from assault only on religious grounds. My gold is the same as any Anglophile's or Sassenach's."

The men stirred. "Truth in that," and one man came at him again. He seized both wrists, forcing the man's arms together.

"There are three guineas in my purse, brother. I can put you in the way of earning ten for a small piece of work."

"How small? Stand, Larr," came a command from the largest man.

"If you are competent to do it without bungling. Death is your business—are you good businessmen?"

"We manage to support ourselves, man of no allegiance."

"There is a man better off in his coffin, and I care little by what means he reaches it. Ten guineas."

"Among three men?"

"You will have killed a dozen for half the sum before. The three on me you take now, the rest when the job is done."

"All ten before the job is made," said the leader. "I'd not trust my own brother for seven shillings, let alone seven guineas."

McDermott laughed. "Take the gold and scamp the work. Three now, two tomorrow night at this hour, here—and the remaining five when the corpse is cold. If you do not want the commission I can find others to oblige me."

"Done—if you pay once, you'll pay twice. Why not? Who is the corpse?"

"I will give you instructions tomorrow night." He separated three golden guineas from the twenty-odd in his purse and tossed them at the man; they were caught neatly in mid-air. "It is a murder you need not confess—the man is English." He kept his hand on his knife as he turned, but they did not pursue.

3

It would have been obvious to a man of less intelligence than Major Sir Harry Quintain that the colonial officers who greeted him so ceremoniously in fact harbored mutual resentment for his presence. The necessary social entertainments of the three days since his arrival had bored him; he was bored now at the Lord Lieutenant's reception. He laid no claim to company graces and with relief reflected that once these initial formalities were over, he would be free to get on with his job. He would have begged off this reception, and damn what they thought of him, but he wanted to see Anne, and she would be here. He might be kept busy later. He had seen her several minutes ago, sitting with an elderly frumpish woman who must be her aunt, and he was still threading his way among the elegantly dressed crowd. She did not see him until he was at her side and spoke her name, and then she looked up with a little exclamation.

"Harry! I looked for you, but Mrs. Langdon said you were not come as yet."

"I have been here an hour, and been haled about to all the important officials to make my formal bows."

"Ah, that is why I missed you, then! Have you a few minutes to talk?"

"I will take them."

"Then you must meet my aunt, Lady Courtenay—is it not odd that I should have such important acquaintances, Aunt Alice?—Sir Harry Quintain. Harry, you are becoming fat, do you know it? You should take more exercise."

He made his graces to the aunt and accepted a chair at Anne's other side, smiling. He had known Anne all her twenty-one years, and she had always treated him as frankly as his sisters, while he had suffered her as one of them and felt much the same toward her as he felt toward Bella and Emily and Sophie. He was fond of Anne.

"You do me an injustice—it is the latest fashion, the padded waistcoat."

"As though you ever paid notice to fashion! It is good to see you." Her hand was warm on his. "Aunt Alice, will you forgive me if I take Sir Harry off to myself? I must hear all his news from London." The aunt was a nonentity who simpered; a moment later Anne was leading him to a more private corner.

"You are looking well," he said at random; in the half-year since he had seen her he had almost forgotten how pretty Anne was. One might not think her so, seeing her silent and grave; animated, talking, laughing, she had a fresh charm. But it was Anne herself he liked, her directness and honesty.

"Oh, I am always well. Tell me about Emmy, Harry—and is Sophie betrothed as yet? When I left London she was quite to pieces over Ralph Cheyney, but Bella said——" He laughed and told her that it had come to nothing.

"You know Sophie—but I leave it all to Bella, and as for Archie, he dare not open his mouth, being so much in Bella's keeping. Yes, the children are quite well, the infant a great nuisance by now, running all about." He went on talking about Bella's London household, where his two unmarried sisters had also lived since his father's death four years ago, but it seemed to him that Anne listened with half-interest. Even the account of Emmy's infatuation with the young poet drew only brief comment from her, though Emily was her greatest friend.

"How amusing. I warrant Bella was furious! Harry——"

"My dear?"

"I—I do not like to disturb you with my affairs—I hear you are come on some official business——"

"I have, but do not let it worry you. I have still time for my friends." He smiled at her bent head. There was a large gilt mirror on the wall opposite; he saw their reflections against a blurred pattern of background figures, a changing gleam of satin and taffety. The tall, grave man and the girl in pale green silk . . . no pretension to social graces: his servant dressed him in the conservative garments he chose with little thought, and for the rest he was—as he was; appearance did not concern him. But in that moment it came to him with a slight shock that the man in the mirror was no longer quite young. Tall and well-made, and the fair hair still thick even without powder, but not twenty—not thirty. Emily was seventeen years younger, and that was Anne's age. Before now those seventeen years had given him a pleasant feeling of superiority, when he thought about his family; now they stretched like eternity between him and this girl.

If he had married Rosamond Hope he might have had a daughter not much younger than Anne.

"Do you remember, Harry, once you were funning with Emmy and me, and said I must not wed without your consent, more than Emmy should?" She lifted her eyes to him with a small smile. "Well, so I ask your consent now."

"Anne! Do not tell me—you are betrothed? But——"

"Well, not quite as yet. But I believe I shall be soon, if my aunt and Sir Julian can persuade Uncle George. Of course he is my guardian and must be consulted, but you know he would make no serious objection if it is agreeable to me. It is not as if he is at all concerned with the money, though it is in his care until I marry. I—you see, it seems my uncle Sir Julian had hoped I should—be agreeable to the match, and when I came on this visit he——"

"Had a bridegroom chosen and waiting?" Quintain could not fathom her expression. "And are you agreeable, Anne? It is somewhat sudden—you have not been here long."

"Do not be stuffy, Harry!" She laughed. "The sum is, I am more than agreeable—and a good many people are going to call me a fool." Anne never hedged at words. She looked at him frankly. "So are you."

"Why so?" He cocked an eyebrow at her.

"Well—" she gave a little sigh. "Let us set it out plain and have the worst over. I need not mince words with you. Sir Julian is a dear old man who sees no wrong in anyone, and my aunt you have met." He nodded. "They have no children, and Sir Julian takes great interest in young people—Dennis most of all."

"Dennis?"

"Dennis McDermott, Harry. Yes, he is Irish. Sir Julian's lawyer in Dublin. He is a fortune hunter," said Anne. "He is—how can I tell you? You will meet him. He is a great rake among women, especially respectable married women. He is vain, and charming, and extravagant, and he would be very pleased to wed me for the money I possess. There is the matter."

"A pleasant bridegroom." Quintain frowned at her.

"Very. Not a pretty picture? I said you will call me a fool.

[31]

I am going to marry him, Harry." He said nothing; she put a hand on his arm. "I wonder why I try to explain myself to you—perhaps to satisfy my vanity and tell someone I am not a fool. At least I do not think so. Listen to me, Harry. A woman has little choice of husbands among those eligible, in our class of society, and a woman like myself, with—more than sufficient fortune—even less honest choice. I flatter myself that I am not a frump, but I know all too well that nine of ten of the men who have paid court to me have been paying court to my father's money. If I wed one of them, in London, I should be fêted and presented with gifts and wished very happy, but my husband would still be a fortune hunter."

"Is it so inconceivable that someone should love you for yourself?"

"I really do not know. How could I ever be certain? You see, there is not much for women except—domesticities. But if my fortune can buy me a husband, it will be the husband I want. And Dennis is fond of me—enough. I know that."

"You are talking nonsense," said Quintain exactly as he would have said it to Emily. "A cadging colonial rogue—not even English! Are you out of your mind? Your uncle——"

"Oh, no. I—Harry, can you not understand? I love him so much, and not for the reasons others have loved him—if there can be reasons for love. Not for his handsomeness or his charm. He is not a silly fop, as you are thinking. I understand him for what he is, and either because of it or in spite of it I love him."

"You are childish and wilful as Sophie. The famous Gael charm, is that it? Or perhaps you believe the love of a good woman will reform him? Many a girl has been snared with that little notion! I thought you had more sense—and sensibility."

"Do you think I should enjoy marriage with an English fortune hunter more than with a foreign one?" She smiled. "You have not met Dennis."

[32]

"I should like to," said Quintain grimly.

"Very well," and she took his arm, "come along. But I warn you, Harry. You may treat me as you do Sophie or Emmy, but I am not your sister and I brook no interference from you!" She was determinedly gay now, leading him into the crowd.

4

"—Mr. McDermott."

Quintain accepted a graceful white hand and gave McDermott a penetrating stare. In a sense he was meeting the man in a private capacity, as Anne's friend; but almost immediately he found his attention claimed by a concern at once more and less personal. At the back of his mind as he exchanged convention-alities with McDermott was the thought that this was the first Anglophile Irishman he had met on his home ground, and it was a type he would be dealing with and would do well to study. Also, even in the first few minutes, he was revising several opinions.

"I understand you are on a diplomatic mission of some sort. What is more boring than politics?" A fop's speech, but this man was no fop. Quintain, in twenty years of soldiering and odd, dirty, dangerous jobs about a dozen nations, had perforce become a judge of men: often his life had depended on that judgment. McDermott was too handsome to be anything but a city rake, a woman's man, but he was more than that. How much more, there was no way of telling. The charm was not directed at women only; undeniably it was a real and potent force.

Most charmers were weaklings; this one was not. Most charm-ers were surface-deep; McDermott used his personality with an air of mockery, as if saying, Despise me for a fop and a fool, though I am neither, yet I will persuade you against your will.

The Irish, or only the man? Quintain had met a few Irish, in

London, on the Continent; the qualities he had observed them to hold in common were capacity for liquor and belligerence, but plenty of Englishmen shared those qualities.

Anne joined their brief formal talk and presently carried McDermott away to dance. Anne, and this unknown quantity!—all one could term him. Standards different in a colony, but what of his family background, his situation? A lawyer—yes, he would be a clever lawyer. Quintain looked after them thoughtfully—they made an attractive couple; he began to sway back and forth, heel to toe, and a line creased his brow. Any who knew him would have seen that he was thinking furiously. He was already interested in McDermott, and not solely on Anne's account.

He became more interested before the evening was over.

The deep smooth voice accosted him in the cloakroom. "I beg your pardon, Sir Harry. I scarcely like to ask it of so busy a man—and on such short acquaintance—but I should value a private discussion with you."

"Ah?" Quintain turned. "I am at your service, sir."

"Not here, do you think?" McDermott contrived to look gracefully embarrassed. "I believe—that is, Mistress Deering gives me to understand that you are an old family friend, and you may have heard rumors of—of my hopes in that direction. Your advice——" He broke off as a group of men entered.

Quintain frowned at him. What was the fellow after? "I am at your service," he repeated, "though I fail to see what influence you might suppose me to wield."

"None, exactly, but—oh, the devil!" exclaimed McDermott with his sudden one-sided smile. "I take it you are accommodated at the Chancellor's city house? If we might share a chair——"

"No, I prefer to have my own rooms. I am at the Queen's Hostel in Derby Street. Certainly sir—we shall leave together, then." There was nothing in such an exchange to annoy him, unless it were bewilderment as to McDermott's motive: after a

[34]

few minutes he realized that he was annoyed chiefly because Mc-Dermott had subtly implied him to stand in avuncular relationship to Anne. Damn the fellow! thought Quintain with a smile. McDermott was no schoolboy himself—and why should that implication trouble him?

It was near an hour past midnight when the company began to drift away. He kept the servant waiting with his cloak while he extricated himself from old Plunkett and found Anne. "I will wait upon you when I have the chance. I have some advice for you which you will not take."

"Doubtless," she returned. He thought she looked a little tired, and pressed her arm.

"Good night, Anne." He bowed to Lady Courtenay, and as he turned away, he saw Anne's eyes change expression on a woman just passing. Absently he identified her as a matron he had been introduced to: the name escaped him, no, Hale—Vail. Quite an ordinary woman: a friend of Anne's? And then McDermott was at his elbow.

"But surely you will accept a ride in my carriage, Sir Harry?" Plunkett bleating like a sheep. "Unfamiliar streets—night-men——"

"I have obtained a chair," said McDermott, respectful in the presence of authority. It was evident that Plunkett had no knowledge of him. (How came a young lawyer in the midst of more important guests? Sir Julian, of course.) "By your leave——"

Once they were out of the house, however, no chair was forthcoming. Linkboys and bearers clustered in the street with a good many carriages, but all the nearby chairs appeared to be taken. "Stupid," commented McDermott. "Not five minutes ago I bade them wait for us. You will have a poor impression of Dublin, Sir Harry. Let us try farther up the square." His hand was on Quintain's arm. As they made their way through the crowd and passed from the light of the torches, he added, "There is sure to be one along in a moment; they all hang about an official residence when there are guests, you know." But up to the turning of the street they met no luck.

Quintain was tired and somewhat out of patience with this pushing new acquaintance. "You mentioned some private discussion?" he asked abruptly.

McDermott murmured deprecatingly. "I must not waste your time over a personal matter. It is extraordinarily kind of you——"

Those twenty years of soldiering had instilled in Quintain an instinct for danger, and almost before his brain recorded the sound of footsteps behind, he turned and dodged. The heavy club thudded on the footpath a foot from him, and a hand jerked him upright.

"You take t'other, Larr—Hugh, here!" A muffled shout from McDermott, the sound of a blow. Quintain struck out at random; a club landed on his shoulder. His fist met flesh and he heard a grunt; then a thousand stars exploded in his head and he felt himself falling.

Three

I

Quintain cursed and flung off the wet cloth. "Damnation, I'm in no need of bandages! I've had worse heads from Spanish wine! What is keeping Adams?"

"He'll be coming, don't fret."

His mouth relaxed to a reluctant smile. "Do you never grow tired of showing me patience, Kitty?"

Kitty Cantwell wrung out the cloth and replaced it on his forehead. "If I was off to do that, it'd've been afore now. Bit late to try and change you."

"True." He lay back and watched her move about the room, tidying away a few garments, setting the tray with the remains of his meal outside the door. "Broadmoor would do that, you need not trouble."

"It's just I like to be busy."

Watching her, he thought idly that if he had not changed in ten years she had. Not outwardly—she was still the magnificently Junoesque figure he had first known, not much different at thirty than at twenty; despite her low birth she had never been a slattern. A big woman, brown-haired and brown-eyed, everything of her generous, and a calm strength in her. But she had softened a little, acquired some semblance of gentle manners. Never be a lady, naturally, but she suited him as she was. "How do you like Ireland, Kitty?"

"It's no worse than Spain, or France, or anywhere else we've been," she answered serenely, coming to sit by the bed with her mending. "Places are alike."

"Been a many places together," he said, "have we not? I wonder you've withstood me so long—junketing about to wars and foreign towns."

"Talking nonsense again. Truth is, Harry, I like it better than bein' in England. In England you've to put me apart somewhere like any gentleman does a doxy. Other places we can be together."

He chuckled sleepily. "You should have seen old Plunkett's face when I rejected his hospitality. I was out of patience with all his pomposity and did not trouble for euphemisms—very kind of my lord, but I travel with my own retinue and he might find it awkward to accommodate my mistress in the Chancellery."

"Harry, you never did!"

"I did." He smiled. "He agreed in almighty haste. Kitty?"

"M'mm?"

"That McDermott who was just here, what do you make of him?"

"That Irish? Yes, an' that's something else, going and getting yourself knocked on the head afore we're here a week. Like a green countryman in town the first time."

"I am wondering if it was altogether an accident," said Quintain slowly. "It seems almost too fortuitous. We were not far from a lighted street—nightmen ordinarily——"

"Irish'll do anything. What about him?"

"Why, little Mistress Deering has him for a suitor—and is dead

[38]

set on wedding him, though she admits she knows him to be a fortune hunter." He moved restlessly. "Damnable nonsense—no affair of mine, of course, but I'm fond of the child. It might be Emily or Sophie."

"Nothing strange in that," said Kitty.

"In her desiring to marry a rogue? Mind, she knows him for what he is——"

"Certain." She bit off the thread and smiled at him. "You're a man for men, Harry, but you don't know first rules about women. We got to take what an' how we can. Deering, that'd be Miss Emily's little friend from London. She's here?"

"Yes—visiting some of her father's people." Naturally he never mentioned Kitty's existence to his sisters; naturally they knew of her and never mentioned her to him; but he often spoke of his family to her, and sometimes thought she knew them—only by name—better than himself. Certainly she had given him some useful advice on that occasion when Sophie threatened to elope with young Prior. "The devil of it is, her uncle in London is a vague old fool and would not interfere. There's no one to put a foot down and stop her ruining herself."

"It'd be the money he's after. You said——"

"Yes, there is a very respectable fortune."

"Then let her spend it how she wants," said Kitty, holding her needle up to the light to thread it. "Is she pretty, Harry?"

He did not answer immediately; she looked at him. "Not fashionably so——" All the fashion now was for dark girls with aquiline features, a bold exotic type. "She is no beauty, but has a—a fresh charm. Yes, she is pretty."

Her sewing lay neglected in her lap as she studied him, and the familiar cold fear caught at her heart. Often and often she had told him he should marry, some wellborn lady who'd give him sons. Sometimes he agreed, adding, "Plenty of time," and sometimes he asked if she wanted to be rid of him that she said that. He could not wed any but a gentlewoman, of course. She told herself that she wouldn't mind it, if so be he kept her on, in a little house somewhere nearby—he would still come to her, there was too much between them for him to forget, and it was right he should marry. Even if she had given him a son, and she would forego ten years of life to do that, a by-blow couldn't take the title. There had been times—he was struck with that Diana Cheyney in London, and the French lady two years back, not that he'd be likely to wed a foreigner, but she was a lady and he could have.

He was a gentleman, but aside from accepting the fact she'd never treated him that way. She'd treated him just about the way she'd have treated that Jem Cullen as wanted to marry her all that while ago, or any decent husband of her own birth. She'd followed where he went and made a place for him as she could, some almighty awkward places too, from battlefields to dirty foreign towns, and many the time helped tend his wounds, and set meals for him when there was no servant like he was used to.

It wouldn't make any manner of difference if he wed some lady just to be wed and get a son for the title. No. But suppose he got struck on a lady romantic-like, a lady he could marry? That sort of business there'd never been between them, he never made pretty speeches to her. Times she thought he'd kept her for ten years only because it was convenient, always having a woman to hand, and him traveling about as he did. Oh, he was fond of her, certain. He was used to her. It stood to reason there couldn't be nought like that in his feeling for her—a London trull, and no innocent when he first took her . . . but they'd none of them been like him. It wasn't just that he was gentry, she'd bedded with gentry afore and it wasn't any different. It was him being Harry. Funny how they said words like "trull" and "doxy"; you'd think anybody with sense—even a man—would know a woman'd rather have one man permanent-like than a hundred to come and go. But you had to take life as you found it.

"She's a sweet child," he said, sounding angry. "I'd not like to see her squandered on that—adventurer."

"Maybe she knows what she wants best. If I was a lady with a lot of money, and no way to be sure if a man was lying did he say he loved me, I'd rather buy the husband I wanted even if it was a sham. He'd at least have to pretend, Harry, and times a man married don't even try that, even if he loved her afore."

"That's queer. Anne said something like that too. I don't understand it, I should think——"

"Oh, well, women are queer," she told him comfortably, "an' that's the truth if nought else is."

"But what did you think of McDermott?"

"Only saw him a minute. Daresay he took me for the chambermaid."

"Very likely. Well?"

She gave him a quick look. "Is it on this girl's account you're interested in him? Or something else?"

"I don't quite know . . . it was an odd affair. I don't know. What did you make of him, Kitty?"

"If you're to have dealings with him," she said slowly, "don't you go thinking he's less than he is. Just because he looks like an actor and talks smooth, it's easy to think he's nought but a clever rake. He is that. A woman can't help noting him."

"So I am given to understand. Did he set your heart going faster for his handsomeness?" He was teasing now.

"I always mistrust a man that's too handsome. A many women'll have found reason to mistrust him. But there's more to him than that."

"I had the same notion."

"And he's an eye for money. I never saw a man with those long thin hands hadn't."

"Well, he's a lawyer," said Quintain. With sudden energy he flung back the blankets. "What am I doing lying in bed? What

[41]

the devil has happened to Adams? He said three o'clock. Call Broadmoor, Kitty. I must dress. Yes, yes, my headache is much better. Do you go down and see if Adams has arrived, there's a good girl. I cannot waste time here!"

2

"A hellish piece of bad luck!" said McDermott savagely. "Christ damn his iron Sassenach skull! Ten guineas, for the worst head-ache I ever recall!"

"Let it be a lesson not to act precipitately," said Burke. "Where was the necessity?"

"Deliver me from fools! No precaution is ever wasted. He may be dangerous—better to remove him before the danger is acute. What could be more innocent, two gentlemen set on by night-thieves, perhaps a little nearer crowded streets than nightmen usually venture, but what of that? One gentleman unfortunately dead, the other beaten unconscious. For the love of God, have you any more laudanum?"

The jeweler laughed. "You are commendably ready to sacrifice yourself for the cause! I say again it was unnecessary."

"It was a golden opportunity that we may be sorry failed to succeed. I had to mark him for them, did I not? God damn his thick skull—and those bunglers who rely on clubs instead of steel! If I had not told them to put me down as well, I might have had a knife in his ribs before aid arrived, and who the wiser?"

"You make too much of it."

"I like my plans to be carried out." But McDermott grinned reluctantly. "I still say it was a useful idea. By rights he should be dead as Cromwell."

"Whereas he is very much alive—for an Englishman."

"There are English and English," said McDermott. "This one

[42]

is no fool, which I could not know before I met him, but which increases my regret that he lives. No fool at all. I should be in bed nursing this headache, but under the circumstances I thought it expedient to call and offer my condolences. You should have heard me being apologetic. He did not take to me in the beginning, but he likes me even less now."

"What, he fails to respond to your celebrated wiles?"

"A man's man, John, an upright bold-hearted British officer, and—if you want my opinion—he has no small interest in my intended bride."

"The English heiress? So you will marry her?" Burke looked at him curiously.

"Yes, an excellent arrangement. We can use the money I take from her, can we not? I always said——" He broke off as the door opened, and Burke hastily pushed forward a case of gems on the table between them. But it was only the clerk, Slade. His face was white and frightened.

"I ask pardon to intrude, but it is Father Devin and——" He dodged back to admit the old priest and the enormous figure of Liam Calhoun.

"Will you see us all hanged?" McDermott sprang up. "To come here in broad day——"

"It was necessary," said the priest somberly.

"There was a man from Kerry"—Calhoun spoke quick and harsh—"bringing two boys recommended. We discussed it ten days ago, you recall. He was to deliver them to Burke or Slade, on exchange of certain words, in King William Street yesterday, and they were to stay with Father Devin until a ship came. They were so brought, and were with him since then. An hour ago the guards came to the house—he was fortunate to see them and get away, but they have the boys."

McDermott let out his breath in a little hiss. "The man from Kerry."

[43]

"He never came to the house. Few men know my lodging."

"Your landlord," began Burke.

"He is an honest man and a good Catholic, I trust him. But he is absent on a visit to his sister in Galway, and he did not know about the boys. There is no one else in the house."

"Slade," said McDermott. They were all speaking tersely, coldly, under this sudden blow.

"I saw the man myself," said Burke, "and took the boys to Father Michael. It is not a busy district, I would know if any followed."

"There is a traitor amongst us," said Calhoun. "It was too close a secret—if the intent was to betray the boys, and Father Michael only incidentally. None knew but ourselves the boys would be here at this time."

"Who was at that meeting?" McDermott sat up with a jerk and called the names one by one. "We four here. Nealy. FitzHugh. Kelleher was in Wexford. McCarthy was there—he was to leave for Connacht yesterday. Joyce. Ferguson—he had delayed departure to see FitzHugh on some matter. Eight men knew, aside from yourself."

"A moment," said Burke. "Did all those men know your lodging, Father?"

The priest shook his head helplessly. "I cannot tell you. They are all old friends, we talk of many things at our meetings, they may have known."

"In fact," said McDermott, "I am the only one of you with an alibi! I do not know Devin's lodging because I am agnostic and never have occasion to seek out a priest!" His eyes were dark with anger.

"We know each other in this room," said Calhoun. "It does not lie among us. I would as soon suspect myself as any of you."

"Do we know each other?" McDermott asked softly. "Do we, Liam?" In a little silence four men sought one another's faces and looked away.

[44]

"But it is incredible! No high agent would risk himself for such a little betrayal, the standard reward of five pounds for a priest and a pound a head for the boys!" Burke shook his head. "I cannot believe——"

"No man knows the depth of evil in the human heart," said the priest.

"Whatever the truth, we must plan. They have the boys, and they may have your description, Father. Perhaps there will be more treachery. I think you had best take ship——"

"I have lived here twenty years under them. I will not flee now."

"I will never believe it was an agent," muttered Burke.

Calhoun sat down at the table. "What are we to do about it?" And again a silence fell.

3

Quintain bowed out the minister from London and shut the door thankfully. He had a constitutional dislike of officials, long-tongued pompous bastards, having suffered much at their hands. Turning with a grimace, he asked, "Have you ever reflected on politicians, William?"

"Now and again," said Captain Adams with a grin, "which is why I am in the army."

"Wise man! This isn't so interesting as that affair in the Low Countries. But at least we're less likely to get a knife in the ribs."

"Don't speak too soon, major. The Irish are excitable."

Quintain laughed. But it was, he thought, the very devil of a job to give a man. Give these colonial officers their due, they were doing the best they could in a difficult position; and he saw their point of view.

Smuggling—what else was it? But a damned queer sort. He had not realized that the penal laws set up by Cromwell a hundred years back were still rigidly enforced here in Ireland. Many of the provisions had fallen into disuse in England; but here, of course, there was reason to retain them. The original intention had been the destruction of Irish Papism; that, in this century, was no longer the real issue. The laws penalizing native Catholics were enforced for economic advantage, not as religious oppression. With seven-eighths of the native population prohibited by law from owning or leasing land, from entering any trade or profession, from living within five miles of an incorporated town—from, in fact, being anything other than tenant-farmers—a continuous supply of cheap labor was assured. Little wonder that the natives resented it, with half the crop due the landlord, tithes due the Church of England, and that other legislation limiting the amount of profit; but even in England few farmers could own land, and in any case it was the law. England's way was to keep the law unless and until it was changed.

And God knew, he reflected grimly, there had been need for it at the time, to keep the natives chained to the land while the population was built up again. What were the figures? Two million and more dead in the massacres and sacking of towns and churches. Old Oliver believed in the scriptural maxim, Whatsoever thy hand findeth to do, that do with all thy might!

Adams was saying now, "But, damme, major, it's a queer situation at that. All this intrigue over a gaggle of schoolteachers! I can't recall bein' so anxious to learn my letters."

"Nor I," smiled Quintain. Yes, that was the cardinal point of the Penal Laws. The economic benefit to England, of all the other provisions, depended upon enforcement of the prohibition against education and the practice of the Catholic religion. The London minister had said dryly, "A man with even a little education will look further than the handle of a plough." True. But likely the natives were less concerned with education than with rebellion against authority—any authority. Irish!

[46]

"Thing is," Brigadier General Randall had said, "like those damn' dikes in the Low Countries. Plug a leak here, there's another somewhere else. Somehow they get out and get in again. Smuggle the boys out for education abroad—France, Spain, Papist schools anywhere. Some priests, some schoolmasters, back they come. Colony's riddled with 'em, spreading sedition. We hang 'em when we catch 'em, but we don't catch many."

"Not all come back," the minister said. "There are thousands of Irish living on the Continent—the King of France has an entire division of Irish troops. It's a crime for natives to leave the colony, but we can scarcely attach the persons of those living abroad. Those who return——"

"Organization!" Thus Lieutenant General Gore. "This damned smugglers' organization has been at work near a hundred years. We catch 'em here and there, but it always goes on. And whoever the leaders may be——"

"Yes, I see," Quintain had said, concealing impatience. Whoever the leaders were, they must be Anglophiles, free to move about, to earn money. Any native Irish who renounced Catholicism for the Church of England was Anglophile, and free. And seldom more to be trusted than non-Anglophiles.

Now, looking about the dingy office they had given him in the rabbit warren of the Judicial Court, he laughed resignedly. No one could do more than the officials here, against this secret trade in smuggling men. Watch foreign shipping, but how mark any individuals for suspicion? Any Anglophile in the colony might be concerned. Scarcely a day passed that some man was not arrested for this or that minor lawbreaking: a professed Anglophile who was secretly Catholic, a shopkeeper with one scale of prices for natives, another for Englishmen. Little criminals. For the leaders of the important organization, no clue.

The ultimate annoyance was that he knew no one really cared. Gore had put that concisely: "Damn' foolishness, eh? Stupid peas-

[47]

ants, learning letters do 'em no good anyway. When they commence t' smuggle guns and powder instead of priests and teachers,
I'll commence t' worry for it."

The effect, thought Quintain, would be a long-range one: the
coming generations, if sufficient education were smuggled in,
would not lie so meekly under the economic yoke. But if he
guessed rightly, none of the Crown officers here or at home took
that view; blindly they kept to the law because it was the law, and
criminal activities deserved punishment. This recent hue and cry
over lawlessness in the Irish colony had been raised to cover some
machination of Pitt's, and he had been sent on this mission here
when no one cared greatly whether he accomplished anything or
not. It would sound well in a report to the King—Major Sir Harry
Quintain dispatched to investigate—and that was all.

He swore to himself. At the same time, he was not sorry he had
come to Ireland, because of Anne. Anne and her rogue of an
Irish fortune hunter. He would like to think of some way to stop
this marriage, but women—— Well, they were queer, as Kitty
said; that certainly applied to the lot of them.

He swore again, absently, thinking about McDermott.

Four

I

In eleven years of living what was in effect a double life, Mc-Dermott had accustomed himself to shelving the one part of his life for another at intervals. It was not in him to reveal himself wholly to anyone, but with the men who shared his allegiances he need not put on any great pretense. With others it was a game he played, and whatever he might tell himself, that was why he had returned to Ireland from France—only in lesser degree had race loyalty, desire to aid the cause, swayed him. A man in his position had a much shortened life expectancy, but the promise of almost continual excitement. Ordinarily the game afforded him a good deal of amusement.

Now, as sometimes happened, he found himself unable to shut off the one life from the other on necessity. As he made his way through crowds of fashionably late afternoon shoppers toward FitzWilliam Square, his mind was worrying furiously at this crisis, and at the same time the old nightmare of hatred consumed him, a primitive physical thing he was usually able to keep in control but now possessed him utterly. The top of his mind was sanely, coldly considering the facts; beneath he was a seething caldron of blind ugly emotion.

Wait, Calhoun said. Nothing to do but wait. Gather all the agents and confront them with the treachery? Any man black enough to betray would be bold enough to conceal guilt afterward. Wait, and watch. One of themselves. What was done once could be done twice, and a row of gallows as long as Derby Street needed to accommodate those betrayed—more important, the work stopped, for a time at least. Wait! His hand touched the knife under his coat.

It had been voluntary treachery. There was seldom any subtlety in the English; if by some chance they had dropped on one of the agents, they would have him dangling at the end of a rope before any shrewder head thought to press him for information with a promise of mercy.

Burke. FitzHugh. Calhoun. Nealy. McCarthy. Joyce. Ferguson. Himself. Seven men and a traitor. Which?

His mind went over it coldly, but most of his consciousness was occupied with the hate, helpless, blind, overpowering.

An Anglophile gentleman he was, and his life spent among people he despised. The Pooles, Vails, Fothergills, their silly long-curled women he seduced out of contempt and to prove the lie that gentlewomen were honest. The clients he flattered and cheated. No words for his contempt of them. On the surface, their lives were—a glittering thin bright crust at the top of life, and in their careless cruelty what did they know of what lay underneath? Five hundred years of thievery and murder filled his mind.

The factor saying, "That's five shillings lacking for the rent," and the family turned off the land to starve. The constant ache in bellies never quite filled. The hounds out on the track of a discovered priest—schoolmaster—outlaw. One-half the crop to the landlord, one-tenth to the Church of England, and to hell with the farmer—he has sired enough sons to take his place on the land when he dies. The wives and daughters raped, only native peasants.

Prohibited upon pain of death from owning land . . . their own land, and they paid rent to the usurper. *From entering any trade* . . . *From residing in any corporate town* . . . Chained to the land they could not own. *From contracting legal marriage—from bequeathing property—from receiving bequests from Protestants.*

The earth-floored hut, and one blanket among a family, and the smell of peat smoke on a cold morning. The ache in the arms, cutting the wheat—cutting the wheat for an Englishman. "You say 'sir' to the factor, boy, or you'll have us in trouble." The landlord owned the mill and his wheat was ground free, but it cost the farmer half his profit.

From earning a profit on the land rented amounting to more than one-third above the sum of rent . . . Six pounds a year for a farm, two acres of Lord Desmond's five thousand. "Might be we could spare a shilling for Father Hugh this year, Ellen, or leastways sixpence." The priest, the schoolmaster, in continual hiding, with no means of existence but what they were given, or earned as laborers. The patched shirt passed on a dozen times to younger children . . . and the first time he wore shoes, in France, they made him lame.

From exercise of the Catholic religion . . . *From any education in letters* . . . The cave on the hill, and the children reciting in a whisper. The date, Dennis, you must learn and remember the date—let me hear it again—that is correct, the year of our Lord four hundred and thirty-two, and Ireland has been a Christian nation since that year . . . Irish missionaries who Christianized England and Scotland . . . Gaelic was a written language five hundred years before any other tongue in Western Europe, and our literature reaches over fifteen hundred years. Dennis, you will take Sean's place on guard that I may see how much he remembers of yesterday's lesson. Crouching in the bracken, watching, listening for any approach lest it be English—and if it were, and the master unwarned, another head on the spikes outside the military station. Standing guard with others, too, while the Mass was celebrated in some cave or wood covey.

Two women brushed by him there at the corner of the square. "—A dead bore, my dear, I was quite exhausted, I promise you! I said to Robert afterward——" He did not hear them. At the end of the square a line of cavalry, in the gay buff-and-green of colonial troops, turned smartly into England Street and vanished. He did not see them. He saw a rude gallows with a man hanging, and heard his mother scream. No! Not again! Push that away, a thing finished and done twenty-three years ago, in another life. Nought to do with an elegant Anglophile gentleman with gold in his purse and a horse to carry him. He had brought himself to another place than that.

Where was his place? He was rootless as his father's corpse, condemned to hang in chains until it rotted away.

Enough! He was full of foolish fancies today. At such a rate he would be betraying himself. Hatred was a useful emotion if kept inward and nourished in secret. Allowed to explode, it scattered like birdshot and did no harm.

He ran up the shallow steps of the house and pulled the bell. After a moment the door was opened to him.

"Good day, Wood. Is Mistress Deering in?"

"Yes, sir, and expecting you. Come in, sir. Your cloak, sir?"

2

"But, Dennis, how dreadful! You are sure Harry is not hurt?"
"He must have a skull of iron—I called just now to apologize,

in a manner of speaking, for I feel it was my fault. I'm an old Dubliner and should know better than to invite the attention of nightrunners! Sir Harry is quite recovered."

"And you?"

"Ah, I wondered if I was to get any sympathy! A headache, that is all. I have taken some laudanum."

"And no wonder," exclaimed Anne, her fingers at his temple. "Such a bruise! It is a mercy you were not killed! Did they take much?"

"A guinea or so from me"—knowing nightmen, he had taken care to have no more on him than he owed the rascals—"and eight or ten from Quintain, I believe. It certainly might have been worse—but is that all the sympathy you extend?" as she moved away. "Such lovely cool fingers! Continue to soothe me, I beg."

She snatched her hand away. "You deserve no more, being so foolish! Now behave, Dennis! I should have encouraged my good aunt to chaperone us at tea." At his look of mock dismay she laughed and relented. "She too has a headache and is unequal to greeting company, but very kindly said she trusts me to behave with propriety." Her glance was demure.

"I do not see how we might behave otherwise with the door open and the servants going in and out. It might be attempted, of course——"

"Dennis! Now——" But she responded to his kiss. "Sit down and behave yourself, I hear Wood coming with the tea. And I do not wear lip-rouge in the afternoon, you are not marked." He obeyed her, smiling; the manservant entered with a tray and Anne indicated the small table between their chairs. "That will do, thank you, Wood. I will pour it."

McDermott watched her preparing the cups and felt again an upsurge of triumphant anticipation. Yes, this one was the choice; this one would do very well. He had always meant to wed an heiress one day, but heiresses seldom had anything else to recommend them and he was a fastidious man. No need to be in a hurry. It would necessitate a few changes in his life, marriage; a wife would be dull, and moreover want excuses when he went elsewhere for pleasure. He could have had the Forsythe girl—Forsythe would have taken any suitor for her, and small wonder, downright ugly as she was. He could have had Sally Rankin; she was betrothed to a man in England, but if he chose he might have had her head over heels in love with him, and Rankin easy to persuade—a substantial endowment there. Still, with every possible choice he had hesitated, reluctant to commit himself. Only sensible for a man in his position, the best match he could contrive. But a wife——

He was glad now he had waited. Everything about this choice was right. It was last year Sir Julian had first mentioned it. He had spent a good deal of effort on Courtenay since acquiring him as a client; the old man had no immediate family and there was the chance of obtaining a sizable legacy; Sir Julian liked young people and was easily flattered . . . "A good wife, m' boy, some wellborn quiet gel who'd be an asset in society, eh? No harm if she brings a little money with her. We must look about for you!" —and a nudge, a wink. And later: "M' wife's niece, charmin' gel, just lost her father, y' know. Alice don't much fancy her livin' in London with her uncle. A bit vague he is, and doubtless let her to marry the first fortune hunter who lays suit." "Oh, there is an estate, then, sir?" "Very definitely, Dennis, quite a little fortune there." And: "Alice wants to have her over for a visit," and a speculative glance, a significant cough.

He had not actually to decide about it—it was so obviously the best that had come his way. From the moment he first saw her he knew this was the one. Two acquiescent guardians, ten thousand a year—and Anne. Yes, Anne would not be hard to accept as a wife. He would not mind the loss of freedom for a little, with her, and when he tired of her she would be easy to lie to, easily satisfied with surface attention. But that was all in the future; he felt that she would keep him amused for some time.

Really absurdly easy, but then most women were. She was no country miss fresh from the schoolroom; from the first she had been ready to respond lightly to flirtation, parrying the social repartee that was often broadly suggestive. He had played her well, but the knowledge of Sir Julian's benevolent influence, and her own directness—and possibly something more, his awakening interest in her as a woman—had made him a little bolder earlier than he would otherwise have been. This was not the first time he had kissed her, held her . . . all arranged in a way, but for the formalities.

"Sir Julian has written to my uncle in London. That is what you wished to hear, was it not?"

"But he told me he would—of course I wished it, to add weight to my own letter." He put down his cup and took her hand. "Anne, are you too precipitate? You have not known me long. You will not be sorry, if we marry?"

"No, Dennis. No, I should never be sorry." She looked at him gravely. "One does not need long to love."

"As I know." He kissed the hand. "But your uncle——"

"He will accept Sir Julian's knowledge of you as satisfactory. I have discussed it with Aunt Alice, and we think the wedding may be at Christmas, if that is right with you. It is most wrong that I should talk of it with you like this, alone," and she laughed, "and I know it seems early—but three months. But this is not London, and my aunt says it will be quite proper."

"My love—my love. It seems incredible that I have such good fortune. But I would not press you, Anne, if you desire more time. I——" He hesitated, bit his lip, looking at her frankly. "Sir Julian and Lady Courtenay have been very good to me, but I fear they—overestimate my virtues to you. You know that Sir Julian wished for our marriage."

[55]

"Yes, of course." She smiled, withdrawing her hand. "We can scarcely pretend we met by mere chance, led by Venus."

"Anne——" His tone was troubled. "Anne, it is about that I want to speak. I—it is difficult to find the words, I am not accustomed to—making a show of myself." Her glance was inquiring; he rose and bent over her earnestly. "My dear, I—I can scarcely deny my situation. I am not a wealthy man, I have my living to get. It is true I am wellborn, but what does that count for, after all?" It was an artistic little tale he had concocted, of the country-gentleman father impoverished through no fault of his own, the gentle mother, the childhood in France, the Italian tutors, the tragic death of his parents, his return to Ireland to make a fresh start. No one was likely to challenge the caste of an obvious gentleman . . . "A good many people will say I am marrying you for your money."

"I know that, Dennis. Do you think I am so bird-witted?" Her hand on his arm was gentle. "If I do not mind, why should you?"

"I do mind, and I will tell you why—though it may turn you from me." Small danger, he knew that; this was the time for this little drama. "Listen, my dear, I will make you a confession. When we first met, that—that was in my mind, the money. But then I began to love you, Anne, and it would not matter if you had not a farthing. You must believe that—I do love you, and have these many weeks. After that first little while I never thought for the money, and it is no lie when I say I wish you had nothing—you would believe me the more, and none could call me fortune hunter. Anne——" His hands on her shoulders turned her to him urgently; he took the cup from her hand and set it aside, lifted her and sat down holding her across his lap. "Anne, say you believe me——"

She studied his face for a moment, resisting his attempt to pull her closer, and then drew in her breath with a little sharp gasp. "How could I not believe you, Dennis?"

[56]

"My darling," he said, and set his mouth on hers. Passive at first, she strained up to him suddenly, her arms insistent, her mouth opening eagerly. "Dennis, Dennis, do not ever stop telling me lies—or truth—or whatever you please, so that you do not leave me, ever! Dennis——"

When he lifted his head to breathe the second time, it was with a curiously detached shock he realized how hard his heart was pounding. She spoke his name again faintly, her breath warm on his cheek; and then his heart gave a great leap and he was weak with the aftermath of terror. They had been on his tongue, the damning words, the Gaelic endearments: in one moment he would have said them. Fury at himself choked him; he began to kiss her again to crowd back the traitorous words.

"Dennis, there is Wood—he must not——"

When the manservant entered McDermott was seated in the opposite chair, leisurely filling his pipe. No one but himself could feel the jump of his pulse; no one but himself knew the thought in his mind. A half-forgotten old proverb: *A man prays and makes love sincerely in his own tongue.* He was out of his mind.

One must imagine the emotion well to act it well, but no need to carry it too far. English, she was English. No woman worth a real emotion, and an Englishwoman least of all. To feel even a little love for an English—he would be as much a traitor as that one among the agents they must discover.

3

He was undressing when he heard the sound at the door. His servant was out; the watch had just passed, crying eleven of the clock. He took up his knife from the bedside table, went into the sitting room, pulled back the doorlatch.

"Slade! What the devil—— It is all right, the servant is out, but you know better than to come——"

"Your pardon, sir." Slade breathless and hurried. "I had a story to tell if you'd not been alone, to make it right. Mr. Burke has need of you—they've got the two boys the guards took, and you said a ship—tonight——"

"Christ," said McDermott resignedly, "no peace for the wicked. Very well." He dressed again quickly in dark garments, snuffed the candles, slid the knife under his belt. "You left it late enough —an hour to the tide. Dubois sails at midnight."

"Yes, sir. It was a chancy thing, Mr. Burke not knowing aught was afoot. It was Calhoun got them, with some hired nightmen, from a troop on the way out of the city north."

McDermott swore under his breath. "My bold Liam! And a hue and cry out in consequence."

"Not so far, and it'd be away from the docks," offered Slade timidly. They were down the stairs by then, moving quietly in the darkness. "The watch has just passed."

"I know." McDermott pulled the house-door open. He had kept this modest lodging in a quiet street because it was convenient if not elegant. Another little difficulty his marriage would cause, the necessity of excusing these night journeys. He would contrive something; the thought only passed across his mind. "Where is Burke?"

"The right-hand side of Water Street, a square from the end, sir."

"Very well."

Slade vanished in the darkness, his work done. McDermott walked rapidly, hand on knife, making east by the widest streets. It was late for nightmen in these increasingly poorer districts toward the docks, and early for harlots; he went unaccosted the half-mile to his destination. The sea was only a hundred yards distant, but buildings and ships obscured any gleam off the water; the street looked blackly deserted. He paused in the shadow of a building at the corner, and a hand came to his arm.

"Good man," said Burke, low. "I am sorry to call you from bed. I trust you were alone?"

"For once," returned McDermott sardonically. "Why all this indecent haste? Liam might have warned us."

"And so he might, but the chance came suddenly. Can you make the ship? Here are the boys." Two smaller shadows at his side.

"We can try." His voice slowed and gentled a little. "An exciting visit to Dublin you have, my lads."

"Yes, sir."

"I am not English and you need not call me 'sir.' Do not ever call any man 'sir' again."

"No, s——" The word was bitten off. He started toward the docks, keeping in the shadow, and Burke followed close with the boys.

"Peter Ryan and Joseph Gorman."

"Peter—Joseph. You are not frightened now. Out of Kerry you are, I remember." He went on at random in a whisper, the little reassuring talk he had made so often, and his nerves alert for any hint of danger. "You know why you are here. Your lesson-masters think you very clever, worthy of good education. It is hard to leave your homes, but you are going to friends who will look after you. Do you know, I once went from home like this, to France—you are going to France?"

"Lumiege, s— Is that in France? Joseph is going to a place called Marseilles."

"Yes, that is in France. So you go to Lumiege to become a priest, perhaps. Your mother will be proud of you." He stopped. "Why are you trailing us, John? You can get home to your wife now." A whispered chuckle from Burke.

"I live a dull life—give me a chance at a little excitement. I

[59]

will wait to see if you make the ship . . . I can hear the tide."

"And I. Very well. Joseph, Peter, stay close and try to make no noise—we do not want to attract attention. Now, you will like this shipmaster. His name is Dubois and he likes boys. He has five of his own. You will like France also, it is a fine place. . . ."

There had to be organization in this business, and safeguards where possible. There were many agents within Ireland, acting as liaison-contacts among the priests and schoolmasters of every district, but those agents, whose responsibility it was to see that every community had its schoolmaster, were not all known to one another and none of them to those abroad, the churchmen and scholars who aided the cause in other places. There were too many; it was a loose conspiracy at best, gaining and losing members every week. So there had to be a clearinghouse for uncensored letters, money going out and coming in, and some safeguarding of the principal agents' identity from the hundreds of men they must deal with on the Continent. All the communications from abroad passed by one of two contact-agents, in Dublin and Belfast, the two largest ports. Few sympathizers abroad, save personal friends, knew any other names than those, nor did the various foreign shipmasters hired to carry renegades to and from the Continent: they were far more likely to be venal than Irishmen, or churchmen of any nation—and enough of those men had turned traitor. The last contact-agent in Dublin had died three years ago of old age; the two before him had been hanged, and the one before them had died in the torture room under Dublin gaol.

"A fine place," repeated McDermott. "You will have plenty to eat, and warm clothes." They were at the waterfront now, at the junction of Water Street and the docks. A tangle of masts made a blurred mass against a moonless sky. The *Belle* used this wharf— he could identify her by the men on the deck readying the ship to sail with the tide. The plank was still down—they were in time—and then he froze.

Two men strolled slowly back and forth across the front of the wharf. There was just enough light from the water to show them, in one place at the center of the wharf as they crossed from shadow to shadow.

Dockhands hoping for work loading? Not at this hour, with the ship ready to take the tide. No reason for any men to be about except the crew of the *Belle*—it was evident that no other ship nearby was sailing tonight. They might be spies where no spies should be without information, or innocent sailors looking for a berth, or strong-arms looking for sailors to press into service, but it was little matter; there they were.

"Damnation," he said quietly.

"Would they be port-guards?" suggested Burke.

"Possibly. There will be a hunt out for these two after they escaped the military."

"That was why I thought it best to get them off tonight if we can."

"It might be safer to keep them under cover." He heard the shallow excited breathing of the two boys. "There is a ship they could take in four days."

"Aren't we to go in this one, s——? With the captain you told about?"

He made the decision with a mental shrug. "Why not? You can be of some use after all, John. Get up to the end of the street and make a disturbance to draw them off. Quick! We will try the oldest scheme on them." He did not see Burke move away; he said to the boys, "Take my hands—so—and be ready to run!" They were twenty yards from the wharf, protected by the shadow of a stack of empty crates on the dock. The plank still down from the *Belle* to the wharf, but at any moment it might be lifted aboard. The two men crossed the patch of light again. They carried them-

[61]

selves like soldiers; one had a hand at his belt. Port-guards always vigilant, but——

From the street corner a hundred yards away sounded a sudden loud cry. "Murder—thieves! In God's name, you bastards, loose me! Help! Murderers——" And what sounded like a woman's hoarse scream. The two men on the wharf halted and jerked round, but did not at once move from the spot. On the heel of another outcry a window was raised somewhere along the street and a voice demanded to know what in the name of Jesus and Mary was the yelling. Another scream, and the two men made up the wharf at a trot; as soon as they were past, McDermott started up the wharf, running as fast as he dared without making undue noise, pulling the boys at his side. Twenty yards, and they were again in shadow. The plank was still down from the *Belle*.

He landed on the deck panting, at the feet of a surprised sailor. "The captain Dubois," he gasped in French. "I have the passengers he is expecting." By the time the wiry little captain approached he had recovered his breath. "I apologize for the unceremonious arrival, Dubois."

The shipmaster laughed, extending a hand. "Those two queer ones patrolling the dock? I have been watching them. They are here since three hours, monsieur, and it is my thought they are English spies. Of no innocent purpose, certainly. There has been trouble?"

"A little, yes." Spies, then, a new system of port-watch; that would be Quintain's doing. Something else to worry for. "You are about to cast off?"

"Yes—I had given you up. So these are my passengers?" He bent to the boys.

"Peter Ryan, Joseph Gorman."

"Ah, these so-difficult names! Peter, Joseph"—in his thick English—"you like to sail with me, eh? You will not be frightened?"

"Oh, no, sir." A muffled giggle from one of them. McDermott, whose head was still aching from the blow of twenty-four hours ago, grinned ruefully to himself. An exciting adventure it was to them, and no consciousness of danger. Later they would be home-sick, and undergo the exasperation of learning a new tongue, know loneliness among foreign strangers; now it was only excit-ing. The same for him, and he not much older than these at eleven, twenty-one years ago. No matter. Here were two more, good or bad, who would have the opportunity—refute the Eng-lish creed that Irish were all stupid animals of natives fit only to till the land.

"You would better make haste off before they return, monsieur. Your contriving, to draw them away?"

"A very old scheme. You will deliver the boys to the abbey at Calais, where arrangements have been made. Stay—have you any money, lads? One should not set out on a journey penniless." He found a guinea for each of them hastily. "All good fortune. Pay attention to your teachers and remember your race not to shame it." Two brawny sailors were waiting to lift the plank; he ran down it and started up the wharf rapidly.

At the junction of street and dock the two men passed him, going back toward the ship. He let them see him start nervously and clutch at his cloak as if he thought them nightmen; they turned to look after him only briefly, and it was dark, the distance too great for features to be made out.

He was a good quarter-mile away when a shadow fell in beside him. "That was a near thing," said Burke.

"It was. Did you lead a chase?"

"Not far, in the dark. I never thought I should be up to such antics, a respectable tradesman of my age. What of those men?"

"Dubois said they had been there three hours, watching. If there had been other ships loading or readying for sail nearby, they would pass unremarked among others—and the port-guards.

As it was, he noticed them, the regular guard having already inspected the ship."

"Spies—or special guards."

"The point is, had they specific information about the *Belle*, or these two boys, or myself? Or is it only a watch on foreign shipping for reasons connected with our trade or anything else from illegal brandy to press gangs? Who can tell?"

"Who indeed? Well, I thank you for the evening's entertainment," and Burke turned off in the direction of his shop-premises.

.

Five

I

"We have been here a month," said Quintain with a sigh to Adams, "and already I can see myself growing old and gray at this job. I like to feel I am being of some use, William."

"Yes, sir. It's a fact a thousand men couldn't do much against this."

"And no one cares greatly in any case. Easier to punish the individuals where they are found than prevent the whole organized crime. Well, to work. Let us have the sergeant in."

Sergeant Polwhistle entered behind his enormous guardsman's mustaches and came stiffly to attention. "You may stand at ease. Have you anything useful to report?"

"Depends what you mean by useful, sir." The sergeant relaxed only slightly. "I've detailed patrols, pair an' pair about like, for all foreign ships in port, to take note of any that goes aboard, an' Sergeant Hamm's made up a list—well as he can."

"What did you draw?"

The sergeant looked pained. "'Undreds, sir. Just 'undreds.

From harlots to gentry, an' beggin' pardon, sir, can I or any of my men go walkin' up to a gentleman an' ask, 'Hexcuse me, sir, what might you be adoin' of 'ere?' 'Alf the time we 'ad to hask around for the name, an' Corporal Bly got a facer from one old party he asked 'oo 'e was. Upshot is, sir, you got nearabout five 'undred souls goin' aboard the six foreigners in port this fortnight, an' it don't mean so much as a good swear, sir. One of 'em was the Lord Lieutenant."

"Good God," said Quintain.

"Yes, sir. Went aboard the *Venutti* out of Genoa. Seems 'e was expectin' a shipment of some foreign wine an' it was that important he 'ad to see the captain personal."

"Well, tell Hamm to let me have the list. Continue the patrol. There you are," he added to Adams as the sergeant saluted and went out, "nothing to get hold of! It is the obvious place to look, there must be someone making contact with Continental shipmasters. But am I to inquire of every dockhand and trull at the waterfront as to their reasons for being aboard a ship in port?"

Adams grinned. "You'd get short shrift from the harlots. But gold has a loud voice."

"Yes, that must be tried too. Every foreign shipmaster and sailor lying over in Dublin must be informed that there will be a substantial reward for information."

But when Quintain left his office shortly afterward he was not thinking of this business; he was thinking of Anne. He had seen her only once since the reception, and then not privately; he had thought she was looking out of spirits. He had thought also that she regretted speaking to him as frankly as she had, about McDermott. Which was understandable. It was really nothing to do with him, but he was fond of Anne; he'd not like to see her make such a disastrous marriage. He decided to call on her now, hoping for private talk.

But when he came to Sir Julian's city house in FitzWilliam

Square, he found McDermott before him; it was necessary to be polite.

"I hope you are recovered from our little adventure, Mr. Mc-Dermott?"

"Oh, yes, the damage was slight."

"Do sit down, Harry," said Anne. "You shall be the first to hear officially, and the first guest invited. Sir Julian has had a letter from my uncle George, who consents to the betrothal." All the appropriate excitement was in her voice. "My aunt is to have a formal dinner for me to announce it—you shall have a card, of course."

"We have been somewhat on tenterhooks, as you can imagine," McDermott added to that. "After all, such short acquaintance, and Mr. George Deering never having met me—I am surprised at my own temerity. But Sir Julian's voucher—I feel like holding a private celebration, I assure you."

"I can believe that," said Quintain not too cordially, but it was necessary to add, "My congratulations, of course. Is it decided when the wedding will take place?"

"At Christmas, Harry. I know it seems early—I never thought, when I came here, I should——" Anne laughed a little breathlessly. "And there will be a great deal to do——"

"Flurries of feminine fripperies," said McDermott. "Why is it, Sir Harry, that women place such importance on clothes for a wedding? From the sensible viewpoint, the contrary would appear——"

"Dennis, how outrageous of you. Of course I am interested in my clothes for the wedding. I have just now sent off a letter to Emmy, Harry—will she not be green with jealousy at such a romance?"

"My love, I must go—I have an appointment with a client. Do not forget our theater party on the Monday, and you will wear your yellow gown for me. No, do not trouble to call Wood, I can

[67]

let myself out—I am late already, but that is your fault for being so lovely." McDermott kissed her wrist gracefully. "Servant, Sir Harry—I shall see you soon again, I trust."

She accompanied him into the hall; Quintain sat and listened to a murmur, a little laugh, a silence, before the house-door opened and shut. And what was it about men like McDermott that so fascinated women and so irritated men? Society anywhere could show men who had graceful manners, were credits to their tailors, by chance possessed good looks. It went deeper than that. With very little logical reason he would like to have an excuse to use his fists on the man, destroy that perpetual one-sided smile.

"Well, Anne," he said abruptly, "so it is arranged."

She seated herself opposite him and he studied her. McDermott's compliments were perhaps somewhat fulsome; Anne could never lay claim to being a beauty. He was as accustomed to Anne's appearance as to his sisters', and as with them there was a blurred jumble of memories in him of just-tottering infants, hoydenish youngsters swarming over a half-forgotten nursery, prim schoolgirls, shy maidens grateful for support at their first balls—Anne had been about his father's house freely, a motherless only child. Since he had been out in the world himself, he had not precisely watched Emily and Sophie and Anne grow up, but on all his visits home, there they had been, and he felt much the same emotion for all of them. Now for the first time he was trying to see Anne as another man might see her. Not fashionably pretty, he had told Kitty—but pretty. Delicate features, soft chestnut hair in an intricate arrangement of curls piled high and curls falling over one shoulder, fresh color, a fine white skin. Her eyes were her best point, large hazel eyes with a little smile in them.

"Have I a smut on my face, Harry, or are you hinting for an offer of wine?"

"Your pardon indeed. I—yes, thank you, I will take a glass of wine. I was but trying to read your thoughts."

[68]

"You never could."

"You will be sorry for this, Anne," he burst out, knowing this was the wrong way to go about persuading her but unable to help himself. "You are in love with a handsome face, a seductive voice. He will take your fortune and break your heart, if that is romantic enough for you! It is not for nothing women cannot marry without a guardian's consent; you are all likely to play the fool like this!"

"I must turn you out if you talk so, Harry! I was in a mood when I said that to you about Dennis, and it is not true, not at all. We shall be very happy." She was trying to convince herself, he knew. Women!

"You confessed you knew him for a fortune hunter!"

"I will not defend him to you, he needs no defense! I was only being stupid." But her eyes were downcast.

"Have you any notion," asked Quintain, "that he will be faithful to you?"

"Oh, Harry," she said wearily, turning away, "that is childish. Yes, for a little. Does it matter? How many upright gentlemen you know stay by their wives for a lifetime? I will tell you one thing. He will see I never know of it, and he will always be charming to me—and that is worth some of my money."

Quintain said soberly, "That sounds very unlike a pretty young girl anticipating a romantic wedding." She turned blindly and he saw the tears on her cheeks. "Oh, my dear, I did not mean to make you cry——" He held her as he would hold spoiled, wilful Sophie, smoothing her hair, patting her shoulder. "There, my dear, it's not too late, you are only hurt a little. Take my handkerchief——"

She pulled away, mopping her eyes. "How s-silly to think it was you made me cry! I was being foolish like all women, take no notice of me, Harry. There, I hear my aunt coming, Wood

[69]

must have told her you are here." She was quite herself, dry-eyed and calm, when Lady Courtenay entered.

2

Quintain studied his reflection in the glass absently, wondering if he were at all feverish. He was certainly not himself, with this wild notion in him.

Anne!

Emily's little friend, the youngster he remembered in the nursery. Well, youngsters grew up. Damnation, he was but a few years older than McDermott . . . He had always coupled her in his mind with Emmy and Sophie—Bella being older, of course—but she was no remote kin; it was only that she was used to him, trusted him. No family of her own—the mother dead, the father occupied with hunting and business until his death last year.

The fact remained, he hadn't felt brotherly with her slender rounded body against him, her hair brushing his hand. Not a youngster now.

"It's chill," said Kitty. "Come to bed, Harry."

"Yes, at once." He made sure the window was shut and snuffed the candle. Crossing the room, he barked his shins on the two steps up to the high bed, and swore. "Kitty"—on impulse—"what would you say if I told you I was about to acquire a wife?" He slid under the blankets, conscious of her familiar comfortable warmth waiting for him, and reached out to pull her closer. "Told me often enough I ought to marry."

"That you should, Harry. There's the title."

"Two or three cousins to ensure it."

"That's not the same thing. I've said it, and I mean it, you ought to have a wife and family."

"I believe you really do mean it. Would you mind, Kate?"

[70]

"I—" she said slowly, "I—don't have a right to go an' feel that way, do I? Right kind you've been to me a long time now."

"I'd always look after you," he said. She was silent. "It's not as if I'd be turning you out altogether." And she turned on her side against him.

"You wouldn't? It wouldn't be different—that way?"

"Well——" This was senseless haggling over a very hypothetical event. "I wouldn't want to deceive a wife over that. I don't know, Kitty. I'm talking nonsense—there is no wife and probably never will be."

"Why'd you ask then, Harry?"

"I don't know. Forget it, it doesn't matter." He lay on his back staring into the dark, aware of her presence but not thinking about her—thinking about Anne. Wondering about Anne. It was not, considered detachedly, such a wild idea after all. He had an estate to match hers; she could be sure it was a sincere offer. She was well-bred, young, pretty. Any woman might lose her head over a handsome rogue, but by that little scene today she was already experiencing regrets. If Deering were not so complacent—but even now she might be persuaded to withdraw from the be-trothal, suspecting the man for what he was however he fascinated her. Anne would make a good wife in all respects. Well, perhaps —but one did not expect to find a wife as companionable a bed-mate as other women. Kitty, for instance.

He thought she was asleep; she had put her hand on him as she always did in sleep, as if to make sure he stayed while she slept; then she stirred. "Harry. You got it in mind—there is somebody. You never talked about it so afore."

"It is not likely to happen. Very well, yes, there is, but she is already promised. I was woolgathering—it amounted to no more than being sorry for the girl. Little Miss Deering. She is unhappy with her charming rogue, and too sweet a girl to be so hurt."

"You'd marry her—if she'd have you?"

[71]

"Why talk about it? A little late to persuade her. . . . Have I worried you, Kitty? I did not mean to. I'm a fool. To exchange you for a meek, dutiful wife!" She answered to his kiss eagerly, and her passion was more vigorous than usual.

3

But the notion stayed in his mind, and the remembered feel of Anne's slim shoulders. In love with her? Well, there were different kinds of love. Once it occurred to him to think of her that way, the feeling kept growing in him. He had begun by being indignant at her folly, a vicarious indignation like that he would feel on his sisters' behalf, but now his anger was directed more personally at McDermott.

No, it was not such a wild scheme. If he was to marry at all it would answer very well. A sweet child, Anne. Much too sweet to be victimized by a clever fortune hunter.

By the following week he had come to a decision on it. He left his office early one afternoon and went back to his hotel for his perch-phaeton and pair. Expecting to be in Dublin for some time, he had acquired the perch and pair from a dealer Gore had recommended: "Honest enough as any tout, if you know enough not to be cheated. Nealy, Owen Nealy in Ransome Street, he's your man." Certainly no fault could be found with the bays, a middling good match and prime-mouthed.

He left his groom walking the horses in FitzWilliam Square and inquired of Wood if Mistress Deering was in. In a few moments she came downstairs to him.

"Dear me, you are assiduous! I should have expected you to be too much occupied with affairs of state to wait upon me so often." She gave him her hand. A little to his own surprise he found his heart beating faster.

"Can you accompany me for a drive, Anne?" He indicated the phaeton waiting in the street. "It is such a pleasant day, I thought you might enjoy——"

"It is kind of you, but I had best not; we are expecting Dennis for tea."

"Please come—I will not keep you out long. There is something I wish to say to you."

"Well——" She hesitated. "That does look a spanking pair! I suppose you would not let me take the reins? I am quite accustomed to handling my own pair in the country, you know."

"I will not! Come, fetch a cloak and let us be off."

"Only half an hour, I must be back." She did not keep him waiting; in five minutes he was handing her up to the high seat.

"You need not come," he told the groom, and gathered the reins, turning down the first street west to avoid the crowded shopping districts. After a little desultory talk he fell silent, and Anne glanced at him, smiling.

"What is it you wish to say to me? There seems to be something on your mind."

"I confess I am a little downcast to find you so cheerful. When I saw you last——"

"Oh, I was being missish—I told you to pay no attention."

"You need not hedge with me, Anne. I think I understood your feeling. You know I sympathize, but for—another reason than friendship, if I may so put it. . . . You will think me a pompous fool."

"Not at all, but I do not——"

"Well, you see, Anne, I have suddenly discovered that I do not want you to marry anyone—anyone else," and unable to take his eyes from the lane of traffic he freed one hand and laid it over hers clasped in her lap. "I know it will seem precipitate that I say that——"

"Harry!" She turned to face him; he snatched a glance at her

[73]

and saw her mouth trembling with suppressed mirth. "What are you leading up to? Do not tell me you are about to offer for my hand?"

"There is no occasion for humor," he said stolidly. "I would be greatly honored if you accepted me as a husband. You need not be embarrassed when I add that I am aware you are not altogether content in this betrothal. It would occasion no surprise if you decided to withdraw, my dear—that is no disgrace, particularly in the circumstances. It all arose very suddenly as it was——"

"Most unseemly haste, in fact." She was staring at him.

"As you say. I know it may be difficult for you to look on me as—aught but a friend, but you can at least know I am sincere."

"Are you feeling quite well, Harry? That blow on the head——"

"Let be, Anne! I have said I know it would surprise you. I —it surprises me. I had not thought—but there it is. Would you wed me, Anne? I should do all in my power to make you happy."

She began to laugh, checked herself. "Harry, my dear! Indeed I am cruel to laugh at you—forgive me. But let us speak plainly— you are being chivalrous. You have it in your head I am unhappy, and I am not at all. I spoke foolishly to you, and I am sorry now. You really need not make such a sacrifice!"

"If that were the only thing in my mind, your betrothal, would I ask that?" he countered. "I know it is sudden, but I am very fond of you, Anne, truly. I do not seem too old to you? I would not——"

"Well, not *very* old, Harry. Do tell me—you love me passionately? You are chafing to call Dennis out only for being my affianced husband? You must try to sound a trifle enthusiastic, you know!"

"Vixen," he said, "you think to taunt me just as Sophie does. I am not funning, Anne. I ask you seriously."

"Very well, then I take it seriously." She put her hand on his arm. "You are good, but I know you are only sorry for me, and for no reason. Indeed I am sorry I troubled you with my foolish notions. You are fond of me, and I of you, but not that way. I am quite happy in my betrothal, you know. Dennis and I will suit very well. No, of course I do not quite believe you—how should I?"

"You will not have me making passionate love to you in public, in broad day. I might convince you if——"

"No, nor anywhere else," she laughed. "No, no, I am not miscalling you! You do not really want to marry anyone, Harry, though heaven knows enough fond mamas have pressed their daughters on you! If I may go by gossip, you are quite content with your mistress."

"Anne!" He was outraged. "Mind your tongue!"

"It is not all that close a secret, that you have a mistress? What unmarried man has not? Though I own, if Bella is right, it is somewhat unusual to keep the same one for ten years—is it that long, Harry?"

"I will not discuss such a matter with you, it is most improper."

"You are very stuffy," she told him warmly. "Well, I thank you for your kind offer, but you know I cannot take it seriously. And, please, you must drive me back—I should not be late."

He turned the horses and then pulled them to a stand. They had left city streets for quieter lanes, almost into the country, and no one was about, no house near. He pulled her unceremoniously into his arms and kissed her hard. "So you cannot believe me!"

"Let me go—no, Harry——" Her voice was frightened. Suddenly ashamed, he released her. "It is indecent—how could you? How could you?"

"Forgive me, Anne, but you angered me."

"Yes—I am sorry." Still breathing quickly, she was in command of herself again. "Please—take me back." And as he moved the horses on, "I—I did not imagine you to be in earnest." She sat upright, away from him, looking straight ahead. "I cannot conceive that you are. I am sorry."

"I'm sorry too. I'd not have kissed you if you hadn't laughed."

She said nothing more until they turned into the square again. Then she touched his arm and said, "I really do not know what to say. Do not let it last, Harry—it is mostly because you are sorry for me, and worried for me. You need not be, truly." And then, as they drew up before the house, she added a little exclamation under her breath.

The house-door stood open, and at the top of the steps McDermott was waiting, hands in pockets. Quintain jumped down to assist Anne to the footpath, and nodded at him shortly.

"Dennis, I am so sorry not to be here when you arrive! Harry suggested a little drive——"

"Oh, it is no matter at all." The deep voice was deeper and held a rasp. "Four o'clock, five, what is an appointment? It is only myself, no one of importance you keep waiting while you drive with Sir Harry."

"My apologies for keeping Mistress Anne," said Quintain stiffly. McDermott was very pale, his eyes brilliant with anger. "We did not intend to stay out so long."

"No, indeed I quite meant to be back in time, but we fell to talking——"

"Of course, of course. Did I not say it is no matter? Have you quite ended your talk? Should we not invite Sir Harry to join us, my darling, and cancel the box for the theater, that you may continue your talk in comfort?" He had taken her by the wrist, and Quintain saw his fingers white with the pressure of his grasp.

"I mislike your insinuations, Mr. McDermott."

"I shall apologize if you tell me what they are. I mislike your attentions to my affianced wife, Sir Harry. Rumor has it that you are provided with adequate female company."

[76]

"Dennis, this is absurd. Pay him no notice, Harry, he is a little annoyed at me is all. Thank you for the outing—we shall see you at my dinner on Friday week, I trust." She turned up the steps, but McDermott did not move and his hand held her back.

"In the future, Sir Harry, you will remember that Mistress Deering is betrothed to me."

"Mistress Deering has my sympathy, sir," said Quintain coldly, and took up the reins.

4

She had never seen him angry before, like this. Like every other woman she had sensed something essentially ruthless in him, but he was always so controlled, so mannered; she had not suspected how he would go white with rage, his mouth flat, and the velvet voice so precise and cold.

He had hurt her wrist with his grip. . . . Wood's face scandalized as he pulled her roughly after him into the little sitting room.

"Dennis, you are being absurd! It is nothing to fret over, I am not ten minutes late—I am sorry——"

"You have said that." He shut the door, still holding her, and took her other wrist, his fingers biting deep, holding her prisoned close before him. "Now tell me what you spoke of with that man, why you went with him. Run off so gaily forgetting me entirely! What did he say to you?"

"Let me go, Dennis." She tried to speak coolly, but he always robbed her of all self-possession. With Harry, any other man, anyone else she had ever known, she could maintain her poise in any situation; not with Dennis; whatever emotion was in him somehow communicated itself to her and she spoke what she had no intention of saying. She disliked emotional scenes. But even now,

standing within his hard grasp, the press of his fingers half painful, half pleasurable, she felt her own control slipping away.
"Let me free!" she said sharply.

"Tell me!"

"Do not be a fool. Harry is a very old friend, I look on him
almost as an elder brother. Naturally we have much to speak of
—mutual friends, London——"

"You are lying, you are lying to me. I know what he was saying
to you—what he has said before." A white line was growing about
his mouth. "So you think I am a fool, not to know what all your
friends will be saying—are saying now! Squandering yourself and
your fortune on an upstart of a colonial!—not even English! A
smooth-tongued fortune hunter, an Irish rogue! All your fine
English friends gossiping about it! That was what he was saying
to you, was it not? Warning you against me, advising you to
break off the betrothal! Was he not?" He shook her savagely.

"No, of course he was not—how can you think it?" She struggled against him. "Are you run mad, to say such things, treat me
so? Dennis——"

"I know what he was saying! A bold English gentleman, all
else dirt beneath his boots! And all too likely you listened to him!
Ah, you are charitable indeed—overlooking the fact that I am not
English, so kind, so loving, are you not?" Another shake. "If you
let him persuade you—forget that you belong to me——"

Rising fury lent her strength; she got one hand free and dealt
him a stinging blow to the face. "And you seem to forget you are
not dealing with a trull!"

"There is little difference between trulls and ladies, they are
both women," he said between his teeth; he let her go and the
hand he raised to his face was shaking.

Appalled shame killed her anger. She had never done a thing
like that before, or felt the impulse to do it. He put these new
emotions in her, and that was how she knew she loved him,

though it was not at all like the happy, comfortable love in all the romantic tales. Something immeasurably more immense and hurtful and overwhelming.

"Oh, Dennis, I am sorry. I did not mean to strike you."

He turned his back abruptly. "I lost my temper," he said in a strained voice. "I am sorry too. Forgive me."

"It is all right—it is only that it was so foolish, there was nought like that—— I could not think such things of you."

"I hope not." His hands on her shoulders were gentle now. "You must make allowances for me, I am perhaps oversensitive."

She let him hold her with a long sigh; she felt exhausted with emotion. "I forgive you, if you forgive me. You must not doubt me so, Dennis."

"No—no. It is—I love you so much, I cannot help it." His hand was urgent, trying to turn her face up to his, but for a moment she resisted, resting against him. She thought, he was not acting: he was in a fury. Not for me—not for the reason he gives. No, it is only possessiveness—and greed. A dog with a bone. I belong to him, I am promised to him now, and he would kill any who took me away, and perhaps me as well, because it would hurt his vanity so much. Then his mouth came down on hers and she stopped thinking.

Six

I

Quintain was still angry, cold and inward, that next morning. He was too angry, in fact, to realize that that little drama had taken the effect of turning his exasperation with Anne to McDermott. She need not have laughed at him . . . but she did not deserve mistreatment, and from McDermott's public behavior over it he was not a man would hesitate to beat a wife. He had not blustered, but he had looked—deadly.

So by the time Quintain had gone over the whole scene in his mind, and described the afternoon's events to Kitty in blunt language, striding up and down his chamber and searching his vocabulary for appropriate terms to apply to McDermott, he had forgotten all his anger at Anne and felt himself deeply, chivalrously in love with her, sweet Anne who was betrothed to a brute —and not even a well-bred brute.

He was brusque with Adams, barked at the sergeants, and received Lieutenant General Gore with the minimum of courtesy.

"About your request concerning those boys, Sir Harry——"

"Boys?"

"The two we have in keeping at the gaol. They were taken a month or so back, you recall I told you. In regard to your request to interview them——"

"There is no difficulty about that, I presume. They could afford more information."

Gore grunted. "It is not every day we get our hands on these brats—they're whisked out of the country too slickly, see you. We took these quite by chance—they'd been separated from whatever agent of this organization had them in charge, and were found wandering the streets. Now, Sir Harry, I've been dealing with these people longer than you, and I can tell you you're wasting time on this notion. Of course they've information to give, but it is no manner of use questioning them, not the children. They will never give their rightful names, to start with—knowing that would incriminate their parents in a scheme to flee the country. You'll get nowhere."

"Nevertheless I should like to see them."

Gore shrugged. "As you will. These two are to be transferred today, to an orphanage outside the city. I can arrange for you to see them at the prison now."

But his prophecy proved correct. Quintain, surveying the two boys, thought he had never seen a less prepossessing pair. The older could not have been over eleven, and both were undersized. Their clothes had been poor to begin with, and six weeks in a verminous cell had not improved them. Boys? Brought before the two high officers, guarded by a stolid corporal, they looked like little old men, sharp-faced, blank-eyed. To all questions they maintained a complete silence, though the smaller one wept in evident fear. Quintain was stirred by disgusted bewilderment and pity. This was a dirty trade, trafficking in children taken from their parents to be deliberately trained as inciters of rebellion!

"Waste of time," said Gore. "You forget we have been at this for years. The only information we get comes through informers, not by bribes or threats. We cannot torture children."

"They will be taken to an orphanage, you say?"

"What else can we do with them, not knowing where they belong?" And likely, thought Quintain, they would be better off than with their own peasant families, or exiled in some monkish school abroad. A dirty trade!

The two boys were not, however, destined to end—or begin—their careers under the stern guidance of an Anglican orphanage. They were removed from the military prison early that evening and under the guard of a sergeant and a corporal started in an army-wagon for a small town some nine miles out of Dublin, where the orphanage was located. Along a wooded stretch of high-road the little company was attacked by several mounted men. The corporal was shot dead, but the sergeant lived long enough to talk.

"O'Shaughnessy," said Gore bitterly. "One day we shall take him, God aiding us, and his band of cutthroats with him."

"Who is O'Shaughnessy?"

"Highwayman," said Gore succinctly. "Anything you care to call him. His mob of bandits has worked all the roads about the city for five years—they've an earth somewhere to hide in, and one day we'll find it. This is not the first time O'Shaughnessy has aided prisoners to escape."

That was on the morning after the episode, and Quintain cursed briefly that he had not known of it when it happened. Whatever agency was behind this, they now had the boys again and their next move, presumably, would be to get them off on the first available ship to the Continent. With any luck, being on guard for it, his men should be able not only to prevent that but take note of any suspicious activities at the waterfront.

There were at that time four foreign ships lying in Dublin

harbor, a Dutchman, two Italians, and a Frenchman. Quintain ordered his guard alerted for each; and each was searched by the regular port-guard, without result. All the ships were under constant observation until they weighed anchor, and the men standing watch swore in a body that no boys had gone aboard.

"Not that there wasn't a bit of awkwardness, as you might say, sir. You take it in the day, when there's always a fair crowd at the docks, well, who's to say what lay a man's on 'angin' round a wharf? But like I said afore, and askin' pardon, most parties take it amiss to be hasked their business, an' the ship-orfcers an' crews, they don't like it neither, the men bein' easy noted when the crowd's gorn, an' at night like."

"I realize that, but they would expect port-guards to be about. Any port has men watching for illegal imported goods." But these, he reflected without humor, were exported goods. Unless the boys were being kept undercover to wait for a later ship, they must have been smuggled aboard one of these on that very night, hidden somehow during the search. "What do you mean, awkwardness?"

What could be seen of the sergeant's face behind his mustaches took on an aggrieved expression. "Them Eyetalians, sir. Some of the crew took hexception to our men, an' there was what you might call a ruction."

"Oh?" said Quintain. "What occurred?"

"It were last night, sir. Corporal Williams an' Corporal Jason, they was the ones. I don't know the rights of it meself."

"Send them in here, then."

"Very good, sir."

Corporal Williams and Corporal Jason looked like a pair of traditional clowns playing between-acts in a provincial theater. Jason was long and thin, Williams short and round. "I understand from Sergeant Polwhistle that you had some difficulty upon your duty. What happened?"

"Well, sir——"

[83]

"Them Eyetalians——"

"One of you at a time, please. Williams?"

"Well, sir, it was no fault of ours, certain. Watching that Eyetalian merchant we was as per orders, sir, an' a dull job it was. Yes, sir, excuse me, sir. Reported for jooty at height of the clock, an' took over from Corp'ril Jones an' Private Bowers, sir. She were readying for sail with the tide, all loaded an' crew aboard by ten, an' that's where the trouble started. There wasn't another soul on the wharf, sir, 'ceptin' me an' Adam here, an' we stuck out like a pair of hostriches in White'all, sir——" Williams's military correctness was deteriorating under emotion. "An' the shipmaster come down to hask what we was adoin' of there. Little fat man 'e was, with about three words of Hinglish an' 'e couldn't say those proper. So I says to 'im, we was waitin' for some chaps off the Dover packet what was lyin' next to the Eyetalian, y' see, an' 'e says to me then why was we at the plank of 'is ship hinstead of the other. And then——"

"Get to the point, what occurred?"

"Well, sir"—Jason took up the tale—"then there was about arf a dozen of the Eyetalian crew, they come up be'ind the capting on the plank an' just stood there lookin' at us. An' makin' what sounded to be uncompliment'ry reemarks, sir, in Eyetalian—leastways, I s'pose it was Eyetalian. An' meanwhile, sir"—he coughed apologetically—"I'd been puttin' it off like, but when they didn't go back aboard for quite a spell, I just steps out to the side of the wharf to ease meself, sir. An' one of the crew, 'e says in Hinglish—or what 'e meant for Hinglish—'look at the bastard there,' 'e says, 'pissin' against our plank'—an' I wasn't, sir, I was a good yard away from it—an' they all give a sort of growl, an' the next minute they come down an' piled into us."

"Attacked you?"

"Yes, sir, you could call it that. Six or height of 'em. I see Will here go down, an' I wasn't as you might say in any state to put

[84]

up a fight. Next thing I knew I caught a stunner on the 'ead, sir, an' I couldn't say 'ow long I was hout. When I come to, there was the little Eyetalian captain bendin' over Will, an' the gentleman 'oldin' me 'ead up askin' was I dead."

Quintain jerked upright. "Gentleman?"

"Yes, sir. I didn't arf 'ave a neadache, sir, an' me breeches all unfastened still an' I'd bled all over me tunic, a proper mess I was hin. The gentleman, sir? I don't know 'oo he was, 'e says as 'ow he 'appened along to see the ruckus an' the little captain atrying to 'aul his men orf in case we was port-guards, an' could make trouble for 'im. That's all it was, sir; the crew went back aboard an' the captain made out to apologize for 'em though 'e didn't like us any too much 'imself. We was shook up, but we stayed by the wharf until she sailed a nour after, sir."

Quintain ruined a penpoint, poking it aimlessly into the paper on the table. "I see. I see. You were entirely unconscious, both of you? No telling how long . . . a natural enough little episode, of course—Italians being Italians. Say—this gentleman, had he been aboard the ship, or did he go aboard afterward?"

"Oh, no, sir. 'E just happened by like—seein' somebody orf on another ship, I think 'e said. Quite kind 'e were, sir—'elped me up orf the wharf an' said it was a lesson not to have no dealings with foreigners."

"What did he look like?"

"Lord, sir, I couldn't say rightly, bein' in a daze like—I was sick, too. Not very big, medium-built, sir—it was dark—but 'e had a grip. I'm no featherweight, sir, you can see, an' 'e lifted me up orf the ground like you liftin' a glass of wine. Deep voice 'e had."

"You did not see his face—his clothes—anything to identify him?" And what did it matter? That might have been a contrived scene, that little farce, but it could never be proved—and it might equally have been fortuitous.

[85]

"I see 'im," said Williams. "A gentleman 'e was orl right, sir, an almighty 'andsome gentleman, an' youngish."

The quill snapped in Quintain's fingers. "Say that again!—a very handsome gentleman, medium-built, with a deep voice?" And if that was not Dennis McDermott, what other man was it? And what did it mean? Nothing. He was obsessed with Mc-Dermott. That little comedy might have been produced as a cover for smuggling the boys aboard, or it might be quite innocent, and in either case what was there to connect McDermott with it— even assuming he had been there? Quintain swore. He was over-imaginative; he was letting his dislike for McDermott overrule reason.

"Very well, that is all, dismissed," he said. The two corporals saluted and marched out. Quintain got up and poured himself a glass of wine. Sipping it thoughtfully, he reflected that if he had any hope of winning Anne over to him, he must make amends for his recent discourtesy to her betrothed husband lest Mc-Dermott persuade her to an open break with him. As long as Anne continued to receive him, listen to him—yes, it was but the act of a gentleman to apologize, though it went much against his liking to apologize to that smooth black devil.

He tossed off his wine, slung his cloak about his shoulders, and ordered his horse brought round.

2

McDermott's law offices were on the top floor of a tall stone building in the newer part of the city. A spotty-faced clerk took Quintain's tricorne and set a chair for him. "I will see if Mr. McDermott is free, sir." He expected to be kept waiting until it should suit McDermott to receive him—damn the business that brought him here hat in hand to fawn on the fellow!—but the clerk was not absent a minute when the door of the inner office · opened and McDermott appeared, hand outstretched civilly.

"This is an unexpected pleasure, Sir Harry. Come into my office, will you not?" It was a larger room than the first, and surprisingly well-furnished in baroque style. An ancient but good Turkey carpet, a large table and several chairs with heavily carved legs, a side table bearing two decanters of Italian glass, crystal glasses. "Sit down. May I offer you a glass of sherry?"

"Thank you," said Quintain formally. "I fear I was less than polite to you at our last meeting, and for little reason. I hope you will accept an apology."

"It is not needed, I assure you—rather the other way about. An absurd incident, and you must have been amused at me, the proverbially suspicious lover! I was amused at myself an hour afterward. Why is it that the most experienced man becomes a callow fool when he conceives a romantic attachment for a woman?"

"Human nature perhaps." Quintain relaxed slightly. "I take it then I need not assure you it was quite an innocent——"

"Oh, no, no, do not labor the point! You must make allowances for a man affianced. Would you prefer a light clarry wine, perhaps? No? I have had better sherry, but it is not undrinkable." It was, as a matter of fact, excellent. Quintain sipped and regarded McDermott curiously.

"Mistress Deering has known me all her life—our family estates adjoin, and my two younger sisters are her close friends, you see. It was only natural that I should wait upon her here——"

"Quite natural, and only a man in love could imagine otherwise. Do not disturb yourself for it, I beg." McDermott managed subtly with all this talk to put him in the position of a man asking favors, an anxious apologist. Quintain kept down increasing irritation with an effort. Looking at the other man, he unknowingly echoed a thought another had once had of McDermott. I could

mill him down in ten seconds, he'd be no use in a real fight; he
lacks the reach for fists or swordsmanship. And they never stand
up to an Englishman, any foreigner—they have not that dogged
spirit, whatever their other qualities. He did not think McDermott would be a physical coward, but he was the type always to
avoid physical trouble; his mind did not work that directly.

"I am very glad to hear you say that, sir. It distressed me that
you should blame Mistress Anne——"

"Oh, I did not, not at all, once I was myself again. I would
not make a false impression on you." McDermott had seated himself at his table; now he leaned forward earnestly. "Forgive me,
but as you are an old friend of Anne's I feel I can speak frankly.
You cannot have avoided hearing gossip of me as a fortune hunter,
paying court to the lady for her possessions. Well, I am not a
wealthy man, certainly, but even a poor lawyer may be allowed
some genuine emotions." His voice deepened with sincerity. "I
am sure you can understand how such talk angers me—undoubtedly it makes me all too sensitive regarding aught to do with our
betrothal."

Oh, but he is a clever devil, thought Quintain. If he had no
personal involvement with this, if he had not already disliked
McDermott, that little speech would likely sound sincere, and he
would find himself sympathetic to the man. Even as it was, for
just a flash it was convincing, he saw the proud young man suffer-
ing agonies of love for the beautiful wealthy lady . . . exactly
like the romantic stories all the young London ladies so eagerly
sought for in these new circulating libraries.

He made some noncommittal answer and turned the talk to a
less personal topic. McDermott chatted amiably, showing his
usual flashes of rather ironic wit, gesturing with one long hand.
Himself, perhaps as a soldier, Quintain thought him a touch over-
dressed: he would feel a spectacle in that peacock-blue waistcoat
trimmed in silver braid, but there was no denying it to be in

excellent taste; and the immaculate lace, the smooth satin, bespoke a man fastidious of his person—or a good body servant. He noticed for the first time the large gold seal ring on McDermott's right forefinger.

"You are admiring my ring? A family heirloom." McDermott slipped it off and offered it politely. "Although my father left me nought but a name, we are an old family. He would never part with this."

Quintain examined it with a show of interest. It bore an ornate design of an unidentifiable beast rampant, and the motto in twisted letters *Aegis Fortissima Virtus*. "Virtue is the strongest shield," he murmured. "That is the motto of the Aspinall family of Somerset, I believe."

"Is it?" McDermott took the ring. "Perhaps there is some connection, I do not know."

"I understand, by the way, that you met with a little excitement at the waterfront last evening."

McDermott cocked an eyebrow at him. "What can you possibly —ah, of course, the Italian sailors! How do you happen to know of that? Unless—do not tell me those men were port-guards, as the sailors maintained! Were they your men?"

"I rather thought you were the gentleman, from the men's description."

McDermott laughed. "I trust I have not incriminated myself by being in the vicinity. What was it, smuggled brandy? I wager half the wine in Dublin has escaped the tax—which is why it is so difficult to obtain decent drinkables, for they will swear it is the genuine article out of Rhône or Jerez, and then one finds it colored water—my pardon, now I am incriminating myself!"

"You witnessed the entire incident?"

"Oh, no—no, I do not think so. I had been seeing a client off for England on the Portsmouth mail-packet, and came by as the little Italian shipmaster was endeavoring to calm his crew. I have a few words of Italian, though I am not voluble in the language—also I was curious. I gather the crew objected to having the ship watched, and probably with good reason."

"Probably," agreed Quintain slowly. "Well, I must not take up your time, Mr. McDermott. I am glad you bear me no ill feeling for our little clash." He rose.

"None at all, of course! It was most kind of you to call upon me—MacMurrough!—and I trust we shall meet again soon. Mac-Murrough, Sir Harry's cloak, please. I am a member of Durfee's, perhaps I shall have the pleasure of a game with you there one evening? Good day, Sir Harry, and again my thanks."

3

"Will that be all, sir?"

"No, it will not be all, MacMurrough. You will recopy Mr. Clark's will, if you please. A schoolboy would write more legibly, and there are no fewer than three blots and seven misspelled words."

"I'm sorry, sir."

"You will make a fresh copy at once—I want it on my table by nine o'clock tomorrow morning. Mr. Clark is to come in and sign it at ten. For the moment that is all. Show Mr. Fortescue in immediately when he comes."

"Yes, sir." The clerk went out. McDermott refilled his glass and carried it across to the window, gazing down on a narrow gray street where a light rain began to fall. He studied the authentic amber of the sherry with approval, but he was not thinking about wine. Nor was he thinking about Sir Harry Quintain's mission at the moment, or the implications of that man's visit.

Aspinall, he thought, looking at the ring. Queer, to find out the name ten years afterward. Or it might not have been Aspinall, only some connection. It had seemed a pity to leave the corpse with fourteen guineas in its pockets and the ring on its finger, though it would have been dangerous to sell it and he had not dared wear it for a long time. With the body stripped, the death was put down to nightmen, naturally. A desperate little affair that had been; the man was a fool to charge in alone instead of calling the guards. No time to do aught but use the knife. One of the first jobs he had done for the organization: the first man he had killed. He did not like killing men, even Englishmen. But with a cocked pistol at one's breast there was no choice.

He stopped thinking about the dead man and thought about Quintain. He had let him think he was ignorant of the real purpose of the guards, that it was smuggled cargo they were after. Well, so it was in a way. That was all right. Had Quintain been trying to trick him, with that assumption that he had been there? No reason for Quintain to suspect him. If Quintain had any definite evidence on him, he would have faced Quintain in the military gaol, not his own office.

"I beg your pardon, sir." He turned. "A messenger has brought this for you." Offering the sealed note, the clerk added, "A female messenger, sir."

"Indeed." McDermott gave him a cold glance and he retired hastily.

His name was scrawled across the outside of the note in an agitated hand—probably feminine—he had never seen before. Somewhat intrigued, he slit the seal with his thumbnail. More agitation—several lines of overlarge letters running crookedly across the page. He exclaimed irritably under his breath.

Dennis, I must see you, it is vital. I beg of you, do not refuse me. Despite our parting, despite all, if you once held me in any regard do not fail me now. Come to me tonight, it is in your own interest. I must see you at once—Celia

Several words were underlined twice, and there was a blot of candle grease across the signature. He swore mildly. Now what was at the damned woman? Dramatics—play-acting! When he had done with a woman it was finished, he had no love for post-mortems.

He crumpled the note in his pipe-tray and set light to it, stirring the ashes to black powder.

Seven

With the announcement of Anne's betrothal and forthcoming marriage, a number of Dublin society's matrons had bestirred themselves to welcome her prospective entry into their company with afternoon teas and dinner parties. For all the correct congratulations pressed upon the pair at such gatherings, McDermott could guess at the female talk out of Anne's hearing. *So he has captured a fortune at last, and a deal better bargain than the Forsythe girl. I never believed he really meant to offer for her—a bit too barefaced even for Dennis. Do not be juvenile, cousin; true love does not arrange to strike so fortunately—but whatever he gains by it will be money well spent on her part; a charming husband he will make. I own I thought he should never wed, 'twould cramp his style too greatly. . . . Oh, cousin, pray do not sound so innocent! A number of sober matrons in the city could provide Mistress Deering with excellent references of him. Not that I know any secrets—or keep any, my dear!—but any woman with eyes in her head would know him for what he is. For all his* charm, I'm not certain I'd want him myself. So shaming to have one's husband found murdered in another woman's bed, which is likely how he will end. . . . Poor little Mistress Deering has my sympathy.

Well, let them gossip! He had Anne safe—she would believe nothing against him.

Especially since Sir Julian's patronage of him the last few years, he was acquainted in society circles and a popular guest—hostesses could always count on him for amusing conversation, elegant appearance, and correct behavior. No one suspected how most social affairs bored him, unless he were engaged in some new flirtation or angling after a prospective client.

He had seldom been so bored, however, as at Mrs. Wilde's dinner. As if by diabolical choice, his hostess had included all the most notable bores available in the city; the food was both cold and bad, the wine scarcely drinkable, and Anne was not near him but across the table and far removed, separated from him by two unbeautiful frumps and an explosive retired colonel whose sole interest appeared to be foxhunting. When the ladies rose to withdraw and the butler brought in the red wine, it was only mild relief to find that it was excellent port, to take away the flavor of the other.

He listened with every appearance of absorbed attention to a long monologue from the colonel, and presently rose to excuse himself, ostensibly to visit the cloakroom. He would take good care to linger there until the gentlemen were rejoining the ladies.

But as he came out into the passage and turned toward the door at the rear, a low voice spoke his name and he swung about to see Celia Vail at the foot of the stair.

"Thank God! I was waiting, praying you would come out alone. Dennis——"

"Well, Celia," he said with a mental shrug, "you are grown less discreet, to seek me out in company."

"You did not come to me—you had my note, I know, my maid would not lie——"

"Yes, I had it. You should know how I dislike hysterical women. We were finished some time ago, I see no reason to prolong emotions." He made as if to go by her; she clutched at his arm and drew him into the shadow of the stairwell as two women descended the stair, entered the parlor across the passage.

"You will not get away without hearing me! You must help me, Dennis—it is all your fault in any event!" She held him from turning away, her whisper urgent. "Do you not understand? You have put me in dreadful trouble, it is a child, and I cannot——"

He stared at her. "You do not catch me in that trap, Celia. Too old a game. There cannot be a child—or if so, it is not mine."

"Oh, God, you cannot desert me now! I am telling the truth, I swear it!"

"My dear Celia," and his tone was cold, "I cannot see that it makes the slightest difference whether or not you are pregnant. Certainly it does not to me. You are a respectable—or shall we say erstwhile respectable—married woman. If you suppose all the brats legitimately born are sired by their mothers' husbands, you are less intelligent than I take you for."

She drew back a little. "It is true, I swear it, it is yours, Dennis. I—I do not want it, I am frightened—I must be rid of it! My maid knows a woman who will do it, but it will cost forty guineas. I dare not ask Reynold, he is forever complaining of my extravagance and desires strict accounts. Please, Dennis, for whatever you once felt for me——"

"I begin to see. Whether it is mine or not you will make me pay for it! Or is it just forty guineas you want, and this an easy way to have it?"

"I always knew you could be cruel. Look at me, I am not lying to you—for God's sake, believe me!"

He looked at her in silence, in the dim light of the passage.

He knew too much about women, and about Celia, to entertain any doubt, after that first instinctive denial. His thoughts ran rapidly. No, it was not possible, he had been too careful. One or two occasions—but further back than the nine weeks since they had parted. Yes—just possibly. He put a hand on her shoulder.

"Very well, I believe you. Are you telling me you can be so certain it is mine? I am not that great a fool. If you have not cheated your husband at least once in these nine weeks I know nought about females. Yes, that touches you, does it not? You would find Vail a dead bore after our little games together—and you were not ready to be done with me then."

"No—I swear it, I have——"

"Who was it? Well, no matter. In any case you could not shut your husband out of your chamber. Three choices, then—Vail, or your new lover, or myself—and the chances favor one of the first two."

She was silent, breathing quickly, and then said again, "Dennis, do you think I do not know—that a woman would not know? It is yours—I know it. It is over ten weeks by any reckoning. I tell you I know."

"Women!" he said. "So you know. What is the difference? Vail will be pleased."

"But I do not want it, I must be rid of it, you must help me! Soon it will be too late. Forty guineas is not much; it is only that he is so finicking about the accounts—I might even contrive to pay you back in time, but please, you must let me have it——"

"You forget I will not be married for another month or so," he said sardonically. "At the moment I am but a poor lawyer, and I find forty guineas quite a considerable sum."

A little sob escaped her. "Please, I am desperate, I have foregone all my pride to ask you—Dennis——"

"Have you tried your present lover?"

"I'm not the loose woman you think me!"

"Or perhaps we could make it up between us. There is no reason for all this drama; Vail is complacent enough. You are playing the fool, Celia, a silly woman having the vapors! Why should you not give your husband an heir?"

"I tell you I must be rid of it!"

"Well, look to it yourself, then, I'll have no part of it!" He went on down the passage; she made as if to pursue and then retreated as another group of women came down the stair.

Post-mortems! He surveyed himself in the mirror on the cloak-room door, exasperated, rueful; and laughed again. There was no one else in the room; he whispered in Gaelic to himself, "Little English bitch." But no. Any mongrel she-dog had more heart and brain. So she was frightened!

He went on looking into the mirror without seeing the reflection of the elegant gentleman in satin and lace. He saw a tumbled pallet-bed on the earthen floor of the little hut's one room, his mother's heaving ungainly shape, some neighbor-wife bending over her.

He said in the same harsh whisper, "Not forty pence, damn her!"

2

Wait, Calhoun had said; what else was there to do? In this business every man was dependent on the integrity of those he worked with. It was no new danger, the threat of betrayal—it had only come a little closer over that affair of Father Devin's near capture. Only very young men, in the first flush of idealistic patriotism, credited all compatriots with utter loyalty; McDermott had known too many informers to trust any man on his race or faith or past record; but it seemed incredible that it could have been an agent.

These men, two dozen or thirty of them, constituted the high council of the organization in Ireland. The church had a separate council, composed of the bishops from each county. The agents, all men with excuses for traveling about the country, oversaw their own districts, were responsible for the masters of each community in those districts, and decided upon boys chosen for education abroad. They were the links forming the chain of conspiracy, and only men whose records and characters were blameless—from the patriots' view—could be elevated to such responsible positions. Take himself—when old Dyer died and Calhoun recommended him for the new contact-agent, the council had interviewed every man he had ever worked with, written abroad for references from his teachers in France, the priests who knew him, even the Bishop of Paris, and examined the record of every job he had done for the organization in eight years. They could not afford to take chances.

But any man might be tempted to turn traitor for gold. McDermott despised sentiment, and told himself he was a fool to absolve any of the suspectable men even in his mind; but he could not bring himself to believe it would be possible for Burke or Calhoun to turn Judas. He knew them too well. Any of the others, not those.

It had been at Burke's suggestion that the story of treachery had not been told to any of the others. Only those four knew it who had heard it first. "If one of us betrayed Father Michael," said the jeweler, "it will be of little use to discuss plans to investigate it among ourselves. And if all the agents knew, we should have a holiday of accusation and suspicion, personal grudges starting quarrels right and left. I see no benefit in that."

"Nor I," seconded the priest. "As it happens, no harm has been done—or very little. We have rescued the boys, thanks to quick action on Calhoun's part, and I am safe enough."

"And I cannot believe it was one of ourselves——" Burke kept repeating that doggedly.

"We must wait," said Calhoun. "When one is unsure what to do, do nothing and gain time to plan."

They had overruled McDermott, who would prefer some action taken; but as he had said, he was only their messenger boy, subservient to their decisions. These last six or eight weeks when he went to the docks to meet foreign shipmasters and accept letters for renegades within the country, or dispatch another boy on the way to a foreign school, or tender letters destined for men abroad, he went expecting challenge and arrest, and each time when he regained his office or his chambers after such an excursion he was faintly surprised. One betrayal often led to two, and thence to a hundred. But September had given way to October and November came in and grew old, and still all went smoothly with no hint of trouble.

Except for Quintain's guards, of course. But if that was all the man could do—and that was nothing new either, the obvious defense; the regular colonial authorities kept port-guards posted as a matter of course, and if Quintain's special force was a trifle more assiduous, being fresh on the job, it was not a serious obstacle.

There was no regular time appointed for the agents' meetings— two or three of them would be in Dublin once a month or so, and call at Burke's, who would summon McDermott to deliver the latest communications from abroad and take whatever instructions the agents had for him. On the last day of November, as he left his offices, in the street outside Slade brushed past him with a low murmur: "Tonight at nine." McDermott went on to Durfee's clubrooms, where he engaged first Vail and then James Fothergill at cards, apologized for winning their money, and finally dined early. At half after eight he went back to his offices, empty and locked now. He crossed the dark anteroom to his inner office, lit one candle in the branch on his table, and pulled out the lower drawer. The false bottom lifted easily for all it fit well; under it lay a neat pile of letters. He transferred them to the inside pocket of his coat and departed for Burke's.

The clerk let him into the darkened shop. In the private room at the rear Burke, Nealy, Ferguson, Kelleher, and Father Devin were waiting for him. "Gentlemen," he greeted them, "—and Mr. Nealy," and Nealy laughed. "When was a horse dealer ever a gentleman?"

"You are still bearing a grudge for that bay gelding. I maintain it was your own fault. I never claimed he was a racer."

"A long way off it, Owen." He sat down and Burke offered him the decanter. "I expected to find Calhoun here." Calhoun, whose district was Ulster, had gone north seven weeks ago and should be in Dublin again soon.

"Likely he is on his way south now," said Burke.

"Well—" McDermott set down his glass and produced the letters, sorting them out rapidly. "Not too many this time. The Bishop of Kerry, Father John O'Brien—your districts, Thomas. An important-looking document for the Archbishop of Connacht" —tossing it over to Ferguson—"something for you, Owen, perhaps it is from your boy at last. Who knows a Patrick Shea?"

"He is a master in Waterford," said Kelleher. "I will take the letter."

"Good. The Bishop of Leinster, Father Fitzryan, Joseph Mc-Allister—all in your districts, Owen. I believe that is all—yes, the rest are for other destinations. I——" They all looked up as the door opened.

"It is Calhoun, sir."

"Ah, Liam, good to see you. We wondered if you had reached Dublin."

Calhoun advanced to the table in silence. He did not seat himself, but looked about the group slowly, and all greetings died at his expression.

"You have bad news." They all knew a look like that. News of a priest taken, news of a master hanged—of information laid, a man beaten and dead in a cell, the hounds baying on a desperate man's track. They waited for him to tell it.

"Bad news," said Calhoun. His voice was so altered that Mc-Dermott scarcely recognized it. "Bad news I have." His eyes came to rest dully on McDermott and he said "Dennis" with a queerly painful gasp. McDermott went to him instantly.

"What is it, Liam?"

Calhoun raised his head. "There is a thing—I must tell you all. My shame makes me tell it—I do not want to. It concerns—a treachery. John—Dennis—you know what I mean. Tell them. We said they should not know—until we knew for certain. Tell them now—I cannot."

Burke asked quietly, "You are sure? You know the traitor?"

"I have come to tell you his name."

"Very well." Burke turned to the others. "You will understand the reasons a few of us withheld this from you. Calhoun asks us to speak—I will tell you what is behind this." In a level voice he recounted the events of the priest's betrayal, with all their implications of an agent's involvement. A few murmurs and indignant denials punctuated the story; Kelleher fixed a dark stare on McDermott. "Calhoun tells us he knows the informer. Liam?"

Calhoun had remained motionless, standing, while Burke spoke. Now he cast another slow glance about the table.

"Well, let us hear!" Nealy was on his feet. "Is the traitor present?"

"I know who it is," said Kelleher softly.

"Yes—I will tell you. I came to tell you—as soon as I knew. I am the traitor," said Calhoun. He took a step toward them. "I betrayed Father Michael."

[101]

There was dead silence in the room. McDermott put a hand on Calhoun's arm, and the touch seemed to rouse the big man from a daze.

"I—do not know what you will think for it, if I should no longer act for this company. How could it be in my mind? I could not know—a man does not wear a mask with his first-born son."

"Sean!" said McDermott.

"Sean it was. Why would I guard my tongue with him? My own son, and would I not stop in Swords to see him when I came south?—spend a night, talking of old times——" Calhoun raised one hand in a violent half-completed gesture. "Yes, I told him of that, in idle talk, unthinking, as I might tell such a thing to one of you."

"He knew Devin's lodging——"

"Sean Calhoun knew my lodging," said the priest, "because I had been his confessor when he was in Dublin. You cannot take his sin for him, Calhoun. It was no blame of yours."

"It was—the reward," said Calhoun. "Seven pounds. You understand."

There was another silence, a murmur of ugly-sounding talk from Nealy and Ferguson, before McDermott said, "If a man will turn traitor, he will turn traitor for seven pence or seven hundred. And every traitor has a sire. We know you, Liam. It was no blame to you."

"I sired him," said Calhoun.

"He told you?" demanded Ferguson. "He boasted——"

"That he would not do. He was a little drunk, and indiscreet." Calhoun spoke remotely now. "Today—this afternoon it was that I was in Swords. I kept at him until he confessed the whole. And I came here to tell you. That is it."

"You need not have done that," said Burke gravely. "It is your credit you have spoken. No man here blames you."

"What of the traitor?" demanded Kelleher suddenly; and Calhoun moved.

"The traitor is dead. . . . I gave him life, I had the right to take it from him, did I not?"

McDermott looked about the group. "Get out, all of you, leave him to me. This is not a drama in the theater for an audience." And at Burke's nod all the men rose quietly. Kelleher was the last to leave; he paused at the door.

"I ask your pardon, McDermott." He got no reply.

As the door closed Calhoun sank down in a chair. "I had the right—I had the right."

"You had the right," said McDermott steadily. "It is finished, Liam. Do not think about it again."

"Mary's favorite he was . . . and thank God she is dead. Any other crime, how could it come between father and son? But he took English money for information given."

"Put it out of your mind. It is done, and you saved him further sins to pay for."

"He was the first-born," said Calhoun. "He used to sit on my knee and beg for some old tale."

McDermott gripped his shoulder. "Do you forget, Liam, I knew him too. I have slept in the same bed and shared the same bowl with him. But the traitor has cut off from old loves and all memories." Calhoun buried his face in his arms across the table, and as the muffled, wrenching sounds of his grief filled the room, McDermott turned his back and stood before the little dead hearth, bitter memory welling up in his own mind.

It needed courage for a man to choose the life Liam Calhoun led. He might have held a respected position in any university in Europe, but he had come back to Ireland to be a renegade schoolmaster—posing as a tinker with his horse and cart, up and down all roads, and if he had ten pounds a year to call his own it was a good year. But he had married a wife and raised up six children, and many more than that had reason to remember him.

Himself most of all, perhaps. . . . A bad year for crops that had been, and when the landlord's half was cut, there would be barely enough to last the family through the winter. Brian McDermott was ill a day or so and left it standing after the owner's half was carted away; just past the start of the hunting season that was. He remembered the yell of the hounds, the excited cheering of the gentlemen riders, the scream of the fox which they brought to bay and killed in the cornfield, the wheat all trampled and spoiled—and his father running out like a madman, driven mad at last by them, and the military officer from the garrison lying on the ground with blood on his face. Overt attack upon an officer . . . and so they hanged him, and put the family off the farm because there was no longer a man to work the land. It was four days' walk to his uncle's house, and his mother heavy with child, and his youngest brother dead of cold before they reached that place. That was a famine year—one of the famine years—and all of them dead before it was over: his mother and young Brian and Bridget and John and the baby, and very likely he would have died too except for Liam . . . they had been good, Liam and Mary Calhoun, taking him in with their own brood. The year after that he had been sent to France, one of those chosen for education; and in the end was it not Liam who had much to do with his decision to return, ten years later? Liam's still-burning idealism for the cause of freedom?

This was a bitter thing to come to a man like Calhoun.

He turned back to the table and filled a glass with Burke's good aged *uisgebaugh*. "Liam. Liam, take this now—it will help. And listen to me. You have two good sons and three honest daughters left to you. This will pass. Drink—that is right."

Calhoun said, "I held him when he took his first steps."

Eight

I

He woke with a great start, drenched in sweat, his heart pounding. The aftermath of terror held him motionless, and then with a gasp he turned on his side, only beginning to realize it had been no more than a nightmare. It was very dark—and then an unsteady vertical line of yellow light grew across the room, and his heart leaped again. He made himself move, sit up, reach for the knife on the bedside table—and, fully awake, damned himself for a fool.

It was only Kincaid, his servant, with a candle, opening the door stealthily, peering in.

"Mr. McDermott? Beg pardon, sir, I thought I heard you call out."

"Yes, it is all right—I was having a nightmare." The man came into the room holding the candle high, a vague white ghost in his night rail.

"Lord, sir, you're white an' sweating—a nightmare it was for certain. Will you take a glass of something?"

"No—yes, I——" He put a hand to his head, pushed back the tumbled blankets. "I will not sleep easily; you had best bring me some brandy."

"Yes, sir." Kincaid came to the bed, kindled two of the candles in the standard on the table. McDermott watched him out and sat on the edge of the bed, feeling his heart gradually cease its pounding. . . . He did not wholly trust Kincaid; he must be on guard with him. A good servant, but prying—meddlesome.

A child, a foolish frightened child, to wake with a nightmare! He would have a glass of brandy and smoke a pipe and then he could sleep again. He got out of bed, put on the exotic-embroidered silk dressing gown, went to the window and raised it for a breath of clear air. Cold dampness blew into his face, the hiss and splash of a heavy rain.

"Will that be all, sir?"

"Yes, that will do." He turned. "I am sorry to wake you."

"It's no matter, sir; it's my duty to serve you. Good night, sir."

He began to fill his pipe. He did not want to think about Liam, and Sean whom he had known; he thought about Kincaid. No reason to mistrust him, except that he was another of those who aped the English, even in servitude . . . wherever one turned, English!

That sorry business of tonight, the nightmare of remembered terror it had brought him, the correct Anglophile servant, all brought the hate welling up into his throat like vomit, until he must crush the wineglass in his fingers or smash his fist through the window or scream like a hysterical woman—anything, to express the hate. He stood still and let it have its way with him, playing on his body as a harpist on the strings. It ran darkly along his veins and hammered against his side seeking an outlet, the beloved hatred.

English, English, English, all his life. Thieves, killers, rapists— English! The arrogant strong English, Saxon for brawn and Norman for greed, taking—destroying. When the Britons ran savage in the woods, painted blue, and worshiped stone idols, there was civilization here. This was the first nation in Western Europe to have a written language, national law, literature, Christianity. Ireland was known for her scholars over a thousand years of history . . . but England wanted more land, and peasants to work the land when it was stolen.

English! Slave-keepers, woman-stealers—English!—and makers of traitors! Where was it to end? Five hundred years of nothing but the lowest labor, how could it not change the race? That was Liam's dream, the dream of the men who began and carried on this work, in secret, without pay, at the risk of their lives—that learning should not be killed among this people, the knowledge of a great past not be forgotten, the flame be kept alive and the memory of freedom and the hope of freedom never die. But would it?

English! With their caste-arrogance, stupidity, insensitive, careless strength—the destroying English! There would have to be an eighth circle in hell to hold the whole race.

He savored the hate like fine brandy on his tongue, willing it down to stay quiet and grow ever stronger without expression. And something else slid into his mind.

Celia. Anne. Remember your race not to shame it. Jesus, Mary, and Joseph, to think of a son of his half-English! A perversion of his manhood.

He carried the candle-branch to his sitting room, sat down at the table, found paper, ink, the little box where he kept money. His penmanship was something less than his usual graceful hand; the pen scratched hastily across the page.

Celia—I have reconsidered the point and find myself in agreement with you. Here are your forty guineas—speed the abortionist's hand, and let it be a warning to you for the future. I shall contrive to win it back from your husband at cards, but if I fail, it will still be money well spent.

It made an awkward package, sealed twice over for security, coins and notes folded inside. He would have MacMurrough take it round in the morning, and damn what he or the Vail servants might speculate. He could not afford to take chances.

And he would take care that Anne had no children.

2

"Good God, John, do you take me for an English lord to fling money about like that? I am not married to her yet."

"They are very fine stones."

"I daresay, but I cannot afford a hundred pounds."

"Call it an investment," advised Burke. "An extravagant wedding gift will pay you dividends in tenderness—or if you prefer, complacency. Any woman would admire this—observe the fine craftsmanship——"

"None of your wiles. I cannot afford it," repeated McDermott firmly. "You have no idea what expense this involves me in. A wardrobe of new clothes, a year's lease of the house we have chosen—— I had to assume that, in my role of the proud young lover loath to accept his lady's money—I can allow her to persuade me after we are wed—a bevy of new servants, a series of dinners for all the men I know, and now a wedding gift."

"One would know you are out of Ulster, and it overrun with Scots for ten generations. You do not convince me. You could take a hundred pounds off any garrison-officer any evening in the week, with their passion for deep play."

"Miscalling me a cheat?"

"Oh, saints, no," said Burke. "They are asking to be taken when they face you across a card table. Now just look at this again—one of the finest pieces I have ever——"

"No. Besides the price, I do not like it for Anne. Sapphires are too cold a stone."

"Emeralds——"

"Now be sensible, man. Nothing over fifty pounds, and none of those vulgar large breastplates you call brooches."

Burke put the sapphires away resignedly. "Garnets," he suggested. "Here is an attractive design—the brooch can also be worn as a necklet on a chain, you see, and the ear-hoops to match. There is a bracelet as well——"

"How much?"

"One of your female ancestors dallied too long with one of those Ulster Scots. Forty pounds for the set."

"M'mm—garnets are right for her. Yes, I think so. It will do very well. A velvet-lined box, mind, and see they are well polished." He laughed. "Do not grumble! Think of the dividends, John. Ten thousand a year she has. If I cannot coax a couple of thousand from her every year I am not the man I think I am, and the most of it will go to the fund abroad."

Burke was polishing the garnets with his handkerchief. "Rather yourself than myself. Whatever you take from her you will earn. It is not a way I would want to earn my living, marrying a rich English wife."

McDermott shrugged. "Women are women. Not so unpleasant as you might think—she is young and pretty."

The jeweler made a derisive sound. "One of these scrawny cold Englishwomen!"

"Make haste," said McDermott abruptly, "wrap them and give them to me—I am to be with her for tea."

Anne was delighted with the garnets. "My very favorite stone, Dennis!—how did you know? And it is a charming design. Thank you, my darling."

He returned her kiss and helped her fasten the brooch to her bodice. "I wish I might afford a more valuable gift, Anne."

"Ah, fudge! I like garnets much better than more precious stones—especially as you give them to me," and she smiled up at him gaily. "Come now, sit down and let me talk seriously before Sir Julian and my aunt come to interrupt us. I am glad in a way you said that, I have wanted to discuss it with you."

"What, my love?" He sat down beside her on the sofa. Anne began to pour the tea and arrange cakes on each plate with careful attention, not looking at him.

"Why, the money. I have had a letter from Mr. Mackie in London, the lawyer who looks after it, you know—and of course he is also a trustee until I marry, but he suggests—he is a very cautious man, you see—he says that as most of the capital is invested in England, and you—although you are a lawyer also—perhaps are unfamiliar with such investments, doubtless it is best that he continue to administer the estate, and pay me the income as he has been doing."

"Mr. Mackie is quite right," said McDermott promptly. An income-return of ten thousand a year—if Sir Julian's estimate was right, and he saw no reason it should not be—was quite sufficient to go on with, and the shrewd Mr. Mackie would undoubtedly see that the income did not dwindle. "I am relieved he suggests it. You know, Anne, I have heard enough gossip that I am marrying you for your fortune without giving your friends more foundation for such talk." He gave her a rueful smile. "It is only natural, perhaps, but—ah, you know how it angers me, why must I talk of it? I have no care for the money, it is yours."

"But, Dennis—no, let me say this, please, though it may make you angry with me." She took his hand in both of hers tightly, still not meeting his eyes. "I—I do not know precisely how much money you have, but it does not seem fair to me, when I have all this of my own, that you should bear all our expenses, when we are married, for the house and servants and so on. I——"

"That is my responsibility," he interrupted stiffly, "to make a home for my wife. I own it may not be what you are accustomed to. I cannot afford——"

"Oh, do not go all proud and masculine for it, I beg! I do not want to quarrel about it. I—I should like you to feel that it is our money, Dennis, to share and enjoy."

"That is generous of you." His tone was grim. "I am to accept my living from you and make all the gossip true, is that it?"

She flared up at him instantly. "Well, if they say I am buying a husband, at least you might give me value for my money and be more amiable!"

He pulled her into his arms contritely. "There, my love, I did not mean to snap at you! I am cross-grained, indeed, to take all you say wrongly! Forgive me. You will do whatever you like about the money, it is none of my affair." As yet, he added to himself, and kissed her. She made a little murmur and pressed closer . . . he thought of Burke's description and smiled.

Coldhearted the English were, but not always cold otherwise. Women were women, and that depended on the woman. It would be amusing—interesting—to have the teaching of Anne.

"Should I remember them all in my prayers, Dennis?"

"Who, my darling?"

"All the other women—who have given you practice in making love so beautifully."

"Jealous, my love?"

"Oh, dear, no . . . you are marrying me . . . m'mm, again, please. I have never understood it," she added dreamily against his shoulder, "why women—very young women, that is—are so fastidious for it, and like shy young men—who blush at a kiss. After all, when one hires a—a carpenter, say, to build a chest of drawers, one wants a man who knows the construction of such a thing—and just where to place the nails—and how to hammer them in soundly——"

"Minx, do not let your proper aunt hear talk like that . . . are you greatly interested in the principles of sound construction?"

"Fascinated, sir, fascinated! . . . and again . . . mind the cups, Dennis! Oh, d-damnation, there is Sir Julian——" They were both laughing as the old baronet entered, and he surveyed them approvingly.

3

"What more can I do?" asked Quintain angrily. "It is not exactly a conventional situation. As it is, I am something less than a gentleman to miscall her affianced husband and press my own suit at once."

Kitty watched him striding up and down the chamber. "She won't hear aught against him, I s'pose."

"She's as good as told me she knows he's a rogue, and then turns and defends him if I say anything out of the way!"

"She's in love with him, Harry, and she knows he don't love her—leastways not as much. That's enough to turn any woman a bit queer in how she acts. You'd marry her, though, if she did get rid of the other one and say she'd have you?"

"Yes," he said. "Yes—though it's a mad thing, falling in love with her like this, little Anne. But where's the sense talking about it? Not likely she'd break with him now, the wedding three weeks off."

"No," said Kitty.

"That bastard!" he said, beginning to pace again. "I swear, Kitty, there's something about him—I can't talk to him five minutes without wanting to get my hands on his throat!"

"Smarmy," she said. "I know the kind. Says things to your face polite as you please, an' an hour after, you wonder all of a sudden if he meant that the way you took it."

"He'll break her heart. She won't see reason. I've tried to make her think sensibly——"

"You'll never do that with anybody in love." Kitty wished he would stop talking about it, but she saw nothing queer in his discussing it with her. He discussed most things with her. A romance between a lady and a gentleman was altogether different from the relationship between a gentleman and the daughter of a London cooper.

"You're a woman," he said, coming to a halt in front of her. "What else can I say to her she'd listen to?"

She looked at him helplessly. She couldn't be like a lady if her life depended on it, she couldn't know how a lady'd feel about anything like this. "I don't know, Harry. I wish I could think of a thing to tell you, but I don't know. If she won't have you, an' you wanting to make her Lady Quintain an' all, well, more fool she, but if she won't, she won't." Why couldn't he have set his fancy on some lady just to marry without going all romantic about it, a lady he'd make a home for and lie with once in a while and have sons by, and still come to her for his real pleasure? She wouldn't mind that. Not as much as this.

"Well, more fool I for falling in love with her like an eighteen-year-old!" He picked up his cloak; she went to fasten the frogs for him. "Let be, I have dressed myself some years now!" He dropped a perfunctory kiss on her cheek and went out.

Ah, that girl was a fool! But women would all be fools at this time and that time. Even if she'd been a lady born, she'd never look like one . . . slim and graceful and swirling in stays and fur-trimmed gowns. He'd never looked twice at little girls like that, afore. That Diana lady had been tall and fine-made, she'd seen her once in the street, he pointed her out. He used to say, What does a man want with a pipestem of a woman who feels as if she'd come apart in his hands? Maybe he'd changed, or maybe it was different with a wife.

But she wouldn't have him, that was plain. Struck deep on the other one, she was. Maybe once they were wed he'd put it out of his mind.

"Fair daft I'm goin'," Kitty said aloud. "It's nought to do with me, save I don't like him to be hurted so."

Nine

I

Quintain sat at his desk and looked at the latest report from Sergeant Polwhistle—six pages of nothing. He swore. This morning he had had another visit from Gore and Randall, who scarcely troubled to conceal their pleasure at his lack of success. They knew well enough no man could do more than they were doing, on their regular routine, at this business.

What was he doing here? Fencing with his own shadow!—while these pompous desk-soldiers smirked in their sleeves at him. "Damned old women!" he said, and Adams laughed.

"Oh, they are. All the same, major, it's a teaser. Nothing to get hold of. In a thing like this, you sit on your arse and wait for the information to come to you. And if it don't come, that's just too bad."

"I'd like to get just one," said Quintain. "I tell you, William, I don't give one **damn** for their colony-law or the whole dirty country—don't know why we took it in the first place—but just to wipe the eyes of these tin soldiers I'd like to show 'em it can be done, and take just one of the leaders for 'em to hang."

"Can't say I'm far behind you. But it's not a promising lookout, is it? What'd the sergeant have for you?"

"Nothing!" Quintain pushed the report across the table. "There's nowhere to start. All the same—all the same, you know ——" He got up to move across the room to the window; he stood, hands in pockets, swaying rhythmically heel to toe.

Adams eyed him alertly. "You've some suspicion—definite?"

"No! I wish it were—I wish it could be. But I can't in honesty call it definite."

When had he begun to have that irrational, teasing idea? It had grown in him gradually, and out of nothing. There was nothing else to base it on, so very probably it was based on his dislike of the man and nothing more. Why else, out of a hundred thousand people living roundabout—actually, two or three or four million throughout the entire country—why else should he drop on one man to suspect? Why, because that man was Anne's affianced husband, and he found him the most almighty irritating fellow he'd ever known, that was the sum of it. So McDermott must needs be put down as under suspicion!

But the idea persisted at the back of his mind. No, it was not all the product of a feverish imagination—he'd never been accused of being as imaginative as all that. The trouble was, he couldn't be sure his personal dislike, his feeling for Anne, was not encouraging him to make much out of little—or something out of nothing.

For the hundredth time he began to go over it deliberately in his mind, putting together all the little incidents and nuances, meaningless in themselves, which formed, he must admit, a very weak support of his suspicion.

Take that business of the Italian sailors. What did it mean? Exactly nothing. Several ships were leaving port that night, among them the Portsmouth mail-packet; what more natural than that McDermott should be at the waterfront seeing a client off for England? Any man—Quintain himself—might pause to watch a fracas among sailors. A number of other men besides McDermott would have been at the waterfront that night; and there was no guarantee that the Italian ship had been the one to carry those wretched boys. But put it down: McDermott had been there.

Then, and this was really too nebulous and irrelevant to think about at all, there was young Lieutenant Percival Ashley Aspinall. . . . Quintain had been made free, by courtesy, as a visitor to the city, of Durfee's clubrooms. He had fallen into the habit of taking a meal there occasionally, and was acquainted with several of the members, although he disliked cards and declined all offers to join their gaming. Sitting one evening over a London newssheet, he had overheard some of the conversation from a nearby table, and was vaguely bothered by some forgotten association. "Aspinall." He had been thinking about the Aspinall family recently—why? Of course, that motto on McDermott's seal ring. He had finished the newssheet, and rose to join the men talking.

"I beg your pardon, sir—Captain Poole, is it not? Good evening, Mr. Vail—Mr. Masterson. I ask pardon for intruding, but you were mentioning someone called Aspinall? I know some of the Aspinall family—an old Somerset name, you know." They were cordial, pressed him to sit down, offered wine.

"I was just saying we should have the watch doubled. Shocking, the number of nightmen about the streets. Chap takes his life in his hands to venture out alone after dark, in some districts. London's bad enough, but you expect it there. Aspinall, oh, yes." Masterson shook his head. "That's how he came to an end, poor devil. Sad waste—only twenty-three, you know. I believe you had an encounter with them yourself, Sir Harry, soon after you arrived."

"I never thought it was nightrunners did for Aspinall," said

Poole. "He wasn't a ladies' man, so it wouldn't have been aught like that, but a personal grudge of some other sort—disgruntled servant, or even one of the men in his command. And I'll tell you for why. Nightmen as a rule don't use knives."

"Who was he and what occurred?" asked Quintain. Poole shrugged and took up his glass.

"It's ancient history—I'd quite forgot it until Robert spoke his name. Plenty of unfortunates done for by nightmen—it was put down to that—and none of us knew the youngster well; he'd been here only a year or so. But I said at the time it wasn't quite an ordinary affair. Aspinall was a wild one, y' see, devil's own temper and no caution at all—charge in and damn the odds, that was Aspinall. Might've made a good officer when he'd settled down. But there were men who didn't like him—he was hard on the troops, and spoke out of turn with superiors, you know the type."

"I do," said Quintain. "They need seasoning and shooting over."

"As you say. Well, at the time he was junior to Captain Twyne, and one of his duties was assigning the port-guards. He was hot on inspectin' the men at odd times, and now and then he'd go down to the docks, maybe thinkin' to catch 'em out lazin' on duty. And one morning the watch found him dead as King Charles on one of the wharves, stabbed."

"Really," said Quintain, only mildly interested. "Had he been robbed?"

"Yes," said Poole. "His pockets were empty, and his servant said there were a ring and neckcloth-pin missing. There wasn't a mark on him save for the stab-wound. But it never struck me as an ordinary job for night-thieves. No one cared greatly—he was a younger son—and any investigation would have been useless."

"When was this?"

"Let me think—it would be almost exactly ten years ago. Thirty-nine, late in thirty-nine, just after the war with Spain began." Masterson began to talk again about the prevalence of nightrunners and Vail drifted away to join someone else at cards. Quintain thought, a ring. Why should that strike a chord in his mind? By God, yes, that seal ring of McDermott's, bearing the motto of the Aspinall family.

And what did that mean? Nothing again. "Virtue is the strongest shield." A common enough Latin tag, if a rather inappropriate motto for McDermott. A man dead and a ring allegedly missing ten years ago; no description available of said ring, which might have been anything from a six-pointed emerald to an antique intaglio—and another man with a ring he claimed as a family heirloom.

He was making this out of whole cloth, only because he disliked McDermott. Assume the very unlikely fact that the ring was the same ring; the only deduction that warranted was that McDermott had purchased it from some hole-in-the-corner shop where thieves had disposed of it, and was passing it off as an inheritance to lend credence to his claim of gentle birth.

—Which Quintain did not believe for one moment, but if he was able to prove McDermott the offspring of a Dublin harlot, what use was that? It was not a hanging offense. He was letting his dislike lead him far astray.

To go back, there was his own adventure with the nightmen. Was he reading too much into that? Only a few days after his arrival in Dublin, and evidently the nature of his commission was commonly known—had it been a direct attempt to murder him? Nightmen usually lurked in lonelier spots. McDermott had sought him out on the flimsiest of excuses, led him away from the lighted street—but not far away, and hopeful lovers seldom had good reason for all their actions, whether motivated by true love or ambition. And McDermott had been injured and robbed too.

What else was there? The French sailor. Richards and his men had done their work faithfully, spreading the word in every waterfront tavern and bawdy-house that liberal rewards would be forthcoming for information leading to the capture of those who aided natives to flee the country. There were enough men who would like to see some of that money, but few who had any helpful information to offer. The first who came forward was duly reported to Captain Adams, who carried the news to Quintain in his office.

"Richards is here, sir, with a man who says he knows something of interest. Your bait has caught a bird, evidently."

"Good—I thought it would. Send Richards in." But Lieutenant Richards had not been able to persuade the man to speak.

"He's a Frenchy, sir, a sailor. He wants his hands on the reward safe enough, but says he won't speak save to 'a very high officer, a man of honor.' Seems to think anybody else would give him away as an informer, and he's scared to death."

"Of what? We're not going to hang him."

"Well, partly of having anybody find out he's given information about these gentry, sir, but mostly of hell." Richards grinned. "He's Papist, of course, and these people are aiding the Papists."

"He may go to everlasting torment for turning informer," said Quintain dryly, "but he'll enjoy himself in this world on the reward money. Very well, bring him in."

The French sailor was young, dirty, ingratiating, and voluble. "I wish to be certain you are a man of honor, you understan' this is not a 'oliday business for me, they are ver' bad to men who betray w'en they find out, an' my name I do not tell, excep' that I swear to you I speak trut'——"

"Perhaps you would prefer to speak French," said Quintain in that tongue, and immediately regretted it, for the sailor, freed of the trammels of English, waxed twice as voluble. "Now let us be orderly about this. William, give him a chair. You have some information concerning persons who are aiding natives of this colony to leave the country unlawfully? Is this evidence you have seen or heard yourself or know from someone else?"

"I see it—three times I see it, myself alone, monsieur. How much do you pay me?"

"Let me hear what you have to tell and I will judge how much it is worth." But this one-sided arrangement did not suit the sailor at all; he pressed for ten pounds and was given five before he answered any questions. "Now, what do you know?"

It appeared that he was a sailor before the mast on a French cargo ship out of Marseilles. She made Dublin, to unload wine and silks and pick up wool, two or three times a year. On every occasion when she lay in Dublin harbor, a man came to see the master in his cabin, the door was shut and there was long talk between them. All three times they had been in Dublin since he joined the crew of the ship, this had happened; and once they had a passenger out of Dublin to Marseilles, a boy of nine or ten years. Once again, when the man was in the master's cabin, he himself had opened the door, bringing some message, and had seen the captain giving the man papers. Papers? Yes, folded papers with colored seals on the outside. Letters, then. Yes. It was evident that this was some secret business——

"Agreed," said Quintain. "Do you know the man's name?"

"Ah, no, how should I? I see only a little glimpse of him three times! Twice he comes at night, it is dark."

"I see. What is his appearance?" This led nowhere; its only informative value was the confirmation it offered that someone—or a series of someones—visited foreign shipmasters, presumably on illegal affairs. And who was to say whether it was smuggled wine or smuggled humans? "Is he old or young, stout or slim, a gentleman—a tradesman? How is he dressed? Have you heard him speak?"

"No, monsieur. He is dressed well, like a gentleman. Dark—a well-looking man, no beard or mustaches, not a boy but still young. The best look I have at him, he is smiling, and his smile is not even—so—more to one side than the other." Further patient questioning produced no more details. Quintain wasted another five minutes assuring the sailor that his part in this would remain a close secret, refused additional payment, and gestured him out.

"Information!" he said to Adams. "All that is not worth five shillings, let alone five pounds. Write out a warrant for a dark young man with an uneven smile, and arrest a hundred to fit the description! And the one out of the hundred who did visit the master of the *Bonne Chance* would prove to have done so to barter for a case of smuggled brandy!"

What had the French sailor contributed? Very little. It added up, but it was negative information—nothing to take action on. What else? Well, to be frankly fanciful, as Adams put it, look at the man's character. You couldn't indict a man on his personal qualities, but if you knew what a man was like in himself you knew what he was likely to do or not do. To begin with, McDermott was a gamester. Quintain had watched him at cards. He was the rare gamester who played not for the excitement of matching wits with an opponent, nor the excitement of victory, nor entirely for the stakes, but—if Quintain read him rightly—to prove his skill, over and over again. He was a cool, passionless player, certainly skillful—and lucky. Quintain had only once seen him rise from the table out of pocket.

He was admittedly a rake. But from all the gossip, and all Quintain could learn, he collected mistresses not because of extraordinary virility, or, conversely, any necessity to prove to himself and the world that he was virile, a common motive among rakes. His known and suspected conquests were all married women of high social standing. Quintain deduced from that a vast contempt for such women, the vain, extravagant, silly women of fashion who lived for gowns, balls, and gossip. He could sympathize in a way if that were true. Did McDermott exercise his seductive powers among that one group solely because of such contempt, or was it something subtler still?

He could not see McDermott standing up to a man with his fists, but he could imagine him using a knife—and smiling as he used it.

But what it came down to was that there was no earthly reason to connect McDermott with anything unlawful. It was only because he disliked him, because McDermott was to marry Anne, that the idea had entered his head to make that connection. Much as he would like to fasten some wrongdoing upon the man, the facts did not warrant it.

And Anne—he could not understand her. Any woman might be taken in by such a man, but when she admitted him to be nothing but a fortune hunter—well! The way she was with him, the way they behaved together—— Quintain swore to himself in a half-bewildered tone.

2

He had met them by chance in King William Street only yesterday afternoon, as he came out of the jeweler's shop where he had, with a heavy heart, been choosing a wedding gift for her. "Harry——" She took his arm from behind. "How nice to see you! Is it not a lovely day after all that rain?"

She looked already a little more mature than he had ever seen her, in an amber-colored gown with marten-trimmed cloak to match. There were garnets in her ears and at her throat. McDermott, suave in dark blue and maroon, with an elaborately tied neckcloth lace-edged, hovered behind her.

"You have no idea," he told Quintain, offering his hand, "how relieved I am to see another male after the afternoon I have had. She has trailed me all about the city looking at gowns, hats, curtains, carpets, Italian glass, Dresden china, French lace—I cannot remember the half of what we have seen!"

"Pay no attention to him," said Anne. "He has been very good, but we have not been from the house above an hour and a half, and he is not at all as exhausted as he sounds. I have been showing him a few of the things we will have for our house, Harry. Such lovely things, I have had such fun choosing them." And paying for them? wondered Quintain.

"I thought you told me the house you have taken is furnished."

"Oh, after a fashion, but we shall not be there forever, you know. Sooner or later we shall want to buy a house, and, besides, I want my own things," said Anne obscurely. "Are you in a great hurry? Perhaps you would join us for tea, we are going to White's Hotel."

Quintain hesitated, looking at McDermott. Damn the man! How was he so irritating, for no reason at all? Quintain, though certainly not vain of his appearance, was accustomed to respectful glances from other men for his commanding height, military carriage, and the breadth of his shoulders. Not only did McDermott not seem to mind looking up at him, but Quintain had the uneasy sensation that the man was inwardly amused at him as if at a hulking line-private, all brawn and no brain.

"I would not intrude—" he began formally, but Anne overruled him.

"Nonsense, of course you could not; only think what prestige it gives us to be seen taking tea with a baronet! If you have the time to spare, that is? There is but one more place I must take Dennis, and it is on the way to White's—it will not take a moment." As they made their way through the crowded street toward the hotel in the next square, she chattered on gaily. "It was the first thing I knew we must have, and I consulted Mr. Brewster about it a month ago. He ordered it especially from England, and it arrived only a day or two since. I have seen it, but I wished to show it to Dennis. Mr. Brewster will keep it until we settle in the house, you see——"

"And what is this very special object?"

"But the harpsichord, Harry! Of course it will mean nothing to you, unmusical as you are—you should hear him try to sing, Dennis, a dog baying at the moon—but it is very beautiful, and I want Dennis to try the tone, he plays better than I——"

"Oh, no," protested McDermott modestly, "you have a pleasing touch, my dear." They were the very model of a loving affianced pair.

In Mr. Brewster's furnishing-establishment an obsequious clerk received them and was brushed aside by the stout proprietor, who ushered them into a rear storeroom, with many apologies for disorder and dust, to display a small rosewood harpsichord newly uncrated and polished. As far as Quintain could see it was only a harpsichord, but Anne exclaimed lovingly over it and stroked the carven cupids about the keyboard.

"Do you like it, Dennis?"

Whatever McDermott's boredom with curtains and carpets, he appeared to be interested in the harpsichord. The shopkeeper hastened to pull forward the little rosewood bench; McDermott seated himself and ran an arpeggio on the keyboard. "The tone is quite good."

"Play me something?"

"If you will sing for me." He played a few measures, looking up at her with a smile, and she laughed.

"You devil, to choose such a song!" Unmusical, Quintain might be, but he could admire Anne's voice, clear and true. She stood at McDermott's side, one hand on his shoulder as she sang.

> Early one morning, just as the sun was rising,
> I heard a maid sing in the valley below—
> "O do not grieve me, O do not leave me!
> How can you treat a poor maiden so?"

McDermott joined his baritone to her voice with the second stanza:

> Thus sang the maiden, her sorrow bewailing,
> Thus sang the maid in the valley below—
> "O do not grieve me, never deceive me!
> How can you treat a poor maiden so?"

"Charming!" said the shopkeeper respectfully. "Charming!"

Quintain wondered and continued to wonder, as McDermott graciously approved the instrument, and they went on to White's for tea. Anne was prettily anxious over preparing McDermott's tea exactly as he liked it, gay over discussing wedding plans. If he had not heard her, before, confessing knowledge of the man, he would have believed her any happy young bride. How could she? He was ready to admit that McDermott's easy charm made him liked by most people, men as well as women; there was just something to the man that made him violently distasteful to Quintain himself. If there was love at first sight, perhaps there was hate at first sight too.

He called at the house on the Sunday before the wedding, to bring Anne the gift he had chosen. Guiltily he reflected that he had paid more for it than for his wedding gift to Bella, but Bella would never know. Anne was pleased, but alone with him for the first time since his attempt to coerce her, a trifle more reserved than usual. After thanking him, she did not clasp the sapphire bracelet on her arm, but laid it away in its velvet-lined box.

"Am I interrupting?" he asked. "I know you are busy."

"Oh, no, I am glad of the excuse to rest for a bit. Yes, there is a great deal to be done. I cannot turn round but the seamstress is at me for a fitting, and there are letters to write. Aunt Alice is upsetting the maids in a flurry of preparing rooms—Emily and Sophie arrive tomorrow, you know, they will attend me——"

"You are too tired to think clearly. Of course I know, and will meet them at the dock. Bella was furious at being obliged to find a chaperone for them at such short notice." But with unaccustomed perception he had heard the desolate note in her voice; and this would be his last chance to argue with her. "Anne, you cannot do this! The man is a rogue——"

"I will not listen to such talk! You are too fond of having your own way, Harry, that is all. And I never knew you had such a powerful imagination! You have conceived this absurd suspicion all from one little impulsive thing I said to you, when I was in a mood—and did not know Dennis so well as I know him now. Please, do you leave, Harry, and put all this nonsense from your mind."

He had tried, at least; perhaps he had expected to fail.

3

Well, it was a fashionable wedding. He could not pretend to enjoy it. As soon as possible he escaped from the merrymaking.

"Was it a nice wedding!" he barked to Kitty's inquiry. "What the devil do you mean by that? If you think I found pleasure in seeing her wed to that man, you are much mistaken!"

"I didn't mean nothing, Harry. Only wondered. I'd like to see a real society wedding some time," she added wistfully. "With all the fine gowns and all." Quintain, after tossing off a glass of the best sherry available in Dublin as if it were common ale, was muttering to himself, not mincing words in a description of the recent bridegroom. "Now that'll do no good," she said sensibly. "They're wed now, nobody can undo that. You'd best just put it out of your mind. And I'm sure I for one hope they'll be happy, and so ought you."

"I've too good a notion what he is to hope for that! By God, I'd like to wipe that smile off his face! By God, Kitty, if I could prove what he really is—ah, it may be a damnation fool idea, but —but——! By God," he said, "she'd be free of him if he dangled at the end of a rope!"

"Now that is a fool idea, Harry. If you feel that bad and want to kill him, you make some excuse and call him out to a duel like an honest man. Don't you want dinner?"

"No," he said shortly. When he'd gone out again, Kitty looked after him with a sigh. She wished he'd told her about the wedding, how Mistress Deering had been dressed and all, but a man didn't take much notice and with him feeling so, he wouldn't care.

Privately she thought—even apart from how she felt about it herself—that it was just as well he'd missed getting this lady. By all accounts she was a taking little thing, but a man like Harry needed more than that. Still, if he'd married her, even being in love with her, and found she wasn't his style in bed, maybe he'd not put her away, herself, like he'd planned to. Anyway, he wouldn't now—not for awhile yet, please God.

And she did truly wish Mistress Deering—no, her name was different now—to be happy with her own gentleman. Because if she wasn't, and Harry there to see, it'd just upset him all the more, and the Lord knew what would come of that.

Ten

I

Anne lay quiet in the dark and listened to the slow breath of her sleeping husband. The more wakeful part of her mind was occupied a little anxiously with the dinner party scheduled for Wednesday week, running over the list of guests—was there anyone else she should have invited? but they could not possibly manage more than twelve in that poky little dining room—wondering whether she could, after all, trust the cook at pastries instead of having a sweet trifle with plenty of ratafia cakes, really plenty, not the niggardly display one so often had at dinners. But the drowsier part was drifting over the events of the last three weeks, wonderingly, comfortably.

How silly she had been, having the vapors like a senseless schoolgirl. She had not suspected how easy it would be, how easy —to forget? Well, to accept . . . She had known in her mind he would make it easy—it was his job to do that, was it not—a wave of half-bitter, half-happy pain washing across her mind with that thought. Even at the last, she had wondered how she could do it,

[129]

how she could let herself do it. But it would be all right. Forever, it would be all right.

Emmy and Sophie. A typical Sophie comment, after meeting Dennis: "I wish I had a shilling for every woman who is envying you, Anne." And Emmy: "He's charming, dearest, you're very lucky, but I wish you were to live in London." Everyone approving of it. Uncle George, vaguely benevolent: "Time you were married, m' dear, and I daresay your aunt has chosen a suitable match. Clever young fella, eh? Yes, yes." Sir Julian beaming; Aunt Alice in such a flutter. Everyone—except Mr. Mackie.

Surprising he had come all that way for the wedding, but there he was on the Plymouth packet with Emmy and Sophie. "In a way, my dear lady, your late father left me *in loco parentis,* shall we say?" A shrewd, lean old Scot appraising Dennis as coldly as he might judge a projected bank loan or a new investment. "I have seen the managair of our local branch, my dear Mistress Anne, and arranged for the account to be transfairred," and all the while his faded blue eyes were on Dennis. "Mr. Gordon is a vairy trustworthy man—may I suggest, if you have any little worries or pairplexities, he will be only too happy to help you." Mr. Mackie knew—but not that she knew. Oh, what a fool she had been to speak out that way to Harry!—regret it all her life. All her life—with Dennis.

It did not matter, she would not let it matter. Damn the money, why should it be of great importance?—though it would be if one did not have any, of course . . . look at Amelia Franklin. The thought of Amelia had given her courage, those last few days. Everyone in London knew that Gerard Franklin must marry money—the family poor as church mice even if well-bred, and a pack of young sisters to find dowers for. And Amelia the only daughter of a wealthy, indulgent father—she might have had her pick of a dozen young men, though she was no beauty. But she had wanted Gerard, and where was the harm in that? They had

had a large fashionable wedding and gone off to the Continent for their wedding journey, and not once in these three years had Anne seen Amelia look remotely unhappy. She had a pretty little house and an adorable infant and Gerard was always pleasantly affectionate to her, in company at least. It was only silly young girls who dreamed of romance. Nine of ten marriages, among gentry, were made for convenience. Yes, look at Bella: "We will suit very well, Archie is of good family and has sufficient money, with what endowment I have. Of course it pleases me, Harry. I am quite agreeable—you may go on and discuss all the arrangements with him—much the most acceptable suit you have offered me." Marriage was like that, no reason hers should be different.

It was easy, easy to accept it—with Dennis. Her mind moved sleepily over these three weeks . . . the journey by coach to Sir Julian's country house in Wicklow, where they would spend a fortnight . . . the smiling servants receiving them. It had rained most of the time, but what was that on a wedding journey? Quite perfect, all of it . . . and then the return to the city, here to their own little house, all the lovely things she had bought for it . . . he had been angry, but only a bit. "Very well, my love, I will say no more; the house furnishings are your choice in any case, and very probably I could not afford those you would prefer." "Oh, Dennis, it is no matter, please do not worry over it—I have enjoyed my extravagance so much."

Never mind that. It was a nice house, for all its small dining hall and having a dressing closet to only the one large chamber, this chamber. Settling into her new life as a matron, all the household duties, planning the meals for cook, directing the maids, receiving the polite afternoon calls of other matrons, sipping tea, looking at the clock and thinking, He will be home in two hours.

She started back to complete wakefulness as he moved and flung out an arm. Was he about to have another nightmare, as he had last night? She half-raised herself on one elbow, peering at him anxiously. No, he was but muttering in his sleep. Not English, and not French, at least no French she knew. She lay back again, faint curiosity at the edge of her consciousness; he was quiet, and presently she slept.

2

It was a small thing, and what matter was it? Those first times when he made love to her, the strange harsh words on his tongue, and the effort of will so violent she felt it stiffen his body, and always afterward silence with his passion. She had even spoken of it, indirectly, hesitantly. "Dennis."

"My love?"

"What part of France did you live in?"

"Paris," he answered absently, and a moment later, "Why?"

"I thought perhaps you had spoken a provincial dialect I should not know."

He turned from the mirror where he was arranging his neckcloth; he wore a frown. "When? What do you mean?"

"Oh, it is of no consequence. You were muttering in your sleep, that is all, and it did not sound like English or French. I only wondered."

He stared at her and then said shortly, "It must have been one of the two. I am sorry to disturb you."

"You did not, of course." There was really nothing queer in it at all, women were always imagining secrets. He had not been thinking of her, nor cross with her, but incensed at his servant for some reason; Kincaid had come in a moment before to carry out the cold shaving-water, and said somewhat in a tone too low for her to hear, which annoyed Dennis. He was ordinarily casual with servants, but autocratic with Kincaid.

[132]

"It's not seemly, sir, for a gentleman to barber himself. I've never had any complaint from any other gentleman——"

"Enough," he said, and smiled at his reflection. "I trust my throat bare to no man—it makes me nervous." He thrust the gold pin into his neckcloth and gestured the man away.

"Dennis, if you do not like him as a servant why do you keep him?"

"Like him? Does one like or dislike servants? He is as efficient as any."

Only because he was subject to moods. She had not suspected to what extent, but she was beginning to find out . . . That day it had cleared in the afternoon, and they had gone out to stroll along the near lanes for an hour after four days of being shut up in the house. As they approached the front steps of the manor again, the old butler was gesturing furiously at a man in the drive.

"This is a gentleman's house—get you to the rear door if you expect charity!"

"What is all this, Walters?"

"I beg your pardon, sir, I'm very sorry. A beggar, sir, at the front door bold as brass——"

"Ah," he said, surveying the man. "But not only a beggar—a wandering musician, by the harp. Do you play it, my man?"

The beggar was a very tall, lanky man with a shock of red hair; his garments were stained and patched, but he took off his ancient cap with a flourish and bowed so low as almost to sweep the ground. "Thomas Kelleher at your service, my lady—and my lord. Not a bite have I had this day, and I says to meself, sure in such a grand big house they'll have a decent meal to spare for a poor man wanderin' the roads, and he the finest harpist ever came out of Kerry, not to boast, your worships——"

"Excellent!" There was excited amusement in Dennis's voice. "What could be more appropriate? You shall have your own private musician to entertain you after dinner, my dear, as the queens of old. Here, man, get round to the kitchens and have your meal. You shall play for us presently and if you are skillful, may earn a shilling or two. Delightful—some of these itinerant minstrels are quite good."

He had the man sent for after dinner when they sat cozily over a glass of claret before the fire in the parlor. "Did they feed you? Good. Let us hear some of your art." The musician stood just inside the door, uninvited to sit, his little carved wooden harp balanced across one arm. He was a strange-looking man, unkempt and ragged. He did not look like a musician. But he drew soft chords from the harp and sang in a clear sweet tenor, in the native tongue.

"You have a good voice. Will you tell us what that song was about?"

"It is a love ballad, my lady. It speaks of a maiden whose true love is dead, and she sorrows for him '. . . my lodging is on the cold ground,' she cries, 'where they have lodged my love to lie.' It is a very old song." Without hesitation he began to sing again, one long dirty hand fondling the harp strings. The first song had been melancholy, but this one was inexpressibly more sorrowful. It was queer music, all the chords unresolved, in minor key. It was disturbing music. It was a wind moaning to itself through the trees at the top of a high hill, and a mutter of thunder coming nearer. She shuddered suddenly—someone walking on her grave. The last note of the harp sent a chill finger down her spine, an unexpectedly high note like a trumpet call.

"What is that song?"

"That is the lament for the death of Shane O'Neill, lady."

"One can hear it is a lament. And who was this O'Neill?"

"A prince of Ulster, lady, a matter of two hundred years back."

"And so well-loved that a lament was made for him. Did he die young?"

"Yes, lady," said the harpist softly. "The English killed him and put his head on a spike over the gate to Dublin gaol."

Dennis stirred at her side. "Sing us something gay," he commanded brusquely. "Do you know *The Rakes of Galway?*" Yes, something gay after that weird, oddly challenging tune. The musician struck up a lively air, posturing and grinning as he sang what were evidently risqué verses, but she liked this music scarcely better. It was gay, but there was something wild about it, something primitive and uncontrolled. She was glad when it ended, and Dennis rose and found a coin for the harpist and sent him away.

"What a queer man! Are there many like him, earning their livings like that?"

"A good many," he answered abstractedly. "Not all of them are as skillful. In another time he would have been chief musician to a king or clan chief—we rewarded artists then instead of penalizing them."

"I had not heard any of the native music before. I am not sure I like it. It—it is not very pretty, is it?"

He turned away to stare down at the leaping flames in the hearth. "No," he said. "No, it is not—pretty music. It comes from the heart, and the secret things of the heart are very seldom pretty."

With a belated little shock she realized the word he had spoken —we. Remotely she heard the echo of Harry Quintain's voice— "and not even English!" No, he was not English. It was hard to realize, when he was such a perfect model of an English gentleman. But there was different blood in him, and it made him different in himself. The thought came to her, absurd a comparison as it was, that he was like the native music, all emotion a little exaggerated, the sorrow too darkly tragic, the joy too wild for permanence. There was no medium of temper in him—he could change from one mood to another in a flash, with a word or ges-

[135]

ture. She had thought she understood him, but she had seen only the surface; she knew him better hour by hour, and she thought with a strange ache at her heart that she loved him the more as she knew him.

And it was that night, after the harpist had been there, that she was roused for the first time to a passion she had not suspected in herself, and for the first time he was not gentle with her, finding that she did not need gentleness . . . "Oh, God, Dennis—so sorry —did not mean to hurt you—" and he was laughing, the taste of blood in her mouth, his hands hard and demanding.

Oh, she understood better now. Loving or not loving had nought to do with this. He pretended very well otherwise, but in this he had no need to pretend—she was a woman.

3

Yes, she had known him for a nervously sensitive man, but until now, when they were so often alone together, she had not realized how nervous. They returned to the city and settled into the house in Sydney Street in the second week of January, and entered on a different daily routine from that first fortnight. He was usually home by six, and since most Dublin society dined at an hour which would be considered early by Londoners, they had finished their meal by eight or half after and sat in the ladies' withdrawing room behind the larger parlor. "Dennis, my dear, can you not settle somewhere? If you wish me to talk or play at cards with you, tell me and I will do so, only do not walk about staring at me—you make me quite nervous."

"I am sorry, I did not mean to annoy you." Half an hour ago when they came into the room he had taken up a newssheet to read; ten minutes later he was up, pacing across to pull back the curtain and look out, fill his pipe from the silver tobacco-jar on the mantel, play a restless tattoo on the back of a chair, take the poker to the fire. For fully ten minutes now he had been walking about the room, hands in pockets, eyes on her, and then when she looked up, glancing away.

"If you wish to go out—" she began doubtfully. Very likely he was reluctant to leave her for the first time, thinking she might take it amiss. Now they were in their own house he would not spend half his evenings at home—few gentlemen did. He would be at his clubrooms with his friends, amusing himself. And if she chose, she would be out too, at feminine parties. "I would not mind if you wish to go out," she said, to put him at ease on that score.

"I did not plan to go out. Do you wish me to leave you?"

"Of course not, Dennis, how absurd." She smiled at him. He took up his news-page again and flung himself down in the opposite chair. After a little silence he laid the sheet down and looked at her.

"Anne, I am sorry to annoy you—what did I do?"

"Why, nothing. I do not like to see you so restless, that is all. Is aught worrying you?"

"No, no, certainly not. What are you so busy over?"

"The dinner party, Dennis. It is awkward—there are at least twenty people we must have, and we cannot have them all at once with the dining hall so small, but I am sure if I invite Mrs. Hazelton before Mrs. Wilde, Mrs. Wilde will be furious—she gave us that dreadful German clock, you know; it was far more expensive than Mrs. Hazelton's damask cloth—and then there are Harry and old Mr. Andrews, and I cannot think which unattached females to pair them off with. There is Mistress Pritchard——"

"Spare me! That hatchet-faced old spinster who talks of nothing but politics? Whenever I face her across a dining table I am surprised that she joins the ladies in retiring and does not ask to share the gentlemen's port."

"She is rather a terror," agreed Anne, "but we cannot have an uneven number, you know. There is Cynthia Fortescue who would do for one——"

"Have her for old Andrews and leave out Quintain. Put him off until another time."

"Oh, we cannot, Dennis! After such a magnificent gift to me, and Harry is really like my own family, you know."

"I know it all too well," he said a little wryly. She looked up from the scratched-out list of names.

"You do not really like Harry, do you? I was in hopes, when you were reconciled after that silly quarrel——"

"Why, it does not signify whether I like him or not, does it? He is your friend, and visiting here only for a brief time."

She abandoned the subject, fearing to begin a disagreement between them. "I should have the Vails also, as he is a client of yours and Mrs. Vail entertained for me, but Aunt Alice tells me she has been very ill and is not accepting invitations as yet."

"Really. The fever?"

"I expect so, there has been quite a plague of it, all this damp weather. Well, that is the best I can do. Aunt Alice and Sir Julian, Mr. Andrews, the Wildes, the Fortescues and Cynthia, Harry and old Mistress Pritchard, and that is twelve with ourselves. The week following I can—yes, that is a splendid idea. I will have Mrs. Hazelton and Mrs. Brownlee and Mrs. Vail if she is about, and one or two others, to an afternoon tea, to make it more an especial affair for them—that should mollify Mrs. Hazelton." She folded the list briskly.

"When is this dinner to occur, by the way?"

"Wednesday week, Dennis. And I pray the cook lives up to her references!"

Eleven

I

Now that she was a matron herself, it was permissible to wear deeper color. She had never liked the insipid pale shades young unmarried women were expected to choose, and Emily was used to say that it was no wonder some thought her inclined to intellectualism, a dreadful charge, by the bold colors she chose to wear. But they were vastly more becoming than delicate blues and mauves. She was especially pleased with this new gown. It was a lovely color, the color of good port wine, exactly matching Dennis's garnets. Small though she might be, no one had ever denied her excellent figure; the bodice was perhaps a trifle low, but she needed no padding like Emmy.

Carefully, leaning to the mirror, she applied a touch of cheek-rouge and reddened her lips. "It is not too much, is it, Susan?"—turning to the maid.

"Oh, no, madam, you look lovely."

"Would you fasten this, please?" She handed the maid the pendant on its chain, caught the tiny gold hoops through her ears, the garnets gleaming as she moved her head. "Thank you, and the bracelet, yes. Is Mr. McDermott not here yet? What is the time?"

"It's just gone half after six, madam."

"Good heavens," she exclaimed, "he will not have time to dress! Where do you suppose—listen, is that the door?"

It was. He came in a moment later, already flinging off his coat, stopping to brush her cheek with a kiss as he made for his dressing closet. "My love, I know I am late, I could not help it— a most tiresome old man who is forever making new wills, and I could scarcely be impolite!"

"You will have to hurry, Dennis. That is all, Susan, thank you. Dennis! The maid is gone, do you come in here." He appeared in the open door, struggling out of his shirt, Kincaid behind him with the fresh one over his arm. "Dennis, you are a disgraceful sight, you must be shaved again before appearing in company. And why you insist on doing it yourself—you cut your chin again this morning——"

"I know, I know, I know! I shall do so—there is plenty of time. Ah, my dear, is not that bodice cut a little low?"

Anne laughed. "Men! If you were not married to me, you would admire it extravagantly."

"I daresay. By the way, Anne, I am very sorry—" he was searching out his razor, wetting his face before the dressing glass. "I shall have to be out an hour or so this evening. I shall be back as soon as possible."

She stared at him. "Out? What on earth are you thinking of? We are having ten guests to dinner!"

"Now how could I help knowing that when the household has been in a turmoil over it for three days? I am sorry indeed, but it is unavoidable. I did not know until today or I should have made other arrangements. It is a client—he is leaving for England

[140]

on a ship sailing at dawn, and consequently I must see him this evening over some last-minute business."

"But, Dennis, you cannot! You cannot simply walk out and leave me alone with our guests! You are their host!"

"My darling, I have apologized—I shall apologize to our guests—but I must. It is important business, to do with some investments I make for him, and I will have no other opportunity to see him."

"But, Dennis! Could you not arrange the matter by letter?"

"No, it is necessary that I have his signature. I am sorry," he repeated. "I know it is awkward, I shall not be more than an hour."

She suppressed a hasty remark. "Awkward is scarcely the word! They will think you a rather cavalier host." Her first dinner in her own home, and he must invite their humiliation like this!

"Then they must do so, I cannot help it." Kincaid handed him the towel silently and he dried his face.

"Dennis—" She bit her lip; she did not want to quarrel before the servant. "Is there no possible way to remedy it? After all, our first guests——"

"I fear not. I am sorry, but I must go. Do not fuss over it, Anne; it is not such a tragedy! Do you go down in the event some arrive early. I will join you directly."

After a moment she left the room without speaking, realizing there was nothing to be done. He was master of the house. She was bitterly disappointed; after all her planning, her anxious arrangement that this should be a successful evening, he had destroyed it before it began. They would think it so odd, and perhaps any apology or explanation would only make matters worse, reminding the snobbish Mrs. Wilde and the old-fashioned Fortescues that Dennis was, however much a gentleman, still a lawyer, a professional man who earned his own living.

There was no point in having a quarrel about it, now or later. It did not seem so important to him, of course. She sat in the parlor disconsolately, waiting for the guests, determining to pass it off lightly, not to let it matter. By the time the parlormaid ushered in the first arrivals she was able to play the hostess smilingly.

He did not come down until after several guests had arrived. Despite his haste in dressing he looked, as always, magnificent in formal clothes—ice-blue satin, a foam of lace at wrists and throat, hair silvered with powder.

And it was not so awkward as she had feared, after all. He made no half-apologetic excuses; he captured the attention of the whole table, telling the story with drama, with many gestures. "What was I to do, I ask? Refuse my client and lose him, or turn my wife against me by discourtesy to our guests? Let the client go hang, I can hear the ladies saying, but I am a farsighted man. I said to myself, my lovely wife I can persuade into giving me another chance—the client never!" He had even Mrs. Wilde smiling. "But there is enough excellent company to entertain one another, and I forego no more time than it will take the ladies to repair their coiffures and lip-rouge and the gentlemen to enjoy their port. At least I trust they will enjoy it. I consider it very good quality myself."

He left soon after the trifle was served, promising to be back among them before they missed him. A good deal relieved, Anne saw that even old Mr. Fortescue was smiling after his host.

"Mr. McDermott must be very conscientious," pronounced Mistress Pritchard approvingly. "Young men nowadays—pah!— no purpose, no integrity! Not such as in my father's time. But your husband seems to be reliable."

"Oh, yes, and he was so vexed that this should occur, but he was adamant even when I pressed him to postpone it."

"Admirable!" said Mistress Pritchard. "Men that are men never pay notice to women—go their own way. Too polite nowadays. Namby-pamby."

"Are you looking at me, Mistress Pritchard?" asked Quintain

from across the table. "I fear I am not so conscientious as Mr. McDermott—I am scamping my work by being here."

"Oh, I'm certain you'd never do such a thing, Sir Harry!" Cynthia Fortescue, overemphatic, flirtatious.

"But I would—I am." He smiled down at her. "I must confess I am disappointed to miss out on a little excitement also. We are in the way of hoping to arrest a criminal this evening, and instead of accompanying my men to clap irons on the wretch, I dine in state with a charming hostess."

"A criminal! But how thrilling! What has he done?"

"Military secrets," said Quintain solemnly. "I can divulge no more. Suffice it that recent information enables us to be tolerably sure the man will be at a certain place at a certain time, and we hope to nab him. I assure you it is a sacrifice for me to miss the denouement! Had it not been such short notice I should have begged off this evening, Anne."

"I am so glad you did not," she returned mechanically, wondering how long Dennis would be absent. If he had not come back by the time they all gathered in the parlor it would be rather awkward, after all; she meant to have cards and Harry never played, or Cynthia; it would make an uneven number. It would surely not require long to obtain a signature? She snatched a glance at the clock; it wanted ten minutes to nine. Say half an hour for the gentlemen to spend over port—she hoped he would be back by half after the hour, if not before.

When the ladies left the dining room and trooped upstairs, she contrived to delay there as long as possible, hoping devoutly that Harry or some other gentleman would keep them talking over the port. But the guests rejoined in the parlor a few minutes before half after nine, and still Dennis had not returned. She would not let them see how vexed she was; she made conversation easily, thankfully seconded the suggestion that Cynthia should play for them upon the harpsichord. By the time the girl had displayed her inconsiderable skill it was nearing ten o'clock and Mrs. Wilde was whispering to her husband. Oh, Dennis, thought Anne distractedly, when you promised! He had gone to talking, forgetting the time, and likely at this moment was sitting somewhere over wine, his business accomplished long since.

At the first chime of the clock a little silence fell in the group, and she was casting about desperately for some further casual remark when the house-door thudded open and closed; a moment afterward he entered.

"I am abject—dare I try to apologize? But better late than never."

"Quite all right," said old Mistress Pritchard. "Conscientious—reliable! But you shall not escape me tonight, young man. I hear reports that you are an excellent hand at piquet, and I have long wanted an opportunity to match wits with you. Will you give me a game?"

"With pleasure, dear lady." Perhaps it was the hair-powder that made him look pale, or perhaps he had hurried on the way back. At all events, thank God he was here and something could be made of the evening. Hastily Anne ordered the tables set out and settled them to play, paired two and two. Harry, of course, would not play, and presently he came up to her as she watched Rosemary Wilde beating old Mr. Andrews hands down.

"I am—relieved," he said in a low tone, "to see you looking so well, Anne."

"Why should I not?" she smiled at him. "Brides are expected to be radiant, are they not?"

"As you say." He seemed a little put out, and he was the first to leave, looking at his pocket-watch, saying, "I know you will forgive my early departure. You understand that—like your husband—I have an occupation too. I am somewhat anxious to discover whether my criminal was taken." Mr. Andrews chuckled and advised him to use care or another criminal might take him on his way. "Yes, indeed, the streets are dangerous at night, I will take a chair." He made formal farewells to the company.

"We were honored by your presence," said Dennis at the door.

"You are too kind. Good night, sir. Anne—" he kissed her wrist.

"Good night, Harry." They had accompanied Quintain into the hall; as the door shut, before the maid had turned away, Dennis seized her arm.

"And you need not be so damnation friendly with him!" he said rigidly. "Your hand on his arm, calling him by name as if you said 'My darling!'"

"Why, Dennis! I do not—" She knew the maid had heard; she was suddenly furious. "A great right you have to criticize my behavior, when you abandoned a houseful of guests for half the evening, as if it were a jest!"

He looked down at her in silence for a moment. Then he said, "You do not know how lucky it was that I returned at all." He dropped her arm and went back into the parlor.

She had not the heart to pursue the argument later, as they undressed and retired. He had not spoken to her, not one word, since the last guests departed and they came upstairs. He disrobed rapidly in the dressing closet, came out with his silk robe wrapped about him, wandered around the room smoking his pipe while her maid helped her with her gown, unfastened the stays, brought out a fresh night rail. He was angry with her: had she really seemed too friendly with Harry? No—that possessive jealousy of his again, wanting to own her—not because he loved her. She thought, If I make an issue of this now it will grow between us all our lives . . . I cannot bear to quarrel with him.

"Dennis." She turned from her dressing table; the maid had gone out. "Dennis, I am sorry I was cross-grained with you this evening. It really did not matter at all, I was foolish." And a voice in her mind said mockingly, Yes, that is the thing, be meek and submissive so he will walk over you all the more, take advantage of you right and left like any autocratic husband!

The triple reflection in the pier glass showed her face troubled, half-exasperated, pale without its artificial color. He looked at her without speaking, and then put his pipe down in its tray and came to her.

"My darling, did you think I was angry at you? Foolish Anne— lovely Anne! I am not at all. I was brooding over a business matter, forgive me," and he lifted her against him. "And I never told you how beautiful you looked tonight in your new gown. You see, already I become a neglectful husband——"

"You never could!"

"But I like you much better without it, do you know that?" He had her in his arms, starting toward the high bed.

"Dennis darling, I have not brushed my hair——"

"Damn your hair for one night."

"The candles——"

"That is easily remedied." He laid her on the bed and went back to snuff the flames. She smiled to herself in the darkness . . . it had been a very successful evening, after all.

2

She had told herself that she must not be surprised, or hurt, or angry, when he asked her for money. He would do that, perhaps soon. She did not know just how he would do it, what excuse he would give, after all his protestation of caring nothing for the money. She must accept the situation as it developed . . . but even thinking about it, it was hard to remember Amelia Franklin, to plan to be wise and sensible.

Already she had paid a few household expenses without consulting him. Of course a man could not be expected to remember such matters as grocers' bills, but if it had entered his head he made no mention of it. Naturally she paid her personal maid's wages, and settled the cost for her clothes, any little trinkets she might purchase.

In London, before she was married, Mr. Mackie had paid a quarterly allowance into an account at the bank; when she wanted money she went to his office and signed an order, and he gave her a glass of claret—a mild lady's wine—and chatted with her while a clerk hurried to the bank and obtained the cash. A lady, of course, would not dream of entering such an exclusively masculine establishment as a bank. Now she would have to ask Dennis to cash orders for her, or Mr. Gordon at his private offices —she might venture there, or stop outside and ask a clerk to go in for her. How did women manage who had no men to arrange these matters?

She decided that Dennis would probably make some excuse to ask for a loan, to buy something ostensibly for them to share: plead a momentary shortage of cash and ask her to pay the bill, perhaps promising to reimburse her. That was a way he could ease into the habit of letting her pay. It was an ugly little suspicion, but she knew him so well . . . and she was right. Only it did not turn out quite as she had expected.

He broached the subject one evening at dinner, abruptly. "By the way, Anne, you know we spoke of buying a carriage and pair. You will want it to go about the city, and certainly when you are out alone of an evening, or even with me, I should prefer you to go in your own carriage rather than a chair. It is safer."

"Of course, we must do that. I shall leave the choice to you; you will know the dealers and be able to select a good pair."

"I have intended to look into the matter, but the truth is——" He hesitated, frowned, and then said, "The devil! Why not be frank? The sum is, I cannot at the moment afford the price of an equipage and horses such as I should like for you. It is false economy to buy cheaply, and—well, that is the matter." He looked away angrily.

"But, Dennis, that is no trouble. I can easily afford whatever the cost may be, you know." She held her voice steady. "If you will tell me what the amount might be, I will write you an order and you may purchase them at once."

"It is not your business to pay for such a thing—I do not want you to." The instant protest she expected.

"But, my dear"—They were like actors on a stage, reciting proscribed lines!—"it is absurd, with all that money in the bank, that we should not have what we need! What difference in whose name it is deposited?" They wrangled amiably about it, and he allowed her to persuade him at last, thirty minutes later as they sat in the withdrawing room.

"Very well, but I mislike it. I will call it only a loan, Anne, and pay it into your account when——"

"Nonsense, there can be no loans or debts between husband and wife! I tell you again, it is our money, Dennis, to use and enjoy." She was anxious to have this little scene over, try to forget it. "How much would it be?"

"Three hundred pounds should be sufficient," he said after an odd pause—it was almost as if the actor had forgotten his lines for a moment.

She went to her writing table, found the book of orders in her drawer. "I will sign it and leave the amount for you to fill in; that will be easier."

"Yes, that will serve—excellently," he agreed. She bent over the table that he might not see how her hand shook as she signed her name. Likely she would never know how much went for the carriage and pair, and how much into his pocket . . . oh, Dennis, Dennis!

He took the slip from her, looked at it. He said, "I do not like it. Not at all."

"You are oversensitive, it is quite all right. Now let us forget it, and tomorrow you will choose me a fine smart pair——"

"But it is not my money!" he exclaimed. "It is not my money!" His tone was angry and—was it bewildered? He strode across the room, turned with a quick gesture.

"Do not make all this upset about it," she began, and then gasped. He was tearing the paper violently to pieces, wadding them up, tossing them into the fire.

"No, I cannot take it," and he did not look at her; his expression was ashamed and troubled. "I will not take it, Anne. But you shall have your carriage, I promise you."

Acting again? Building more good faith in her, to convince her of his love? Oh, Dennis, Dennis . . . all his charm, all his handsomeness, had never been his sole attraction for her. She saw through him, sadly, amusedly, and so to her he was like a beloved child who lied from imagination, not wickedness.

A day or two after that she asked him to cash an order for her at the bank. "Thirty pounds will do. I am going about the shops with Cynthia tomorrow, and there is Mrs. Wilde's card party on Friday—I am sure to lose. I always do, you know."

"Very well, make out the order and let me have it." But when she gave it to him he frowned. "You have not made out the amount. You should always write it out in full, my dear; it is dangerous to sign a blank order. Suppose I should lose it, and some rogue——"

"Oh," she laughed, "I do not suppose you to be so careless as all that! I cannot be bothered—you will see to it then?"

He folded the order away in his pocketbook. "Yes, I will see to it, of course." He said no more about the danger of signing blank orders.

The following evening he tendered the thirty pounds to her without comment except to say, "Here is your money." He had thoughtfully obtained it in several denominations, large and small notes and coins.

"Thank you, Dennis." She wondered what amount he had filled in upon the order. She would never know. Did it matter? If he was really so sensitive as to prefer to take her money in secret, he would never take so much that Mr. Gordon would one day refuse to honor her orders. There should be sufficient to satisfy them both, from ten thousand a year. But it was a hard little lump in her breast, the thought of it.

The day after that he haled her out, when he came home, to admire an elegant city carriage, the body painted in three colors and the seat quilted in silk taffety, a pair of high-stepping matched chestnuts, and a stout coachman in maroon livery with silver buttons. "And a groom, and a stableboy," he told her in high spirits, "who are at this moment preparing the stables. Do you like it, my love? I have thought you might also want a small phaeton, it would be easier to manage in city traffic, though I have every confidence in Ryan's ability—his references are excellent."

"It is wonderful, Dennis—I love it all—and such a beautiful pair! But you said——"

"Ah," he said with a careless gesture, "I had a stroke of luck at the tables. It was not so costly as you might think."

3

He went out that evening, and for once she did not miss his presence. She sat alone in the little withdrawing room and thought about the money. This was an issue she must not dodge, she must be honest with herself if not with him. Amelia Franklin . . . but Gerard was not Dennis. She had married him knowing he wanted the money, accepting it as the condition of having him. She had thought, such a little time ago, that it would be so easy—loving him, knowing him. She had not suspected that his wanting the money and taking the money would come, suddenly, to seem a little shabby.

Well, it was a thing she must face. Perhaps it was degrading and poor-spirited of her, but she could not stop loving him. Harry—how little he knew about people!—she smiled. Love did not exist because of noble qualities in the one loved, or die because of—other qualities.

It was late when she went upstairs, but he had not come in. She could not sleep at once, and tossed restlessly for what seemed eternity; finally she roused, lit a candle, and looked at the clock. It was near two of the morning. He had never been so late home. And then she heard a sound in the passage. A mutter; a little thump.

She got out of bed, put on her dressing gown, and carried the candle to the door. In the passage outside Dennis was lying full length on the floor and Kincaid was bending over him. She gave a startled exclamation; the man straightened and inclined to her respectfully.

"Dennis—what is it, what——"

"No call to fret, madam. He's a bit the worse for wine is all. I'll look to him, madam. Don't you worry over it now. I'll make up a bed in another chamber an' get him tucked up," said the servant soothingly.

"Drunken——" But he never drank too much; she had heard other men chaff him because he was so careful with drink. He looked so white——

"You don't want to be troubled with him," said Kincaid, familiarly, but in her distress she was conscious only of relief that he was there. "Leave him to me, madam, an' he'll be right as rain in the morning—leastways, not exactly that, but sensible anyway." He hoisted the limp figure up with seeming ease and started for the nearest empty chamber down the passage.

She watched until he had got Dennis in and shut the door, and then retreated into her own chamber slowly . . . Drunken! That was not like Dennis—oh, how could she know? However much one loved, it was not possible to know all about a man in half a year. Heavy-hearted, she returned to bed, but she did not sleep until dawn was lighting the window.

Twelve

I

The clerk rose deferentially as McDermott came into the ante-room. "Good morning, sir. A fine day." McDermott grunted. "I have Mr. Wychbolt's contract copied, sir, in duplicate as you ordered——"

"Very well, I will see it presently. For the moment I wish to be undisturbed, MacMurrough." He went into his office and shut the door; he put a hand to his head, which was aching savagely. Overdrinking like a fool, trying to escape that way—he should have learned better than that ten years ago.

MacMurrough, he thought. That was the reason he had hired the boy, his name. It was the traitor MacMurrough who had brought the English into Ireland all those years back. His mind fumbled for the number, five hundred and seventy-nine years—do not lose count, mark it year by year, yes. It had pleased him to have the boy at beck and call, and he had been hard on him, a sharp master. Now suddenly it seemed a childish thing to have done. This MacMurrough had no more to do with that traitor than he himself with some doubtless blackguardly Ulster mac Diarmuid of six centuries back.

He sat down at the table and massaged his temples wearily. Running away, that was no use. The money, the money . . . Anne. Good God, what was five hundred pounds to her? She would never miss it, and a hundred pounds had gone for the carriage and horses in any case. He could not begin to reckon the sum he had taken from the English dishonestly. It was no matter at all, from the English.

But he had never taken money from a woman. What was the difference? She was English.

He got up and poured a glass of wine he did not want. The laudanum he had taken was not helping the headache to any extent.

There was insistent memory knocking at his mind for outlet. What was it? The money—the money. Not from a woman—and so he had gone out and got himself drunk, like a twenty-year-old idealist. Good God, he had married her for the money!— What was the thing at the back of his mind?

Daniel O'Farrell's shilling . . . he had not thought of that in years. He could not have been more than six or seven.

On an errand to the mill for his father he was, and O'Farrell was there to pay the miller. He idled along the bridge as a boy will, postponing return to work in the field, and saw the man come out. O'Farrell was counting over the money left to him—and he dropped a shilling in the grass beyond the bridge.

The boy pounced on it eagerly—the first coin he had ever handled. O'Farrell had gone on, unknowing. A whole shilling!

He carried it home to his mother, excited and proud. "Look, mother, a whole shilling!"

She dropped the wooden ladle in excitement as great as his. "Dennis—it is! A whole shilling! Where did you have it, boy? Some gentleman gave it you?"

"It will help for the rent?" he asked happily. "Father will be pleased?"

"Yes, yes, but where did you have it?" She turned the coin over in her roughened hands wonderingly.

"It was Dan O'Farrell dropped it by the mill, not knowing. And I——"

"Ah," she said regretfully, "then you must take it back to him; we cannot keep it."

He was astonished and disappointed. "Take it back? But, mother——" Father had been so worried for the rent.

She bent over him, pressing the coin into his palm . . . how clearly he remembered Ellen McDermott in that moment! A thin dark woman, her black hair in its smooth knob, her blue eyes smiling a little; she was four or five months along with his sister Bridget; and her hand on his shoulder was firm, her tone a little surprised. "Dennis, boy, it is not our money. It would be different entirely if it was a gentleman dropped it, an Englishman. But O'Farrell is one of us, and for that shilling he worked as hard as your father or myself or yourself. He will be missing it; you must take it back. We are decent, respectable people and not thieves." And as he still hesitated, reluctant to give up the shining coin, she gave him a brisk spank. "Run now and take it back to O'Farrell."

And he had run, if unwillingly, and given it back. O'Farrell had indeed missed it—his wife wept with relief when she saw it. "That is a good boy you are, Dennis, and I thank you."

A little scene he had almost forgotten. A shilling—five hundred pounds. But he would not take money for himself—no! It was for the work, the desperately needed money that went so quickly for school fees, clothes, books, ship-passage, all the necessary bribes here and abroad. The church looked to those who would study for priests, but not all by any means wished to enter the church. The money—the never-enough, damnably important money; gathered painfully, sent out secretly to swell the fund abroad. Sometimes there was a contribution from some man who had the benefit of that fund and stayed on the Continent to earn his living. But it was always short. Another hundred pounds, two, five hundred, meant fifty more boys rescued from slavery, fifty more men of learning to represent this race and thwart the oppression of the English.

Would he take money for himself, when he had seen men die for lack of five shillings to pay the rent?

"She is English," he said aloud to Ellen McDermott. "She is English."

Anne . . . he had married her to take the money . . . women are women. No woman to be trusted—loved. A twenty-year-old idealist—worse. How could he love an Englishwoman? As much a traitor to his people as that old MacMurrough.

Let be! He was a fool indeed, brooding over emotions like this. It was not important—leave it. A traitor. Yes, that was something to think about.

Speak of luck! In another thirty seconds they would have had him. His foot had been on the plank—and then the hand on his arm, the low voice: "You must go no farther, signor. The mate has betrayed and there are men waiting for you in the captain's cabin. They have a pistol to his head and the crew guarded below, but I slipped away—quiet!—men on the deck——" And as he turned swiftly, the loud command, the shot. He knew the streets better and drew away from the chase without much difficulty, but it was a near thing.

The *Amica* out of Genoa, master, Roberto Guido. The mate, the unknown voice had said, but who was to say who betrayed? At all events, whatever letters Guido had carried in secret were in English hands. More luck. If any of them had been destined for him or contained his name, a military guard would have come for him four days ago. And Guido, and Guido's ship, could not be used again; even if he were proved trustworthy, the English would be watching him too closely.

He swore, less at Guido than himself, and started nervously as the clerk tapped at the door.

"I beg your pardon, sir, I'm sorry to disturb you——"

"Yes, yes, what is it?"

"Your man, sir, come with a message from your house."

"Kincaid . . . let him come in."

2

"Oh, God almighty," Quintain had said almost prayerfully. "If it were—if it could be! What I would not give—yes, yes, William, I am but woolgathering! Go on!"

"That was on for seven of the clock, as I say, major, when we posted ourselves to wait. The man—you heard him—swore the captain expected the agent that evening, and of course all those letters we confiscated go to prove it. The *Amica* was to lie in Dublin only one day—she tied up at noon and was making to sail at midnight. If there was to be any contact made with the master, it was likelier to be attempted after dark, as you said at the time. We had bad luck, that was all."

"If I knew the man who gave the alarm——!"

"It was only natural, sir, if you'll excuse it. Richards and I were in the captain's cabin, holding a pistol on him—swearing in Italian he was, like a cat spitting, you should have heard it—and I'd got six men stationed on deck and another six guarding the crew below. What further precautions could we take? The men all had orders to make no move, to let any who came aboard get up to the cabin before closing in. One man seems to have been too anxious for the kill, and warned him off with a challenge. These things will happen."

"Two minutes more and we might have had him! I never knew such luck. You had no chance even to fire?"

"The man who shouted fired one shot——"

"To warn him further!"

"And they heard him running, so of course, like good soldiers," said Adams sardonically, "they left their posts and gave chase, all six. I sent Richards to find out what was happening when we heard the shot. By that time our man was six streets away, naturally."

"And that was at what time?"

Adams looked faintly surprised; what difference was the hour? "Oh, near half after nine, a few minutes one way or the other."

"God," said Quintain softly, "if it could be!" Disregarding Adams's curious stare, he began to pace the room rapidly, thinking. Evidence—it was no evidence at all, only one more fact that might fit in to an entirely unfounded theory. No, it was too baseless even to be called a theory. What did he have?

The night-thieves' attack. The ring, and Aspinall's death—at the waterfront, remember. That farcical affair of the Italian sailors. Somehow, against all reason, something about that said "McDermott" to him: something subtly mocking, a mannered comedy with the stage manager watching from the wings. The evidence of the French sailor. And now the bare fact that at one hour when he knew definitely that someone was calling upon a foreign shipmaster on secret business, McDermott had been absent from his own dinner party. And that was all, and a poor little list of circumstantial evidence it was. Out of a possible hundred thousand suspectable men he had dropped on one simply because he disliked that man; he had four occurrences (the Aspinall business was too farfetched to count) which could be manipulated into four links connecting that man with a criminal organization. But it would take a deal of hammering and forging to make those links solid.

[158]

Pick on any man in Dublin and find similar evidence to connect him with a crime! Go to Gore and Randall: "I have detected one of your rebel leaders, gentlemen. I know he is guilty because he was absent from home on a certain night—because he may be wearing a dead man's ring—because he witnessed a fracas between two corporals and a pack of foreign sailors." Bah! You hate him, Quintain, because he has Anne, and you would accuse him in your mind of any enormity from grave-robbing to matricide, let alone inciting rebellion.

But—but! There were nuances to these things. He was being fanciful—very well, he would not stint his fancy, he would challenge himself to prove it. Bring the suspicion into the open, and he had nought to act on; but he might discover something.

His reputation as an officer had been built partly on his attention to the men under him; he knew his men well. Now he went over the list of them in his mind, deliberately, before choosing three he could trust to do the job discreetly.

"Hawkins—Wells—Daly." Two corporals and a private. "I am assigning you to special duty, and I must impress on you that it is not to be discussed with anyone but myself. I want you to play nursemaids"—he smiled—"to a certain gentleman. He is to be followed wherever he goes, and he must not know he is followed. I think I can trust all of you to accomplish that. I want this man under observation twenty-four hours a day. I want to know where he goes and if possible what he does at all times. You may as well keep to uniform—there are always soldiers about the streets, and it will even afford you an excuse for loitering. But I warn you, the man you watch must not know you are watching him, for there is no evidence to bring against him, and if I am asked, by my own superiors or himself, why I put a guard on him, I have nothing to answer. I have told you so much because you are, I believe, trustworthy men. Do you understand? Good. Now——"

More waste of time, like the special port-guards. Nothing

would come of this. But he had taken the decision; now act on it!

"You will relieve one another—arrange it among yourselves. One of you to report here to me each morning."

"And the man, sir?"

"The man is one Dennis McDermott, a gentleman-lawyer— the house in Sydney Street, his offices——"

And that was five days ago. For five days he had at intervals damned himself for an imaginative fool. Wasting time, his own and that of three men . . . nothing, nothing in their reports. Departed Sydney Street half after nine, repaired to offices. At one of the clock took chair to Durfee's clubrooms; remained one hour and a half; walked back to offices. At five of the clock returned Sydney Street, remained in all evening. Visitors, office: Mr. Fortescue, Mr. Clark of England Street, Mr. Vail, unidentified gentleman who stayed half an hour, second unknown gentleman arrived in carriage with crest on panel . . .

But some obstinacy made him hesitate about calling the men off. Give it a chance. A month, two, three, one day there might be something. And aside from the other business, what would he not give to catch McDermott out visiting a woman, or in any other little peccadillo that might turn Anne against him!

3

For eleven years McDermott had been accustomed to living on guard, keeping every real emotion under cover, knowing that any man—the man who served him wine, the man who partnered him at cards, the man who paid him to draw up a will—any man might be the means to destroy him if he made only one error. A look or a word to make his status as Anglophile or gentleman suspect would be only a little less disastrous to his personal fortunes than direct betrayal of his position as conspirator. So he looked on every man as a potential enemy, and even with his servant he was on guard.

Kincaid had been with him six months; he was an efficient servant, but in that time McDermott had come to suspect that he was that irritating, and dangerous, type, a curious servant.

But he was not concerned with Kincaid at the moment, only with the message the man brought. Against all common sense he had a vision of Anne taken ill suddenly, an accident to the carriage—Anne—and he rose from his chair as Kincaid entered.

"Well, what is it?"

Kincaid turned and closed the office door behind him carefully, a big burly man in his drab servants' suiting, self-effacing, deferential. "I beg pardon to disturb you, sir——"

"Yes, yes, what is the message?"

Kincaid said in Gaelic, "I have got a message for you, but it is my own."

All McDermott's nerves quivered alert. He sat down again. He said coldly, "Keep to a civilized tongue—how am I to understand your peasant gibberish?"

"Well, seeing you talk it in your sleep how was I to know you do not talk it awake?" asked Kincaid in a reasonable tone. "It is not to interfere—I am curious, but a man's secrets are his own and especially in what I think this business to be—but I have information you should know, McDermott." There were no titles of quality in the Gaelic, but his voice was still deferential, almost humble. "I thought it best to come here to be sure of speaking private."

A lightning decision to be made. McDermott looked at him in silence. To gain time he said noncommittally, "Do I not tell you to speak English to me?"

"Well, if you will have it, sir, I know you can't be certain I'm to be trusted." Kincaid dropped his voice. "It's awkward, I see it is, but I had to speak. My confessor is Father Terence Lannery, p'raps you'd know him, he'll give you a good report of me, sir. And might be I'd best just say what I've come to say and you stay quiet, sir; that way you needn't commit yourself. You needn't fear I'd say a word to a soul, a pleasure to serve you if it's the business I think it is."

"I have not the remotest idea what you are talking about," said McDermott, "but I will listen to you a little further. Do you want a rise in wages, is that it?"

"You're a clever one," said Kincaid admiringly, "and you'd never give yourself away in a sensible state, sir. But many's the night I've heard you mutter away to yourself in sleep, an' last night when you was in liquor 'twas all I could do to keep you quiet—shoutin' out some of the finest curses on the Sassenachs I ever listened to, a pity it was I had to miss any of it. I tell you straight, sir, I've been curious. I wasn't with you a week afore I was curious, you talkin' the tongue in your sleep that way. I didn't go to interfere, sir, but I followed you a few times when you was out at night, just to see. And you didn't go to that place in King William Street, or down to the waterfront, after a woman —that much I know. Maybe you're surprised I could do that without you knowing, but I'm quiet on my feet, sir—a good servant's got to be."

McDermott said, "Go on, please." He crossed the room and locked the door, never taking his eyes from the man.

"Before God and the Apostles," said Kincaid hurriedly, "you needn't be feared I'd give you away, sir. If I was off to get a reward from the English, wouldn't I have done it afore? I'd made up my mind to speak, only to ask if there's maybe a way I could help, but knowin' how you'd take it, I put it off. Only you'd ought to know about this, that's why I come now. There's chaps followin' you in the street, Mr. McDermott—regular." McDermott did not speak, but continued to watch him. "Listen, sir, I'd cut out my tongue afore I give away aught to them, you can trust me. I'm out of Tyrone, sir, not a southron. Well enough I know you're Ulster too by the way you talk the tongue. It's not much learning I had, sir, only what the masters could din into me times I hadn't to help in the fields, and it's only like yourself, sir, asking pardon, that I'm Anglophile, so I'll be let to live in a town and take decent work to better myself. I've not renounced the church save to the English, I go to confession regular, Father Terence knows me—they could put me on the rack and I'd never speak. They hanged my father for an outlaw, sir——"

"Then that is a thing we have in common," said McDermott, moving at last. "So my tongue betrays me in sleep. Yes, if you had it in mind to tell anyone, you would have done that without coming to me, would you not? Unless you thought I would pay better than the English." Kincaid spoke his mind, succinctly and obscenely, about the English. "And what business do you think I am engaged in?"

"It's nothing for me to ask into," said Kincaid, reverting to his own tongue, "and I'm not asking. Whatever it is, it's not to the Sassenachs' advantage and I say God speed the work. Let me tell you about these men, now, and be sure you can trust Brian Kincaid's word. I've committed most sins but never yet helped the English. I happened to see this one man, McDermott, outside the house, two days back—a common soldier. In the morning it was, and you were late. I came out just after you on an errand you'd set me in the city, and saw him trailing you down the street. So I was curious, and I says to myself, we'll just see, and I put myself outside your offices when I'd done the errand, and watched. He was there, standing about like any off-duty soldier waiting for a girl to make up to or someone to offer him a drink. But he never moved far from the door, and when you come out and went to your clubrooms for a meal, he was right after you. Well, I came away, but when I knew you'd be coming back to the house I went a bit down the street and hid in an alley and watched. And when you came, here he was behind you like hound after master—big chap he is—only after you went in, he waited round a bit until another soldier came up, and they had a word, and then off he goes and the other one stays. I've kept an eye out since, and there's three of them altogether, on watch at all hours."

"Soldiers," said McDermott thoughtfully, pouring wine. "Surprises are coming at me right and left these days."

"Do you know what's behind it and what they're after?"

"Yes, I believe I do. This is helpful to know, but I wish I knew something else—what to do about you." He looked at Kincaid. "I could murder you now and dispose of the corpse after dark, or offer you a sufficient bribe to keep you quiet until I find it more convenient to get rid of you—or I can take a chance on trusting you, of course."

"I swear by the virgin——"

"Do not trouble, the devil can always quote Scripture. You sound like an honest man. If you are not, I shall surely have to dispose of you permanently—you know too much to be left alive. But then it is also true," added McDermott reflectively, "that if you have been collecting information in the hope of increasing the reward on me, and this is a trick to make me betray myself, then I shall likely have no chance to kill you—you will go straight from here to the military."

"You can put me in chains," said Kincaid passionately, "and keep me under your eye—I swear——"

"I fear the sight of you chained in an opposite chair might startle my clients. I have taken chances before. If this one goes wrong I have still had a good run. We shall see about these soldiers, and meanwhile my thanks for speaking—if it is true. Get you back to the house and I will speak further when I come in this afternoon."

Kincaid, looking relieved, stood up. "A gentleman you are. It is all true, I swear it—you'll see them yourself once you look. And you can trust me, McDermott. I don't know what you may be in to, but when there are English soldiers after a man, that is enough to give him credit with me—or any other honest man."

Thirteen

I

Yes, he had taken chances before; but his life had all too often depended on his judgment of men for him to afford errors in that judgment. Kincaid was probably trustworthy—up to a point at least. Any man who had seen his father hanging in chains was not likely to accept gold from the hangmen.

The soldiers, that was another matter. Trackers meant suspicion, and suspicion meant he had given cause for it in some way—how? Was it Quintain's doing, and not only how but why? This might be serious.

When he left his offices in the middle of the day he looked about casually as he came into the street. Dublin was full of common soldiers; he saw a line-private across the road, a sergeant of cavalry walking with a serving-woman, a troop-corporal idling against the corner of the building. He went on to Durfee's; when he came out an hour later he noted several soldiers about the street, but none of the same men. However, when he left his offices again at half after four, the troop-corporal was having his boots polished by an industrious street-urchin at the corner of the square.

He returned home to Sydney Street in a thoughtful mood. Kincaid had evidently been waiting for him, and forestalled the parlormaid in opening the door.

"If you'll wait a bit, sir—'tis safe enough, the other servants are in the rear—I want to show you the two of them. Come into the parlor, sir; you can watch from the window. I see the same thing happen yesterday."

He let the man lead him into the parlor and stood a little back from the window, Kincaid holding the curtain aside. Almost at once the troop-corporal came into sight, strolling leisurely up the center of the footpath, a man obviously off duty with no particular destination in mind. He paused outside the house, glanced all about, sat down on the carriage-block and wriggled one boot half off as if it pinched him, yawned, stood up and idled a few yards farther down the street.

"You convince me," said McDermott. "I have seen him twice before today—but I would not have if I had not been looking."

"Just wait, sir."

Another man in uniform appeared, walking from the opposite direction; they both wore the blue-and-buff of Territorial troops. They spoke together briefly; then the second man clapped the other on the shoulder, and he turned, striding briskly up the street. The other, after standing indecisively for a little, drifted out of the watchers' vision alongside the house.

"The one's took over guard from the other, sir."

"Seemingly." McDermott frowned. "M'mm—yes. I think something must be done about this. I should very much like to ask one of those two a few questions."

"You're not thinking you'd get the right answers, sir?"

"One never knows. Courtesy works wonders . . . is my wife at home?"

"No, sir, she—the mistress is gone out to some female party, sir."

"Ah. I shall change to the maroon satin for dinner——"

"Yes, sir," said Kincaid, looking disappointed as a child deprived of a promised outing.

"And after dinner I shall have a small piece of work for you to do."

"Yes, sir!"

"And you will further oblige me," said McDermott, "by ceasing to call me 'sir' except when others are about to hear. We are not a subservient race. No man is inferior to another in importance as an individual, although I will admit to you that I enjoy being sirred by Englishmen."

"Yes, McDermott," said Kincaid, grinning.

2

"You will not mind if I leave you this evening, my dear?"

"Of course not, Dennis—so long as you do not overdrink again." She smiled at him, but he thought forcedly. He made a grimace, bending to kiss her.

"Do not mention it! I am occasionally led astray by my wild companions, but it will not occur again. Am I forgiven?"

"Of course, my dear . . . you frightened me."

"Then it will surely not happen again. I shall not be late. Good night, my darling." He went upstairs for his cloak—and to see Kincaid.

"I am going out"—he fastened the frogs quickly, took up his tricorne—"and so are you. Now listen. When I leave the house, do you wait in the shelter of the door until you see this watchdog start after me, and then follow. Do you know England Street— that narrow alley three houses down on the right-hand side?"

"I know it."

"Good. It is a dark night. I will wait inside the mouth of the alley. Close up on the man and we will trap him between us. I have a burning desire," said McDermott, "to ask him one small question."

"What is that—the name of his next kin?"

"No, the name of his commanding officer. Follow me down, and keep close enough to be ready when I move on him." He ran down the stair and let himself out of the house.

The early winter dusk had shut down; Sydney Street was quiet and no chair or linkboys shed light before them anywhere. He stood for a moment on the step, to give the man time to identify him, come up ready to follow; then he set off at a leisurely pace toward the junction of Sydney and England streets two hundred yards away. Although he listened he could hear no pursuing steps, and gave both the corporal and Kincaid good marks.

At the corner of the square he turned left down England Street, crossing to the right-hand side of the road. Where the stone wall of the third house down made a barrier, a little dark thread of alley wound down between the wall and a tall hedge confining the next house; he slipped quietly into it and waited motionless three steps from the footpath.

For the space of ten heartbeats there was silence, and then he heard a faint betraying stir of cautious feet on packed earth—the corporal, unsure of his quarry in the dark but certain he must be somewhere ahead, and proceeding with care. McDermott stepped out of the alley, heard a quick movement nearby at the sound of his approach, and saw the man as a vague blur, blacker in the blackness.

"Stop where you are," he said. "I have a pistol and there is a man behind you."

Whatever else one could say of the average British troop-corporal, he was not noted for timidity. This one, who perhaps had a distorted notion of the courtesy of Dublin nightrunners, evidently assumed it was one of that gentry who addressed him. He growled, "Keep back, whoreson, you'll take nought from me!" and ran straight at McDermott, tugging at his pistol. McDermott staggered back under the unexpected attack and struck out blindly; at the same moment Kincaid cannoned into the man from behind, and all three went down in the muck of the alley.

"Get out from under, I'll take him," panted Kincaid. A fist landed in McDermott's ribs; he struggled free of the tangle; Kincaid rose to his knees and after planting a large fist in the corporal's face, started to haul him to his feet. The corporal, swearing mightily in a Cockney accent all the while, rose up suddenly and swung a wild blow at Kincaid, who promptly landed his fist well and truly on the man's jaw. The corporal's head snapped back and he fell heavily against the stone wall a yard behind him.

"Anxious to start a fight, was he not," said Kincaid.

McDermott said resignedly, "You must be an honest man—only an honest man would be such a fool. I want to question the bastard, not murder him. A fine chance I have of getting aught out of him after this!"

"I ask your pardon indeed"—Kincaid sounded offended—"but he had his hand-gun out; in another second it would have been in your chest." He bent over the limp figure. "What shall we do with him?"

"Gag him first. When he comes to life he will raise an outcry the watch could hear from across the city."

"I think you are wrong," said Kincaid in a different tone. "I never meant it, McDermott, but the man is dead."

"Dead!" He joined Kincaid on the ground. "Good God, do not tell me! He cannot be——" The words died on his tongue. His hand found the broken skull where the wall had battered out the life. "Jesus, Mary, and Joseph!" he exclaimed furiously. "Damn

[169]

you to hell for a fool, Brian Kincaid! Now you have killed him on me and I can learn nothing from him!"

"I am very sorry, I never meant it; it was the wall," said Kincaid apologetically.

"Good Christ, have I not eyes? His skull must have been thin as an eggshell. Now what to do? This is a muddle of accidents——"

"Leave him and come away, McDermott. The watch will put it down to nightmen. We can take the other one tomorrow night," suggested Kincaid, suddenly struck with the idea. McDermott raised his eyes to a moonless sky.

"Heaven deliver me from such fools! Why did I want to question him? To discover who is the principal setting him to trail me—and to warn them I know of the guard. And to have him found dead three hundred yards from my own door! I do not know what is behind this, but I have no urge to find out from a military judge. Good God, what an annoyance! For once I am sorry to see an Englishman dead! Here, help me lift him; we must get him away from this district."

Kincaid obeyed clumsily and they got the corpse up between them, arms dangling limply. "Where do we take him?"

"Anywhere a sufficient distance away. Get his arm about your neck, so—if we meet anyone we are three drunken roisterers—sing, and for God's sake, remember to sing in English!"

3

"Corporal Daly, major."

Quintain looked up. "Good, send him in." Daly entered, came to attention and saluted. "Well, what have you for me? I see you have changed your duty about. Wells has been on during the night, has he not?"

"Yes, sir, but we've not changed. Private 'Awkins takes nine

to five, sir, an' Wells up to midnight, an' then me. But 'e slipped
out on us last night, sir. I'm sorry—it's all that girl, you needn't
go blamin' 'im——"

"Mrs. McDermott? What do you mean, charging—how could
you lose him?" demanded Quintain. "Did he throw you off deliberately, has he discovered your watch? How——"

"Oh, not Mr. McDermott, sir. It's Wells, but I said to 'Awkins,
it's all that girl. She——"

"Begin at the beginning and tell me what you are talking
about!"

"Well, sir, when I come up to take over from Wells, 'e wasn't
there. We had the arrangement to meet at Sydney Street, account
of from the first, barring one night, 'e's been back at the 'ouse
afore midnight. Wells said if so be 'e stayed out later—McDermott, sir—'e—Wells, sir—'d keep on him until 'e came back, bein'
as 'e—Wells, sir—was on short duty. So I waited by the 'ouse,
thinkin' they'd show up any minute, but when 'e—McDermott,
sir—come, why, Wells wasn't be'ind 'im. 'E was with two other
gentlemen, sir. I know one of 'em on account I've seen 'im with
Mr. McDermott afore an' asked around to get 'is name. It was a
Mr. Fothergill, 'e lives in Berengaria Street. 'Oo the other one
was I don't know, but I 'eard their talk as they come up—in a
chair they was—an' Mr. McDermott said somewhat about cards,
so I take it 'e was hat 'is clubrooms, sir. An' Wells wasn't there."

"Lost him," said Quintain. "But did he not come back to the
house to see you and learn if McDermott was at home?"

"No, sir. I'll tell you 'ow it is, sir, an' you needn't blame 'im.
'E's conscientious ordinary, sir, but I reckon 'e just figured, well,
there wasn't much stirring with Mr. McDermott settled at cards
in 'is club, and 'e—Wells, sir—sloped off to see that girl. 'E's got
a girl 'e's struck on, kitchenmaid at a house in Gloucester Square,
an Irish. I reckon 'e's got orf with 'er at last an' that's why 'e's not
showed up to report this morning, sir—if 'e 'asn't."

[171]

"No, he hasn't," said Quintain grimly. "Well, I thought Wells had enough fatigue-duty to his score to obey orders. We'll see what he has to say for himself."

Wells, however, would have nothing more to say for himself. An hour later an official of the city watch presented himself to the officer of the day and asked if any company was missing a corporal. A uniformed corpse had been found by the watch, victim presumably of nightrunners, since the cause of death was a battered skull and the body was stripped of valuables. The uniform? Blue-and-buff. Territorial troops. Quintain sent Sergeant Polwhistle down to the city morgue, and was soon informed that the corpse was that of Wells.

He said perfunctorily, "Poor devil," but unaccustomed excitement stirred in his mind. He repaired to the morgue in person to examine the corpse and question the members of the watch who had found it.

"Where was it?"

"Half into an alley it was in Kinsale Street, major, that's near the east gate, across town. A rare district for thieves, an' you know how they'll wait inside an alley to pounce out on a man walkin' alone. Killed him at the first blow, stripped 'im, and left 'im where he fell."

Quintain thought about that. Quintain wondered. Do two halves of separate wholes make one whole put together? One man out of a hundred thousand possible to suspect—no real reason to pick him as suspectable. The one soldier out of a thousand set to keep watch on him—found dead—conveniently for that man? Who could say where McDermott had been last night, save the dead man? Playing at cards at Durfee's with James Fothergill! For how long? And what did it matter? Kinsale Street was not too far from Gloucester Square. Wells might have slipped his duty, been on his way to see his doxy there. Nothing could ever be proved about it.

But—but! It was one more thing. Quintain swore. Groping in the dark—fencing with one's shadow!

Logically or illogically, one thing was settled in his mind. He was going to keep that guard on McDermott, waste of time though it might prove to be—still in the hope of discovering something definite.

4

After a day's reflection on it McDermott had made some deductions, and while he was not exactly easy in his mind, had reached the conclusion that he was in no immediate danger.

"It is Quintain," he said positively. "I knew we should regret it that those nightmen bungled their work."

"Why?" asked Burke. "What reason has Quintain to suspect you? If he had anything definite, a witness or a document, his men would not be trailing you about the streets but guarding the door of your cell in Dublin gaol."

"Exactly. And one reason I thought to challenge the guard, bring it into the open and defy him to prove somewhat against me or call off the watch, was that fact. He cannot prove anything. Quintain has no love for me on several counts." McDermott smiled. "He dislikes me most of all for no reason—you know how two men will meet and instantly hate? Also he knew my wife in England. He disapproves of her wedding me and suspects I took her for her fortune—which I did."

"I always said you would regret taking an Englishwoman to wife," observed Joyce.

"It is none of your affair. The point is, Quintain has no reason to connect me with the business he is concerned in investigating. He would like to have a reason. If he had anything definite, as Burke says, he would take definite action."

[173]

"The guards are close enough to it for me," said Nealy nervously. "I hope to God you made sure to lose them before coming here."

"I did. One man may be replaced, but not all of you at once. God damn the man—forcing me to creep out by the servants' door! And that is another thing—I had hoped to see Calhoun here."

"He will likely not be south again until late March, the roads as bad as they are. Was it anything of importance?"

"Tyrone is in his district. I want him to look out Kincaid's record." There were ways of checking on Kincaid, people who had known him, perhaps his family. "Not of great moment, no."

He did not hear Kelleher say, "That business of Calhoun's son was a blow to the heart for him. He is changed—aged." He was thinking, trying to plan.

"Awkward is a mild word for this. I expect to die at the end of a rope, but I tell you, not with Quintain at the gallows-trap! I have no love for him either—and I deserve to be hanged if I cannot outwit him. Now listen, John. I will make every effort to meet the boats and collect the letters, and look to the boys too. The incoming letters are nothing—I can catch the masters at a dockside tavern and arrange to meet them later in secret and take delivery —Quintain's guards can stay there forever for aught I care on that score—but these men trailing me, that is another thing. However, I have a trick in my sleeve for Quintain, to settle the affair once and for all." McDermott laughed. "I should not be surprised if Quintain were already calling himself a fool to go so far with no reason."

"I say again, let us not give him a reason," said Nealy. "What is a delay of a few months if it saves all our lives? Better lie quiet and do nothing until those watchdogs are called off you."

"And it may come to that. We shall see."

Nealy swore. "If what you say is true it all goes back to that Englishwoman. Is he in love with her?"

"By Christ," said McDermott, "if I thought that—! No—no. It is only that he sympathizes with her, as another English, and hates me."

"All her fault—I said you would regret it," Joyce said gloomily. "When did English not spell trouble, whether male or female? How any man——"

"Hold your tongue off my wife!" exclaimed McDermott furiously. "It is no one's blame, a chapter of accidents is all——"

"I can speak my own opinion, can I not? You may earn your living as you please, McDermott, cheating your clients or bedding with an English heiress, but when you bring danger on the rest of us——"

"Quiet, in the name of God!" said Kelleher violently as McDermott rose in wrath. "Now McDermott is right, Joyce. It is none of your affair or ours either. I once mistrusted him, and I ask his pardon again, but in this he is right. A man's wife is his own business and nought for any other man to meddle with. What have women to do with politics or allegiances? You hold your opinion to yourself, Joyce."

"Thank you, Thomas." McDermott sat down again, directing a cold stare at Joyce. "If any of you feel I am neglectful of my duty or incompetent to do it, you have the obvious recourse of appointing some other man. I need not remind you it is a job not every man would want."

"Peace," said Father Devin, breaking a long silence. "No one accuses you of incompetence. In any event, you are not married to the woman by church law—only the Anglican——"

"By God," and McDermott sprang up again, "peace yourself, you old fool! I am married to her as fast as law can tie the knot! You will not miscall her in my hearing——"

"Be quiet, all of you!" commanded Burke in a sudden loud voice. "What in God's name are you all wrangling about? This is supposedly a meeting of intelligent men."

[175]

"So why bring women into it? That is what I said," put in Kelleher.

"I cannot see that McDermott's wife has aught to do with our business. And Father, you are in the wrong, you know Mc-Dermott has renounced the church."

"I have not! No man accuses me of renouncing aught to curry English favor! It is not a matter of churches—one is as senseless as the next—I am agnostic, but I do not press my views on others. Let every man believe as he chooses——"

"And this is not a discussion of theology or philosophy!" Burke smacked his hand down on the table as Devin opened his mouth to speak and Kelleher, looking interested, half-rose, while Ferguson raised an admonitory hand and cleared his throat. "God help us, I sometimes think it is that reason we lost our country and fail to win it back in five hundred years—so occupied arguing philosophies and arts among ourselves, we chase round in circles while the conquerors rob us blind! What matter is it? I am with McDermott—every man to his own mind, but I would add the condition, so long as he does not express it! Now let us get on with the business, for God's sake."

"You are right—I ask pardon," and McDermott inclined stiffly to the priest. "It was only that they angered me with talk of my wife."

"Let us forget it," said Kelleher, smiling down at his harp. "Though if you forgive it, I never expected to hear you defending a Sassenach—of whichever sex."

"I am not—it is only——"

"One would almost think he was becoming romantic over the woman," said Ferguson.

"Let be! I am nothing of the kind. How could I love an Englishwoman? It is only that I am concerned about this investigation, and short-tempered. Now let us get on with the business."

[176]

Yes—how could he? A long time and a far way to a day he had believed in fairy-tale romance. If he ever had, wholly. Nothing in life was what it seemed: the priest under his dignified robes a lecher, the statesman behind his honest oratory a thief, and only too often the beautiful lady with her fastidious manners a trull. Very well: take it as it was and expect nothing better, enjoy it for what it was and expect nothing more.

That five hundred pounds . . . once he had her, hesitant to use her—that way. Feeling like a thief—with an English. And, oh, Christ, remembering all the wives he had bedded, the jests about the husbands, and thinking, Not Anne, of course not Anne. No English to be trusted in any particular. No! He knew too much about women, about her, not to know she was his, that he had her fast in love with him. Did he? What man ever knew all about women?

Only last night, that damnable dangerous emotion tricking him again . . . lying warm in the darkness after passion, and her voice soft in his ear. "But, my dear, do you not want children? That is unnatural. I should like, oh, let us say six—are you agreeable to that? Three of each, of course. Let me choose the names, now——"

"Pray do not saddle me with such a brood!" Trying to jest: "Why look so far into the future?"

"But that is what you always say . . . m'mm, of course I do . . . yes, my darling . . . do not try to change the subject now! Am I one of your vain society ladies to think only of my figure? Six, I said."

His sons half-English. Anne's sons. And the treacherous vision in his mind, Anne laughing down at a small boy, a boy with chestnut hair and blue eyes. Celia Vail. Liam—Sean.

"Dennis, you hurt me . . . no, it is no matter—changing the subject again . . . or are we? Dennis——"

No, not to be thought of, not to be considered. Leave it—put it away. There were more important things to think about. Pretend it is not there. Christ, he was a fool . . . and another little insistent memory in him, his mother's voice on an old tale to amuse the children: *And she laid a spell on him, the fairy-woman, that he should think of nothing but her, and cleave only to her for his true love, forever and a day more.* . . .

Fourteen

I

Anne adjusted the cherry-colored velvet hat to a slightly more dashing angle before the mirror in the forepassage and took up her cloak. "Have you ordered the carriage, Kincaid?"

"Yes, madam, it's just coming round the drive now, madam."

At the door she paused. Bother—she had meant to speak to cook about the joint. She was late already and it would waste more time to have cook fetched up to the dining room; she turned and went down the passage toward the service-premises at the rear. It might be unconventional for a lady to set foot in her own kitchens, but she must not offend Mrs. Fortescue by being another quarter-hour late, and Dennis had complained twice about overcooked beef. She opened the door to the servants' sitting room which adjoined the main kitchen.

"—Gentleman? 'Im? Oh, 'e puts on the look of it, but there's no gentry of Irish, my girl. Worse-born than you or me likely. The mistress, now, I'd not say a word against 'er, a sweet young thing, but you know 's well as me 'e took 'er for the money.

Smarmy ways, all of 'em—no proper feeling, it's all put on. An' they like to keep English servants. You note there's not an Irish in the 'ouse barrin' 'is own man, an' I dessay that's on account a decent Englishman wouldn't put up with 'im as master. I wager——"

Anne stood rigid, listening to the slow ponderous voice from the kitchen.

"—That Kincaid, 'e could likely tell a few tales of what Mc-Dermott's really like. Sorry I am for the mistress, 'er wed to 'im as wants only what she can give 'im in coin, not bed. She——" The voice cut off abruptly as Anne stepped into the kitchen. "Lawks—my lady——" The cook and one of the two parlormaids were sitting at the table over a steaming pot of tea.

She was so angry that it was hard to control her voice, but one did not show emotion before servants. "You did not expect to see me in the kitchens, did you——" It was absurd, she did not know the woman's name. "It will not be necessary to give you the orders I had in mind. I want you out of this house within the hour."

"Mistress—I ask pardon; it was but talk, I didn't go to——"

"That is talk I do not care for. I will not discuss it with you. Take your belongings and go. And as for you"—she looked at the maid—"if I hear of any repetition to the other servants, you will go too!"

"Madam—my wages——"

Anne grasped at her vanishing temper. "You will most certainly receive no wages and no reference when you are discharged for impertinence! I will not discuss it, I said. Now go—as quickly as you may." Trembling with suppressed rage and shame, she came out and returned to the front passage. Even the servants gossiping——

Kincaid swung the door open politely. She said without looking at him, "Kincaid, I have discharged cook for rank imperti-

[180]

nence to your master. She is to be gone from this house within an hour, and I desire you to make sure of that."

"Yes, madam." Kincaid sounded pleased.

"As to dinner, something must be contrived for this evening, and I will obtain another cook tomorrow. The maids must look to it tonight."

"Yes, madam. I'll see to it."

She went out; Ryan touched his forehead to her, opening the carriage door. "Mrs. Fortescue's house in Berengaria Street, Ryan." By the time she was set down at her destination she was sufficiently in command of herself to behave as usual, and perhaps that little bout of anger was beneficial, for she actually won seven guineas from Rosemary Wilde, a notoriously sharp player. But inwardly she was still angry—and shamed. Servants talking about them, speculating about them, sniggering.

She could not tell him about it; she did not think she could discuss it calmly. He need not know, unless Kincaid said something to him, and in that event she must make light of it, invent some small impertinence as an excuse.

But she was taken unawares. When she came in he had already arrived home, and was in the withdrawing room reading a news-sheet. He asked about her card party, congratulated her on the seven guineas, and did not mention cook at all, so evidently Kincaid had said nothing to him. She was ridiculously relieved; there was no reason he should ever know anything about it. She went up to her chamber to change to a less ostentatious gown, since they were dining alone, and hoped that Kincaid and the maids among them would contrive the semblance of a decent meal.

The hope was vain. The potatoes were half-raw, the joint over-cooked, the pudding wore a black crust. She waited for him to voice some complaint, but he said nothing. She could not hope he had not noticed; she said, "I fear I shall have to find another cook; this one grows worse and worse. I am so sorry."

"You are not blaming the recent one for Kincaid's defects, are you? He told me you had discharged the woman—was he mistaken?"

"Oh!—no, certainly not. I—I did not know you knew of it." Why had he said nothing before? "I will visit an agency tomorrow and find another——"

"He said you were offered some impudence and were rid of the woman on the spot. What was it, my dear?"

"Nought of importance really. I did not wish to bother you with it."

"Ah, I wondered why you did not mention it. How was the woman rude to you?"

She was unprepared with any tale; she knew from his tone he would keep on at it until he had some account of the incident. She could not tell him the servants were gossiping about their marriage, but neither did she want to lie to him. Unconsideringly, halving the truth like a Jesuit, she said, "Oh, it was not precisely to me; I overheard her making some criticism of yourself—quite familiar, as servants will do, you know. One cannot let them get out of hand, and I——"

"Of myself?" He put down his fork and looked at her interestedly. "I see. What criticism exactly did she make?"

"I cannot recall the words, it was—an aspersion on your character——"

"As a gentleman, a lawyer, or a husband?" he asked. "Yes, I rather fancied that was why you had not told me. Shall I tell you what the servant was saying?" Now he had gone rather pale, and his eyes glittered with cold anger. "The poor mistress, wed to this upstart of an Irish! No more a gentleman than her coachman! Only for the money he married her at all! That was it, was it not?"

[182]

"I—yes, something like that, I really paid little notice save that it was disrespectful. Servants will gossip about their employers, you know. Once she knew I had overheard I——"

"Oh, I see!" he said softly. "Otherwise you would have passed on and let it go—perhaps agreeing with her!"

"Whatever do you mean, of course I did not imply——"

"Oh, did you not? Yes, perhaps you are sorry already. Do you think I do not know what all your English friends write you in their letters—and you reading between the lines? Poor Anne, marrying one of these odd Irish colonials, no background of course, first-generation gentry, no telling how he will treat her! Oh, you pretend well enough, but I know, I know what some of your friends here are saying! So foolish and improvident to wed any foreigner! Yes, you pretend very well——"

"Dennis, I never meant—what has set you off like this? You are but imagining it——"

"—So patient and kind with me," he went on unheeding her, his voice rising with every word; "you must make allowances for a colonial with no background, not a real gentleman! Yes, perhaps you regret it already——"

"Dennis, the servants will hear—you are gone mad to say such things." It was so sudden, so violent, and his eyes were so cold with rage, as if he hated her: for once his anger raised no anger in her, only dismay and hurt.

"Do you? A grand English lady like yourself, to wed with a common Irish! Demean your blood to take any other but a true gentleman—no gentry real unless it is English gentry, of course! You——"

"Dennis, please, I——" She would not weep, she would not give him that satisfaction. He should not browbeat her like this for no reason at all. She swallowed the hard lump in her throat, but in spite of herself her voice shook. "How can you think it! Of course I am proud to be English, but I do not hold myself any better-bred than you, I could not, how can you believe——"

"Arrogance, always that damned bland, blind arrogance! Are we cattle, to have no pride as humans? I know how you think, all you English! Make allowances, suffer him in patience—your crude colonial husband—you must make the best of it now!"

"You cannot believe such things! I think you must be mad or drunken." That black hate in his eyes! Despite all her self-control a little sob escaped her. He flung his napkin on the table and sprang up.

"Damnation! I will not be wept at by a martyred woman!" He strode out of the room and a moment later she heard the house-door shut with a crash. She sat on at the table, staring down at her plate, swallowing the lump in her throat again and again. The servants listening—Dennis, Dennis—and then the service-door opened behind her and she stiffened her back, raised her head.

"I hope everything was satisfactory, madam?" The maid's tone dutiful, colorless, but how could she not have heard?

"Yes, thank you, Elsie." A miracle that her voice was even. She rose unhurriedly, keeping her face averted. "I will see there is a new cook tomorrow." The doorway and the passage were blurred before her with the hot tears welling up in her eyes; she went down to her withdrawing room and shut the door.

A cheerful little room, gay colors in the carpet and curtains, a brisk fire on the hearth, the two armchairs waiting at opposite sides, the gentleman's and the lady's. She would not weep; it was senseless, he had forced it out of nothing at all, there was no reason he should have such ugly thoughts of her. And everywhere she looked, somewhat to remind her—she would never escape from him, she did not want to escape, but how could they build a life together with those thoughts between them? . . . his silver to-bacco-jar on the mantelpiece, with the clock that had been a wed-ding gift, and the little Dresden figures she had admired and he had bought for her. His London newssheet flung across the arm of his chair. The poker carelessly awry in its stand where he had moved it to prod the coals. She sat bolt upright in the chair, hands folded in her lap, and willed herself not to weep.

2

When McDermott came into the clubrooms he was still taut with emotion, anger, hate—and shame, and the pain hurting like passion in him. But his voice was only a little deeper, his smile a trifle more mocking, when he gave up his cloak to the servant, drifted into the large parlor to greet men he knew sitting about the room talking, gaming, reading newssheets. He ordered a glass of sherry and declined to join a game with old Mr. Andrews.

"You must excuse me this evening. I have had a tiring day and could not fix my mind on the cards." Glass in hand, he wandered over to watch a game in progress between two men he knew casually.

A good deal of loud laughter and subdued talk was evident from one corner of the parlor, where a little group sat over wine and a finished hand of cards, the pack still scattered on the table. Captain Poole, that amiable idiot James Fothergill, Vail, young Gerald Wychbolt, one or two others. Presently he strolled over to them and was welcomed boisterously.

"Here is a man can offer a worthy opinion on the subject, gentlemen! Sit down, McDermott. Fill your glass——"

"Not port mixed with sherry, thank you, captain." By the quality of their mirth and the gleam in Poole's eye they were talking women. He smiled around the circle. "My knowledge is at your service—is it a point of law?" That brought another roar of laughter.

"Not likely! Here, let me put it to him, now—no interruption,

[185]

James!—you never could tell a jest right way round. Now listen to this, McDermott. It seems there was a farmer come to the city, first time off the land, see you—and——"

"Is this by any chance the tale about the farmer, the harlot, and the heifer?"

"Yes, by God, that's it—you know it?" Poole repeated the point of the tale in all its simple obscenity and chuckled. "You've heard it, eh? Well, we've been arguin' as to whether such a thing could occur—eh, now? Don't seem reasonable to me, even granting——"

"Oh, anything can happen with a harlot—not that I am a frequenter of them."

"Don't need to be," said Fothergill with his high laugh, "what?"

"As you say. To quote a Frenchman I once knew, when I must needs pay for my pleasure I am no longer able to give it to my mistresses. But as to the point in question—no play on words intended—it is amazing what small details will affect it, this way or that."

"You're right about that. I've been telling Poole so, but these insensitive soldiers——" Young Wychbolt grinned. "For 'xample, take a woman I knew in London—quite the rage at one time, between-acts dancer at the theater she was, damnation, her name's escaped me. Nell—Polly—no, no matter. Well, she used to rouge her breasts, bright red, mind—French fashion I take it, at least it sounds to be—and on my word, I found it downright revolting—couldn't get up any interest at all. I daresay——"

"Yes, it is French, I recall from my days in Paris. Really? I thought it rather provocative myself."

"That should certainly recommend the custom to every female in Dublin," said Vail, speaking for the first time since McDermott had joined them. His tone was jesting, but there was a hardness beneath it.

Sudden savage desire to hurt Vail took possession of him—Vail, anyone, any English! He said, "You are too kind. I am not all

[186]

that experienced; I only offer an opinion. As I say, small details"
—and he smiled at Vail—"can assume interesting significance. I
once knew a woman with an odd birthmark on her right thigh,
a little ring of black moles—ordinarily an ugly sight, perhaps, but
you know, I found it rather stimulating—for a time."

Vail went perfectly white, standing rigid, glass still uplifted
in one hand. And McDermott, in belated self-mockery, thought,
Yes, that was a sensible thing to do indeed: now he will call you
out to avenge the insult to his wife, and you are a dead man—you
have never laid claim to being a fencer or a marksman.

Vail set his glass down carefully on the table and turned to
walk rapidly out of the room. And perhaps blindly: he blundered
into a man in the doorway, who stared after him.

"And what's struck Reynold?" Poole was the last to sense the
sudden tension in the group.

"Good God," said McDermott softly, blandly. "I have only just
remembered that was his wife." And now he really had hurt Vail.
If the man had intended to call him out he would have done it
then, in the first thirty seconds; now they all knew the extent
of the insult, Vail would be branded coward by all who knew
him.

Abruptly, unexpectedly, the little vicious triumph died away
from him and he was ashamed. He looked at them, the men as
suddenly stilled from their earthy laughter, and he knew what
was in all their minds . . . *None of the instincts of a gentleman—
but then he is not English.* He wanted to fling his wineglass into
those shuttered faces; he wanted to curse them in the only satisfactory tongue for cursing, his own tongue. He got up to his feet
and gave them a one-sided, mirthless smile.

"An embarrassing little *faux pas,* was it not? I had best go
home before I make another. Yes, you are all married men, are
you not? Except Captain Poole. Captain, let it be a warning to

[187]

you in your own affairs. Servant, gentlemen." He turned away leisurely.

Damn them all and to hell with their gentlemanly code!—an English code, typical of the whole race—women of high birth sacrosanct, but any other fair game! Never give the underdog an even chance, that should be the judgment history wrote of them . . . English! And Anne—and Anne? No, he would not think about Anne—but he could not stop himself.

He went home to Sydney Street. The parlormaid opened the door for him—he had forgotten his key. He gave her his cloak, laid his tricorne on the table inside the door. "Where is your mistress?"

"Madam's in her withdrawing room, sir."

He walked down the passage slowly, opened the door, went in. She was sitting in her own chair before the fire, not reading or sewing, only watching the leaping flames. She did not look round as the door opened. "Anne," he said.

She did not speak. If she had, if she had said, Have you come to apologize, it was all your fault we quarreled, his anger would have flared up again and he could not say what he must say. But she did not speak nor move. He crossed the room and stood beside her chair.

"Anne—I am sorry. I did not mean it, I did not mean to say all that."

She turned her head and looked up at him; she had been weeping, but not recently. "Oh, Dennis, it is all right. Only you must not think such things of me. I—I have been sitting here thinking of it, and I understand, my dear. You have—been made to feel sensitive—about it—but it does not matter, Dennis, not at all, to me. Please, you must believe that."

"You are apologizing to me—that is what I came to do. It was all my fault. I did not mean to hurt you." He bent over her, not touching her, and she reached her hands to his shoulders to pull him down beside her in the chair.

"It is all right, truly. Let us never speak of it again. Only, please, never suspect I am feeling such things for you. It is not true. I—I do not like to quarrel so with you." She was holding him tightly.

"You were not, it was I. It was I. I am so sorry, Anne, forgive me. I did not mean to hurt you." He kissed her once, lightly. "My darling." And then on an indrawn breath, "But that is a lie—I did mean to hurt you. I did. And I—hurt—only—myself."

She put her palm across his lips. "We will forget it now and it will not happen again."

"No." There was a long silence while they sat holding each other warmly. He kissed her again. "Anne," he said in a low voice, "Anne. Have you ever stolen anything?"

She raised her head from his shoulder in surprise. "Why, Dennis, what an absurd thing to ask me! Of course I have not."

"My love. My love." He kissed her a third time, but abstractedly. "I stole a shilling once."

"A whole shilling!" she murmured sleepily. "Wicked of you."

"A whole shilling. But I gave it back. I promise you I gave it back."

She put her hand to his mouth again . . . "I love you, Dennis."

3

Quintain put down his pen and stared at Adams. "Will you say that name again?"

Adams did so. Quintain gave a soft profane exclamation and then laughed. "Very well, have him come in." He waited curiously.

McDermott entered the office unhurriedly, nodding at Adams

who held the door for him, and turned in the doorway. "Oh—my friend behind me, may he come in also? Thank you. I believe he may have somewhat to say to Sir Harry. Good day," he added to Quintain, who had risen formally.

"Good afternoon, Mr. McDermott. I——" Quintain paused. Corporal Daly, wearing an expression made up of sheepishness, consternation, and alarm, had come in after McDermott. He came to stiff attention and saluted.

"Awkward, is it not?" asked McDermott. He looked about the room. "May I sit down?"

"Please do so." Quintain recovered himself quickly. "You may stand at ease, Daly. I am at a loss as to the reason I have the pleasure of your company in my office, Mr. McDermott, and accompanied by one of my men, but I am at your service." Already he saw the trap he was in. Daly had been clumsy, or one of the others, and had given it away.

McDermott seated himself, crossing one knee over the other, and looked at him quizzically. "I am afraid I have put your corporal in an embarrassing position, Sir Harry. Perhaps I had best assure you first of all that the wretched man is not at fault, not at all. It is not inconceivable that he will have difficulty explaining that to you, since when I approached him in my usual civil manner—you agree that I am not notorious for incivility?—and suggested that as we were traveling in the same direction we might as well share a chair, he appeared able only to open and shut his mouth like a ventriloquist's puppet. I should not like to feel that I was to blame for earning him a flogging, or extra fatigue-duty, or whatever mode of punishment the British army is using these days—for its own men."

"I swear to God, sir," said the corporal hoarsely, and stopped as Quintain's eye fell on him.

"Do I understand that you have some complaint to lay against Corporal Daly? It is quite true that he is in my command."

"Well——" McDermott considered the question, head on one side. "Well, no, not against Corporal Daly." He smiled at Quintain. "Shall we have done with fencing, Sir Harry? I should very much like to know why you have set your men to following me."

"Following you? But how could you imagine that indeed?" said Quintain, ready with the answer. "I have given no such orders, nor have any of my officers, so far as I know. There is no reason for such extraordinary action."

"And that is what puzzled me," McDermott told him frankly. "It still does. I seem to have neglected to mention that Corporal Daly, in his very natural surprise at my addressing him, was not in fact entirely speechless. Upon my pressing him as to his reason for tagging after me like a faithful hound, he did manage to utter the revealing words, 'Major Quintain's horders, sir,' which has brought me to your office when I should be in my own."

"The man is either drunk or lying," said Quintain. "Why should I do such a thing? After all, you are not a common criminal, are you, Mr. McDermott?"

"I hope I am not a common anything, Sir Harry."

"Exactly. What possible reason I could have——"

"Well, you might be desirous of getting rid of part of your income," said McDermott. "Private charity—always so much more satisfactory than wholesale philanthropy, do you not agree? I may not be the most capable lawyer in the world, but I am acquainted with the views of British law on something called defamation of character. If it had been true, Sir Harry, that you instituted an inquiry into my private affairs and had military guards trail me in the street—whereby anyone learning it and seeing such guards might suppose me to be under suspicion of some crime—had that been true, I say, I might have brought suit against you for quite a round sum, and had every expectation of winning it—with an unprejudiced jury."

"Quite so," said Quintain shortly. He turned to the corporal. "Let us get the rights of this absurd affair. Daly, I did not give you orders to follow this gentleman, did I?"

"No, sir."

"Nor did any other officer?"

"No, sir."

"Then at least we establish that. Why were you doing so? You are certain he was?" McDermott smiled and nodded. "Well?"

Daly took on an agonized expression. "I don't know, sir."

"You don't know? Do you mean you were drunk?"

"Sir, I musta been."

"The man was drunk," said Quintain, "and very likely mistook you for some acquaintance, begging your pardon. That is the explanation."

"I had no idea a corporal received such excellent pay. To afford a most prodigious bout of drunkenness, lasting a week! But my thanks for your courtesy. I am glad to have the thing explained to me."

"We must certainly ask your pardon for such an annoying episode. Soldiers," said Quintain, and shrugged, "you understand. I trust you will overlook it."

"Naturally—naturally. So long," added McDermott gently, "as I am assured that all such bewildered souls are restrained somewhere safe and will no longer dog my steps or those of any other gentleman. Aside from the fact that it is understandably irritating, you know, we all occasionally make certain visits or contract certain business we should not particularly care to have broadcast. Innocent little secrets—you understand."

Quintain took his proffered hand. "Most annoying, I entirely agree, and please accept my apologies."

"Thank you so much." McDermott paused at the door and gave Corporal Daly a last thoughtful inspection. "Amazing. He must have tremendous capacity, or perhaps it was some of that watered liquor we have been getting so much of recently—the smuggling trade, you know." He shook his head. "I should never take him for drunk. But there, that is your business. I have no desire to make trouble about it, Sir Harry. I only thought it should be brought to your attention."

"I am very glad you did. We cannot have citizens annoyed by such—little mistakes. Again, my apologies, sir."

"Good afternoon," said McDermott, smiling.

As the sound of his steps died in the passage Daly began earnestly, "I swear to God, major, I never give meself away——" but he was interrupted. He listened admiringly, as did three military clerks, Adams, and Sergeant Polwhistle, all of whom gathered in the doorway with interest. Afterward Daly described it to Hawkins as "nothink more nor less than a heducation in langwidge."

4

"Always remember, John," said McDermott, "that attack is the best defense."

"It was a risk."

"No. Why? I knew he had nothing definite on me or he would have clapped me in gaol on solid evidence. Since he did not, he had none. I held all the aces—and when I played them he was forced to throw in his hand. If I should find him setting watch on me again—which he will not try—do you know what I should do? I should go to the Lord Lieutenant of the colony and register a formal complaint. I am being treated like a suspected criminal, I should say indignantly, and my reputation damaged unwarrantably. Why for? If you suspect me of some wrongdoing, tell me what it is and produce the evidence against me. And of course they could not. Neither can Quintain. He only hoped."

"I hope to God you are right."

"Oh, I am right. I knew that when he was so anxious to disclaim the intention. This was what I meant to do with the first guard, but that clumsy fool Kincaid forced a change of plans on me. It is safe enough now. Quintain will think twice before trying anything like that again."

Fifteen

I

"Sir——"

McDermott looked up impatiently. "What is it?"

"Mr. Fortescue's here, sir, for his appointment—but——"

"Very well, show him in."

"I beg pardon, sir, but the lady—she says it's immediate, and Mr. Fortescue says he will wait, seeing it's—well, sir——" Mac-Murrough was embarrassed. Unescorted ladies were rare in lawyers' offices.

"A lady? Well, let her come in." McDermott was interested; he rose expectantly.

But at sight of the woman his expression altered. The clerk pulled the door shut soundlessly; she came up to the table without speaking and sat down in the chair beside it. He had not seen her in some weeks; she bore evidence of her recent illness. She was thinner, the light-brown hair dull, and the rouge stood out starkly on cheek and lip.

"I ask only five minutes of your time," she said; and he laughed.

"That does not sound like Celia. What else?"

"Do you even guess what you have done to me?" she asked. "I will never know why you told Reynold. But you did, and you have finished me. He has put me out, Dennis, and I daresay I deserve it. He said—I am not worth—even fighting a duel over."

"I think his judgment is excellent," said McDermott. "Have you come here to pour out your troubles on my shoulder? You get no sympathy from me."

"I do not expect it. I—very nearly died, you know. Oh, you never troubled even to inquire, did you? It——"

"I will never believe it was any concern of mine."

She studied him a moment and then laughed sharply. "Well, the point of the jest I will come to presently, but I confess to you now—I am not sure either. I could not be. But you gave me the money all the same." One hand went to her eyes. "I wish I was clever," she whispered. "I wish I knew how—to manage—in life. Women—pushed here and there as their men will. I never wanted to marry him, it was my father's choice. I wanted to be away in a home of my own, but I never intended—to play him false. It was you—brought all this on me, your damnable charm."

"Dramatics will do you no good with me. You know as well as I that nine of ten men are ruled by their women." He came round the table to confront her, pulled the hand from her eyes, made her look up at him. He smiled at her. "No one forced you into bed with me, Celia. It was your own choosing, to play Vail false or stay honest. And no one ordered you to bed with the other man, whoever it was——"

"Poole," she said numbly, as if mesmerized.

"Good God, that was a long step from me, that hulk of a soldier! As I once told you, Celia, whores are honest for it—they do not whine that some brutal man is responsible for their being whores. Only ladies do that, because they cannot admit even to themselves that it is a pleasant way to pass the time, or an easy way to have gifts, or the quickest way to revenge themselves on their husbands. You come here and play-act at me, blaming me for the position you are in, but it might have been any man. Did I force you, Celia? Did I threaten you, kidnap you?" As she moved her head slowly from side to side he laughed again and let her go. "Then do not lay it on me!"

She was silent, looking down at her hands twisting together over the little velvet bag. "Well, is that all you came to say to me? If not, make haste—your five minutes is almost gone and I have a client waiting."

"No, it is not what I came to say." Her voice was thin and tired. "Reynold has put me out, I have nothing. He let me take my belongings, that is all. I am going to my sister in London, at least for a little while, but likely she will not want me either—no one would want me——"

"I see. I have a piece of advice for you, Celia. Over a somewhat varied life I have reached the conclusion that no single emotion is so weakening to the character as self-pity. It is a quicksand from which no spirit can struggle to solid ground." She had not even heard him. He watched her with a smile half-contemptuous, half-pitying.

"I have not—any money. The few jewels I own—worth very little. I must leave at once. I must get away before everyone knows of it—gossiping, laughing——"

"Ah," he said, "I thought we should come to the point sooner or later. You want money from me. Will you tell me one reason I should give it to you?"

"Yes." She raised her head; there was new hardness and resolution in her voice. "I want money from you, but—for value received." She held up her bag, took a slip of paper from it. "I kept your little note, Dennis—when you sent me the other money. Very likely you remember what you wrote. No matter what you say, it is all your fault I am in this case, and you are going to pay for it. You made a fine bargain for yourself, did you not? A young, pretty heiress! I do not suppose you would like her to read that note you sent me." She let him see it, only close enough to identify it. "Especially if I told her it was—somewhat more recently written than it was. After your marriage, in other words. I—"

With no change of expression he flung round the table and reached for the bag. She snatched it out of his way, retreating across the room. He stopped where he was: the worst move he could have made, that first impulsive action telling her that her estimate was right.

"So you agree with me—I thought you would! Listen to me, Dennis. If you come one step toward me I will scream out that you would assault me. There are two witnesses in hearing beyond that door, remember! That would finish you as a fine gentleman! I will salvage something from this at least. I will sell you that note, Dennis, for a thousand pounds. Do not tell me you have not got it—I remember your powers of persuasion too well—you can easily coax it from your loving wife!"

Too late, he laughed. "Yes, she is a loving wife. So loving that she will believe aught I tell her—that you are a poor woman crazed by illness and the memory of your sin, and forge my name to a letter to protect your real lover! The note means nothing, you do not frighten me that way."

"But you want it back," she pointed out. "She would find you difficult to believe, Dennis, with your reputation as a rake!—and your hand is quite distinctive, you know. There was gossip before about us——"

"Exactly," he said coolly. "Half Dublin suspected it. She probably heard the gossip at the time. If she did not care then she will not now."

"An affianced lover is not quite the same thing as a husband. And a liaison is not quite the same as the abortion of a bastard," she whipped back at him. "Oh, she would not like it, Dennis—not at all—your turning to another woman the week after your wedding journey! Yes, I can say it was then, that you returned to me so soon as you were back in the city! You have found it easy to wheedle money out of her, I wager, but if she knew of this she would hold the purse-strings a little tighter lest you spend her fortune on other women. No matter how besotted about you she may be, it would make an awkwardness, would it not?"

"No," he said, and lied as he said it and knew she knew he lied.

"A thousand pounds. Call it an investment, to protect your expectations from her. You can get it from her tonight—tomorrow—and give it to me here. Oh, I will be sure not to see you in too much privacy, without someone near to hear me if you try violence!"

"I am never violent. And there is no need for such drama. Keep the note, it will do you no good." And he was speaking mechanically, knowing he could not convince her, after that first blunder.

"A thousand pounds," she said hardly. "I think I am learning to be clever."

His thoughts ran so rapidly that it was not until later he realized the direction they took; he knew only that he must stop her going to Anne with this. But it was not the money, the money he could take from Anne, nor the sly gossip on his name, nor any of the other dangers it threatened. It was because Anne would be hurt by it. Believing that he had kept on a mistress that soon after their marriage—that ugly, cynical little note would shock her—and a woman like this! Why in God's name had he ever found her remotely desirable? Anne—the way she would look at him.

Thinking that, he betrayed himself; he rasped, "By God, Celia, if you do aught to hurt my wife I will kill you! I——" He turned; his whole body was shaking with rage.

She stared at him and began to laugh. "Why, Dennis! Damn you, Dennis! You are in love with her—the reformed rake in love with his own wife! Oh, this is the real point of the jest!"

"Do not be more of a fool than you can help." It was too late to salvage any pride at all, but he could try; he could deny that at least.

"A thousand pounds. Here, at this same time, tomorrow." She was smiling tautly. "I have you and you know it."

The English had great reverence for a thing they called losing well. Part of their absurd code of fair play, which meant of course all rules in favor of the English. He saw even less sense in it than in most English codes. No man enjoyed being beaten; the cup of defeat was always bitter. Why pretend to lose with good grace? He turned his back to her. He said, "I will have it for you. Now in God's name get out!"

Even when the door shut behind her he did not move, or curse to himself. He began to realize that his thought had been for Anne and not for the money; he thrust the thought away violently. He stood there letting the anger move darkly through him, refusing it outlet, until it gathered in a cold mass somewhere at the back of his mind and he could think clearly again. He drew a long breath and held out one hand; it was steady. He went to the door.

"I am so sorry to keep you waiting, Mr. Fortescue. Will you come in?"

"Not at all, not at all. Only happy to oblige a lady, sir."

2

"—And two of them sail the night after tomorrow. Since these masters have been in port only officials of the customs have gone aboard their ships, barring the crew. Names of said officials——"

Quintain moved restlessly. "Let be, William. Nothing there. Or if there is, we have no way of discovering it." He looked to the window, where a dispirited gray rain fell heavily. "Christ!" he exclaimed bitterly. "This country! A worse climate than England's, which is a long word! Do you know why we English are so restless, traveling up and down the world to make a profit in other nations? To escape the English climate! And if any man can tell me why we ever came to Ireland I should like to hear the reason. This damned, damp, boggy, miserable country! What are we doing here, William, you and I? Like a pair of hounds chasing their own tails!"

"You've not got much," agreed Adams.

"Much? I've got nothing! And never will have aught, except by chance. I am the fifth wheel. No commission could do more against this trade than what the regular officials are doing. It is only by chance we might drop on one of the principals. Luck might lead us to one tomorrow, or we might go on like this for five years and get no more than we have."

"I'm bound to agree. To speak frankly, I can't see that it's of great importance, major."

"It is important," said Quintain slowly, "in a way, as showing the temper of the people under our rule. A temper of constant rebellion—obstinate rebellion. Think of England, William, the average tenant-farmers who work the land—the country tradesmen—the laborers. Do you see them risking their lives to learn the alphabet and study history?"

"Hardly, sir—too much common sense. A man don't need to know his letters to grow corn. But if they wanted to, there's no law to stop it."

"Exactly. Here there is. As I said before, in my opinion if the colony-government made it law that all peasants must be literate on pain of death, the entire British army could not force them to learn their letters! Well——" He rose. "I will leave you to sort out the reports." He found his cloak, went out to the garrison gate and ordered his horse. He was feeling stale and tired. What in the name of heaven did it matter, any of it? This was a thankless job he was on—and a useless one; he was beginning to lose even the interest he had roused in it with his reasonless suspicion of McDermott.

No, by God, there was something, he felt it. Likely he would never get tangible evidence, but he was morally certain in his mind.

And Anne—it was not only the man's connection (better call it alleged connection) with a criminal organization; in a way that was the least of it. It was what he would do to Anne. No help for it? Well, they were wed, of course.

He dismounted before the house in Sydney Street; he said to the parlormaid who answered the door, "Will you have someone send round to the stables and get my horse under cover?" The rain was descending like a river now. "Your mistress is in?"

"Yes, sir, I will, sir." He followed her down to the door of the little withdrawing room.

"Harry, how nice. I was just wishing for some company—a horrid day, is it not? Come to the fire, you are wet."

He obeyed, leaning on the mantel, and the steam rose from his damp garments. "You are looking well, Anne. So you find marriage agrees with you?"

"Vastly, sir. And why should it not? Oh, Elsie, would you fetch some wine, please, the sherry. Dennis says it is quite good, this last he has, and would doubtless like your opinion on it. I do not really care for sherry. I know it is most unfashionable of me, but it is too sour."

"Dry," he amended, smiling. "If your husband says it is good, it is—his judgment of wines is excellent."

She looked up at him with her head on one side. "Now what do you mean by that? You sound almost as if you imply that his judgment in other matters is lacking. His judgment in matrimony, perhaps?"

"My dear child! When I am in love with you myself?"

"Oh, nonsense, Harry, pray do not bring that up again." The maid returned and poured the sherry for him.

"It is very good," he said, sipping, and sat down in the chair opposite hers. "Anne, may I speak to you seriously? After all, you have known me for a long time. I flatter myself that you trust me. You know I have never approved your marriage——"

"It is nothing at all to do with you."

"Not in the strictest sense, no. But whatever deeper emotion I feel for you, Anne, I count myself your friend, and must surely be concerned with your happiness. My dear, will you answer me one question—are you truly happy? Do not smile and give me some glib answer about brides. There is no need to be conventional with me, you know. I want the truth."

"Yes, yes, yes, yes," she said crossly. "I know you do not like Dennis, and for that reason you imagine all sorts of things. I wish you would not. Like a silly schoolgirl, I said somewhat to you when I was in a mood, and ever since, you have been romanticizing on it. To be sure I am happy, and will continue to be."

He looked at his wine and said soberly, "Well, I can but admire loyalty in a wife. The first part of that may be true, but I do not think the second. Can you meet my eye and tell me he has not already had money of you?"

She met his eyes defiantly. "I seem to recall, Harry, that the marriage service has somewhat to say about sharing. There can be no question of possessions between a man and wife—it is held jointly."

"Oh, my God," he said, "do not be such a little fool! Granting you are besotted about him, you still were used to have a trifle more common sense than some women. The man will rob you blind, and evidently you will smile and enjoy it."

"I will not listen to such talk——"

"Now, damnation, let us not quarrel about it. I ask your pardon, perhaps I spoke too frankly, he is your husband after all. I shall probably be returning to England soon, and I wanted to say this to you before I go. My dear——" He leaned forward and took her hand. "Among other things, it is a pity you have married into a strange place, where you have no old friends. Oh, your aunt and Sir Julian, yes, but in spite of the kinship you do not know them well. Sometimes one needs old friends, trustworthy friends, Anne. You must not feel that you are cut off from us entirely. I hope you will make visits to London—and"—he hesitated, and then went on, "and do not feel you have no one to turn to. I will not offend you with more criticism of your husband, but there may come a time when you—when you want to escape —all this. And in that event you will have good friends to welcome you and sympathize. I——"

"What in heaven's name are you saying?" She snatched her hand away. "That I could ever wish to leave my husband? That I am a—a—one of your loose women to fancy one can walk away from duty and loyalty——"

"Sometimes, Anne, amputation is the only way to save life. I would not censure you for it, should your marriage turn out as I expect." He tried to speak calmly, but he was conscious of irritation at this infatuated woman so willfully blind. "You cannot know what will come——"

"True, but I know you are going this minute," she told him rigidly. "To say such things to me! We are old friends, yes, but not to that extent. You pretend to feel affection for me—and then to speak so! To think I could desert my husband, like any common trull abandoning a man she is tired of—coupling me in your mind with a woman like—like your own doxy, a loose camp-follower, little better than a waterfront whore!—who goes from man to man for more money or finer gifts——"

"You damned little vixen," he said involuntarily, "keep your tongue off Kitty—she is worth a dozen of you!" For a moment he scarcely realized what he had said, only that it was unpardonably rude.

"You will please leave," she said coldly. "I am sorry, Harry. I would not quarrel with you, but I cannot listen to such talk."

"I—yes. I beg your pardon." His tone was absent. He looked at her and she was Anne, Emily's little friend, the Deering youngster so much about his father's house she was almost like another nuisance of a young sister. A sweet child, Anne, and he was fond of her, he was sorry for her, and that was all . . . she was not Kitty. He had been in love once, long ago, with a girl named Rosamond Hope, and she had refused him, and so he had thought he would never love again. He had taken a woman here and there, for a night or a week or two, and then he had taken Kitty, and she suited him, and he kept her. He ought to marry and ensure the title, but with every woman who was eligible he found excuses why he should not take that step, even women who attracted him mildly. He was settled into a life he liked, reluctant to change it. He had fancied himself in love with this girl because he had conceived a dislike for her husband—because he was sorry for her—and she was safely tied to another man, so he could tell himself, I will be faithful to an unrequited love and never marry any lesser woman . . . another fine excuse! And then in a little outburst of anger he had said—what had he said? . . . worth a dozen like you.

Kitty. It was true. No lady of high family and fortune could ever mean as much to him. No woman could have been to him what she had been for ten years—sharing the campaigns, making a place of comfort for him always, a home if it was only for one night, uncomplaining, cheerful, tending his wounds on occasion, never asking aught, always ready there to give whatever he asked and needed. There was no more a woman could do, or be, or have. She was as much a part of him as his own limbs. Kitty whom he loved.

He had not seen her or thought of her consciously. She was there, a foundation of his life, experienced without being understood. He was understanding now—he was beginning to understand . . . the man who hunted the world over and found what he sought at his own door. It was the little panic taught him that—"goes from man to man for more money or finer gifts." Kitty? But what would he do without Kitty? What other woman could take her place? Never really thought of losing her; she was there to stay so long as he desired it. Kitty, going to some other man—it would be like a wife deserting him.

Anne was speaking; he did not hear her. He was reliving ten years in a few seconds, everything he had shared with Kitty. Kitty whom he loved. A man could be such a fool . . . but he need not stay one.

She would never be a lady—thank God, no, not one of these bird-witted society females, living for gowns and balls. She was his Kitty, and by God he would not see one thing to her changed, a woman for a soldier she was, no stay-at-home finicking lady.

"Harry! Do you hear what I am saying? I——"

"Yes," he said vaguely, "I agree, Anne. Do you forgive me now, I have—business to see to." He went out to the passage and found his cloak. It was still raining heavily—he seemed to remember he had ridden here—of course, the horse was round at the back; he walked around the drive to the stables and found them deserted, his horse tethered in the first stall. He tightened the girth and buckled the bit automatically, mounted in the stableyard, and set off up Sydney Street at a splattering trot. Before he reached the corner the absurd panic set him spurring to a canter, even on the slippery wet streets . . . get back, make sure she is still there!

He flung the reins at the doorman of the hotel, almost ran through the ground-floor offices and passage toward the stair, took the treads three at a time up to his suite of chambers on the first floor. He burst into the sitting room with his heart pounding, and she was not there. "Kitty!" he shouted. "Kitty!" He made for the door of the bedchamber.

She was sitting by the window mending some garment; she looked up, startled. He stopped on the threshold and drew a long breath. "Oh, God, Kitty," he said.

"Whatever's the matter? You look like as if you'd been seeing ghosts."

He had: the ghosts of ten years. And this was like seeing her for the first time, yet knowing her so well, better than himself. Her fine strong body that answered to him so eagerly, her warm eyes and loose-waving brown hair and firm generous mouth, her competent quiet hands that had soothed and tended him, the calm strength and goodness of her that he knew, that was his. He hurried to her, to have her against him and his arms around her.

"Kitty, Kitty, forgive me."

"What is it, Harry? You're all upset again over something; there, love, don't. Soaking you are, you'll be taking the fever—best change to dry clothes——"

He laughed and felt the hot tears pricking his eyes. "Kitty, I love you so much." He had not said that to her for years, never like that. "Kitty, my darling, I want you to marry me."

She drew away from him. "I can't tell any liquor on you—" doubtfully, and he laughed again, clutching her close.

"My dearest, I was never so sober and sane in my life. Did you ever hear of aught so foolish as a man who fell in love and never knew it for ten years? I cannot do without you, Kitty, and

[207]

I must make sure I'll never have to. You are going to marry me, and be Lady Quintain, and never stir from my side the rest of your life, do you hear?"

"You've gone daft," she said.

"No, sane for the first time! You will, Kitty—you would not leave me, you——"

"I'll stay with you the longest day you want, Harry; there's no need to make all this jesting for it. Making out I'd need a wedding ring to do it, even if so be you could wed me——"

"I am not jesting, and I am going to wed you. So soon as we return to England—if you will have me," and he took her face in his hands, smiling down at her. "Do you love me, Kitty, will you have me as husband?"

"Daft," she whispered, and consternation grew in her eyes as she began to believe him. "You couldn't do such, Harry—a gentleman like you—why, none of your family or friends'd ever look at you again——"

"Don't talk silly," he said in her own vernacular. "Look at old Squire Penworthy, wedding his own cook—sensible man—and he's still squire, isn't he?—men still touching cap to him, and he's still Master of the Trevelyan Hunt. There's no law says I can't marry the—the Queen of Russia if I desire it—only I'd much rather marry you, and that's what I'll do. So you'd best set your mind that way, for it is settled."

When his mouth let hers free she said dazedly, "—Won't let you do it, it's daft, it's all wrong, you can't——"

"Be quiet!" He began to kiss her again.

"But, Harry"—a long time later when she could speak—"the title. You need sons, a wife who'd give you a family—not so young any more, I'd maybe never——"

"Then we shall let Cousin James inherit the title, and good riddance! Talking silly again—tell me, Kitty! Tell me yes—tell me you love me——"

"Why, Harry, you got no need to hear that," she said almost resignedly, almost calmly. She drew back and studied his face; he saw a little fear in her eyes, and bewilderment, and all her love for him quick and strong. "Harry, love, I'd never leave you, not the longest day, but you can't do such a thing——"

He stopped her mouth the easiest way. By God, it would be a shock for Bella—and all the hopeful mamas with marriageable daughters angling for a fortunate match! He was going to enjoy their expressions and remarks when they all knew of it. Kitty shouldn't be hurt, no, he'd never mingled much in society anyway; they'd be in the country when they weren't abroad. Best thing he'd ever done for himself, it would be—his arms tightened about her triumphantly. The devil with what they'd all say! With Kitty he'd want nothing else . . . oh, by God, he would enjoy asking the snobbish Bella to his wedding!

He laughed to himself. Times, he thought, times in a man's life there was a deal of satisfaction in being—a rebel.

Sixteen

I

Anne knew there was something wrong, something worrying at him, as soon as he came into the house. He might conceal his moods from everyone else, but not from her. He said nothing when she told him Harry had been to call upon her, and that in itself was odd. "He expects to leave for England shortly, you see——"

"Oh?" He turned from warming himself at the fire. "This—business of his is completed, then?"

"Evidently. You should change to something dry, Dennis."

"Yes, let me get warm first."

"I hope you did not have to go out in all this weather."

"No, no, I was at my offices all day." He answered absently and soon went off upstairs.

At dinner he was rather more silent than usual, twice failed to hear her when she spoke, and pleaded preoccupation with a business matter; but she knew it was not that. He had been at home every evening this week and she had expected him to go to his clubrooms tonight, but instead he came into the withdrawing room and settled in the opposite chair. And abruptly he was talkative, relating some amusing incident with a client, gesturing, laughing. It was not long before he had her laughing with him.

"But how ridiculous, Dennis——"

"Not ridiculous at all, I assure you, a most dignified man, in a brown bagwig at least half a head too large for him—perhaps he keeps his valuables in it as well as his hair—and a really wonderful waistcoat, I meant to ask the name of his tailor. Quilted at the edges, my dear, and gilt buttons——" He broke off, his face alight with mirth, and came over to her. "How lovely you are when you laugh, my darling—did you know that?" He lifted her and sat down in the chair holding her across his lap. "My lovely wife—quite the loveliest one I have ever possessed."

The amusement died in her and she returned his kiss, but her body felt cold. She always saw through his conscious charm; now for the first time she knew when it was being deliberately used against her. There was something he wanted of her.

"Lovely Anne, beautiful Anne. Do you love me at all, my dearest? Only a very little? Tell me!"

"Dennis——" He had felt the slight stiffening of her body; he bent his head to kiss her, and she evaded him, trying to laugh. "Good heavens, Dennis, wed all this time—near three months now, do you know that?—and still asking if I love you! There is no need to keep laying such passionate suit to me! Yes, of course I do, my dear. Now do be good and let me go. I must finish my letter to Emmy." He let her go and went back to his chair; he was hurt, she knew by his manner. Very probably he was putting it down to the endless foibles of women. What was the matter with her? A month ago she would have responded to him without thought.

She sat at her writing table laboring over the letter, uninterested in it. He prodded the fire, and then she heard the lid of his tobacco-jar lifted; he was filling his pipe. Presently a fragrant blue smoke arose; he sat down again and made a little rustle with his newssheet, put it aside, went to the bookcase. "Oh, Anne."

"Yes?"

"I knew there was somewhat I meant to tell you. Today at Durfee's I met a most interesting fellow, a private importer from Dover. Mr. Wrayburn—Mr. Henry Wrayburn. I was particularly interested in his talk of this new business he is engaged in, importing various items from the American colonies. It seems there is a tremendous profit to be made when one has one's own ships, as he has. The original cost is so low, you understand——" He went on talking about the importing business, walking about the room smoking, not looking at her. "He impressed me as a very straightforward, honest man. A small investment, he says, would——"

So it was money he wanted. She should have seen that at once. All this elaborate tale, made up out of whole cloth likely, to have money from her. Oh, God, she thought, I should despise myself because I cannot stop loving him, when he is like this. She interrupted him in the middle of a sentence, the calmness of her voice surprising her.

"Do you mean you would suggest that I invest some money in this company?"

He had halted before the fire, his back to her. She waited; he was silent. At last he said violently, as if his answer came as an interruption to impassioned speech, "No! Most certainly not, I was not thinking of such a thing. Why should you believe I meant that?" He looked at her, and she saw that his forehead was damp with sweat. "I have—nothing to do with your money," he said roughly.

Uneasily she watched him pace the room. He was nervous this evening. He had a book in his hand, but he did not sit down to read it.

"Anne."

"Yes?"

"I am—sorry to disturb you. I wanted to ask——" He was hesitating, fumbling for words—Dennis! There was a white line about his mouth; he put his hands in his pockets, took them out. "I—find I am in—a rather awkward position——" He was trying to ask directly for the money, and he could not do it; she saw him try, and fail to bring the words out. She felt the effort of his body and will, and was touched by a queer pain not her own. She could not bear to see him standing there struggling to strip himself of all pride. Dennis! Dennis always so smooth and self-confident!

She was sitting sidewise in the chair, pen in one hand, the other to her cheek. She started obviously and half turned. "Did you speak to me, Dennis? I am sorry, I was thinking of my letter . . . oh, Dennis, will you fetch me some money from the bank tomorrow? I will give you an order."

"Yes," he said in a low voice, "yes, I will—be glad to oblige you."

"I will just sign it now." She found the book, extracted an order, and signed it without filling in any sum. "Oh—ten pounds, no, twenty. Thank you. What was it you were saying?"

"Nothing—of any importance. It is no matter." As he folded the slip away she saw his hand shaking.

But—Dennis? When it was the reason he had married her? He would not feel—this was none of his acting. A man might feel that—if he truly loved her. If he——

Fairy tales again! Deluding herself. She had not heard him come up behind her; she started as his hands closed on her shoulders, pulled her upright to his arms. "Anne, Anne," he said in a muffled voice against her. He did not move or kiss her, but stood holding her tighter and tighter while she felt her heart beginning

[213]

to pound. If it was true—if it could be true—if it might be true—
oh, God, let it be true——

He sat looking at the money spread out before him on the table.
One thousand and twenty pounds. And if she had not offered
him that blank order, what would he have done? Told Celia to
go to the devil for her money? He could not have asked, invited
Anne's contempt so. Damnation, he had married her for the
money . . . though he had not planned to give it away to other
women. Perhaps there was always one last thing a man would not
do.

He remembered an Italian Jew he had known in Paris. They
had talked of religious persecution, a topic in which both of them
took understandable interest. "I will tell you, young man," said
the Jew, "the first thing you must do is seal up your pride, when
you must move among those who look down on you. Do not lose
hold of it, for pride is the thing that differentiates men from
beasts—but lock it up and forget about it, in business hours. You
cannot afford pride among the overproud. Ingratiate yourself with
them, fawn on them, the while you use every skill to trick them
and cheat them, for that is the only way to conquer the conquerors
—my people knew that long ago. Cleverness will always conquer
brute force, which they use against us. Is it not more humane
to steal a man's money than to club the life out of him? But you
will keep your pride intact, to take it out and look at it in secret,
for only that way will you be able to save yourself from being
smirched by the things you do. Who can return good for evil?
No man with life in him." And he had smiled. "Your people and
mine, we begin to have much in common. If a few more centuries
you labor under oppression, you may grow as clever as we. But

the oppressed race that keeps no pride in itself is doomed. Whatever the slyness we use on the persecutors, it is imperative that we maintain integrity among ourselves."

Yes; that was true. But the Jew had neglected to add, what he doubtless knew, that like anything covered over and left with no outlet of expression, the pride would double itself in the dark. The races which had known oppression had always the greatest pride, a fierce defiant pride to take as insult the lightest word, to take as degrading the least important act. Good God, he was scarcely the first man who had married a woman for her fortune! Why must there be all this soul-searching about it?

Yes, he could lie and say he bribed Celia for that note to protect his own interests, to keep Anne believing in him, that he might take money from her—if that was too little reason, to serve the cause of his people with that money, a loyal patriot disinterested in his own fortunes. It was not true. It was to keep Anne from being hurt—to keep her loving him, wanting him. No other reason, only because he——

No! An Englishwoman, the enemy. He could not feel that. It could not be true.

With a sudden decisive gesture he swept the money into a pile, separated the twenty pounds she had asked for, put the rest in a drawer of the table. Christ, he was a fool. With all his experience, all his knowledge, caught between two women like this!

He swore to himself aloud. Women! Why in the name of God had he entangled himself with any woman at all, ever? Better off if he had turned priest as that old fool Monsignor Defevre had wanted—better off if he had died in a ditch with the rest twenty-three years ago. At this rate, he would likely soon be dead in any case; his mind playing him tricks like this the English would take him like a first offender . . . and it was some comfort that his crimes against English law would call for hanging rather than mere transportation to the Americas. He would not fancy field

[215]

work again, and hampered by chains at that, in a tropical climate.

"Mr. Clark is here, sir."

"Very well, let him come in. And, MacMurrough, I am expecting a lady, the same lady who was here yesterday. Will you show her in to me at once, please."

"Yes, sir."

He had got rid of Clark by the time she came. The clerk held the door for her and she thanked him with a demure smile as she entered. McDermott rose as his only concession to formality.

"Good day, Dennis. I trust you had no difficulty inventing a lie to tell your little bride?" She seated herself uninvited; she was entirely in possession of her wits today, cool and confident. He opened the drawer and laid the money on the table without speaking. "You surprise me. I quite thought you would try to argue your way out of it."

"A little late for that. Give me the note, take the money and go."

"What, you want no fond farewells? After all that has passed between us——"

"I want nothing, particularly humorous conversation. Nothing but the note."

"Not so fast. I will lay my hands on the money first," and she laughed.

"You will give me the note before you touch it!" He took up the money in one hand, held out the other.

"You forget all your courtesy to a lady. I have made the bargain, have I not? We could argue back and forth all day. Come, let me have it, you will have the note in a moment." She opened her bag. He separated the roll of treasury notes in two.

"Here is the half—now give me the paper." She took the notes, wadded them into her bag; slowly she brought out a folded slip and handed it to him. He let her take the remainder of the money, unfolding the paper impatiently.

[216]

"I am so sorry, Dennis. I fear I have given you the wrong paper," she said softly. He was already crumpling the blank page furiously, advancing on her. She backed away from him toward the door. "No violence, remember! Your clerk is in hearing if I scream!"

"Bitch," he said between his teeth, "give it to me! I have no time for jests."

"Oh, nor have I." She pretended to search her bag. "Indeed I am sorry. I fear I have left it where I put it for safekeeping, in my jewel case. And all my baggage packed ready to leave! I sail on the mail-packet for Plymouth this very night, you know. You must forgive an addlepated woman, Dennis, but I will send it to you, I promise."

He made two steps and took her by the shoulders; she opened her mouth and he let her go. "That is better," she smiled. "I am only beginning to find out what power a woman has. There is really nothing you can do about it, is there? You are caught indeed."

"Damn you," he said tiredly, "so you have tricked me—again. Very well, so you have. Do not provoke me by further gloating on it."

"But indeed I mean to be honest with you! That was your complaint, that I was not honest? I will send the note to you from England."

"We both know what you will send from England—a letter asking for more money and threatening me again. So long as you have that note you think to milk me dry before handing it over—if you mean to do that at all." And the most of his anger was for himself: going senile, to be taken by such a trick!

"Well, you know, my dear, I must contrive to support myself now my husband will no longer do so."

He looked her up and down contemptuously. "I could suggest a means for you to earn your living, Celia, but I fear you would not be a great success at it. Not only must a woman possess some semblance of a warm nature for that profession, but she must begin it when she is a good deal younger."

She took a step and slapped him across the face hard, her expression unchanging. "You chose the wrong profession yourself," she said. "You would have made an excellent whoremaster."

With difficulty he restrained himself from reaching for her. "I warn you now, you will get no more money from me. You may do what you please with that note—and I remind you I can manage to intercept letters to my wife—but you will not get another penny! Now get out, and let this be the last I see of you!"

"Hasty, Dennis—you would best think it over a bit more. You have put in half a year and more of hard work to reach your present position as husband of an heiress—you would not like it all destroyed at one stroke?"

"Get out," he said; he could not trust himself to say more.

She smiled at him slowly. "It is unkind of you to suspect me of such low dealing. I made the bargain with you for a thousand pounds—you shall have the note. I was but jesting, after all. It is true I have not got it with me, but you shall have it in your hands before I sail, I promise you."

"Do you expect me to believe that? I am not such a fool. Once, but not twice. Get out, Celia. You have had your jest at me, for God's sake go!"

"As you will . . . you may not believe it, but it is true all the same. I intended it that way from the first." She made him a mocking curtsey and pulled the door open. On the threshold she turned and added gravely, "Good day, Mr. McDermott," for the benefit of the clerk.

He sat down and put his head in his hands. He tried to think, to plan, but all his old cunning for intrigue had deserted him. All he saw in his mind was Anne's face, shocked, dismayed, hurt, turning to him with disgust and contempt.

The money, the money . . . damn the money. "Christ help me," he whispered into his palms. "No, it is not true!" An English . . . Anne. He had not taken her, she had taken him. He was in a trap of his own building.

Seventeen

I

Quintain flung his cloak and riding whip down on the nearest chair and uttered an exasperated oath. His junior looked up with a smile.

"Tiring of the job, major?"

"More than that—I am finished with it," said Quintain emphatically. "I was cursing at those pompous idiots in the Chancellery. I have just come from making my first—and last—report to Randall. He was almighty pleased with it."

"You surprise me," said Adams solemnly.

"Would he not be pleased? What I had to tell him I could have told him a month after we came here—no man could do more at this affair than what he and his aides are doing on their regular duty. Damnation, William, this was a senseless commission from the beginning. To cover up some of old Pelham's political intrigue," he went on bitterly, taking up the bottle of wine and finding a scant glassful left. "A hue and cry raised, and all of us sent off to kick our heels here! Well, it will not be much longer."

"You'll end the business?"

"I have. Thanked them all round with my best company manners for their co-operation, promised each ministry a copy of my report to Parliament, complimented them on their military establishment—and a slovenly, shabby one it is!—and listened to their fatuous compliments in return. I have but to write my report and we may go home to England for a little. And I hope"—he raised the glass to the gods of destiny—"we will be rewarded with an active campaign soon. God, how I loathe penwork!"

"You are in a temper over it indeed," observed Adams mildly. Quintain laughed and stretched.

"Not really, William. As a matter of fact I was never more content in my life. I have found one good thing in Ireland, at least . . . and that I brought with me, but I did not know it at the time. However! No, I am incensed at myself in a way. I've no interest in preserving their damned colony law, but I'd have liked to show up these fat desk-soldiers. But it is a matter of pure chance, not careful investigation. Well, I shall spend a day or so on this report, and we will get off at the end of the week, say."

"So soon?"

"Yes—I have business in England. Personal business . . ." He lay back in the chair, smiling to himself. Kitty. The fool of the world he had been. Thinking of Kitty, he felt a pleasant warm peace settle over his mind. That was the only real importance now. . . .

Adams, seeing him apparently drowsing, and sympathetic for the lethargic effect of official meetings, forbore to speak. Presently he went out to superintend the afternoon change of sentries, and when he returned to the office Quintain had gone. That was how it happened that he did not remind Quintain of the port-guards posted to watch foreign shipping, and ask if the duty should be suspended. He knew it would be, today or tomorrow, but he would not issue the order without Quintain's affirmative; he had an engagement that evening with a redhaired dancer from the theater and could not be troubled to seek out his superior then, and in any case a day or so would make little difference.

Quintain himself, most unusual for him who seldom neglected details, had quite forgotten about Sergeant Polwhistle's patient detail of guards, and as Adams spent the next morning in bed after a full night of drinking and lovemaking, no one thought to remind him. So the guards remained on duty, observing the comings and goings on three foreign vessels lying in Dublin harbor, all that next day and evening.

2

McDermott could not concentrate on his work, and left his offices before four of the clock. He went straight to Sydney Street, uninclined for cards or wine or desultory talk. When he let himself into the front passage one of the parlormaids was polishing the gilt frame of the mirror beside the door and admiring herself in the glass.

"Is your mistress at home?"

"Good afternoon, sir. Yes, sir, she's in her chamber having a fitting for a new gown, sir."

"Ah." He went back to the withdrawing room, found the fire low, and prodded it to life. He chose a book at random and tried to settle himself to read, but he was restless—uneasy. A high wind had got up after the rain, and its wailing about the corners of the house was like that of a *bàn sidhe,* the old woman of the fairy people who warned of all calamities coming to men.

Kincaid came to him presently to ask if he would change his garments. Full of superstition like all simple men, he remarked on it. "I can hear a *bàn sidhe* the other side of that wind, McDermott. Bad luck coming——"

"English, English," said McDermott, who was leaning back in his chair with his eyes shut. "How often must I tell you to use English? With half-a-dozen servants creeping about the house to hear."

"Your pardon." Kincaid was impossible to offend. "But it is an omen all the same."

"It is nothing of the kind, Brian. It is only wind. The *sidhe* are all dead long ago, do you not know that? The English drove them underground and they all died."

"Not they," said Kincaid positively. "They are still about. And no telling ever what they'll be at. Sometimes to hurt and sometimes to help. But when an old hag of the *sidhe* goes to shrieking like that it means no harmless pranks. Bad luck coming, McDermott."

"Cassandra," he said, and Kincaid took it for an unfamiliar curse; he laughed. "I hope to God you are wrong. I have had quite enough bad luck for one day. Yes, you may pour me a glass of wine, thank you." He could not sit still; when Kincaid had gone he wandered about the room glass in hand; he went down the passage, looked into the cold dining room, opened the door to the front parlor and walked about there. All the rooms felt oddly empty, not because he was alone but because Anne was not in them.

He went over to the little rosewood harpsichord and picked out a scale with one finger. The notes rang unexpectedly loud and flat in the silence, as if a ghost played in a house empty of life. The keys made little soft chocks as he depressed them one by one.

> Early one morning, just as the sun was rising,
> I heard a maid sing in the valley below—
> "O do not grieve me, never deceive me!"—

He sat down on the bench and heard himself curse in a whisper.

Bad luck! He had that already—there was no need for any *bàn sidhe* to howl about his door and tell him so.

He heard the knocker, and a moment later the maid coming up the passage to answer it. A low murmur of voices, approaching steps. "Yes, madam, I'll tell the mistress you're here. Will you wait in the parlor, madam?" He sighed and stood up. A caller for Anne, and he was caught here—he must make polite talk.

"Oh, I beg your pardon, sir, I didn't know as 'ow you was here —" as the door opened. He put on a courteous smile of welcome, stepped toward the door; and then he stopped. "I'll tell mistress, madam."

They looked at each other while the maid's steps died away up the stair. "Celia—what are you doing—what——"

She had recovered herself more quickly than he. "Well, I scarce expected to find you home at this hour, Dennis. Did I disturb your mind so greatly that you found your work bothersome? Or perhaps you reckon that as you have married into sufficient money, you need not pay too much attention to your profession?"

"What do you——" He advanced on her, and at his expression she retreated, laughing, holding up a hand.

"Plenty of witnesses here to come rushing in at a scream and discover an outraged lady—and servants, who would embroider the tale for me! Keep your distance. It is too late, Dennis—your wife will be here in a moment. And on the whole I am rather pleased that you are here. I will see how she looks at you instead of imagining it. I promised you should have the note today, did I not? But I always meant your wife to have it first."

"Damn you—damn you, Celia——" Impotent to say anything else; he would not plead with her. After all his experience, teaching him that no woman was ever to be trusted in any particular!

"I wanted more revenge on you than a thousand pounds of your wife's money," she told him viciously. "You have alienated my husband from me and brought me to this state, and I think there is scriptural recommendation—an eye for an eye. Yes, I meant from the first to do this—you will not find her so amenable when she has heard what I have to say!"

And even as the fury and panic filled his mind, he knew she lied about the reason. He knew too much about women to think it was Vail, or aught to do with Vail. It was because he had left her before she was ready to let him go—an insult a woman felt deep; and she had been smoldering ever since.

He said, "Give me the note, Celia; give me the note——" walking toward her quietly, forcing her to step back away from him. "You will not do this—I have paid you—give me the note——" She had it with her now; he made a lunge for her little bag and got her by the throat with his other hand. She struggled with him.

"One way or the other, Dennis," she panted, "will you have it your public reputation or only your wife's opinion? I will scream——"

"Give it to me——"

"And what is all this?" Anne in the doorway, her voice startled. He released Celia and turned to look at her once . . . the last time. She had dressed hurriedly, in a morning gown of sprigged muslin, and her hair was slightly disarranged. He thought he had never seen her look more beautiful. "Mrs.—Mrs. Vail, how pleasant——" Bewildered, unsure, she went on mechanically speaking the words she had ready to say. "You must forgive my appearance. I—what is this, Dennis, you—are, you were——"

Celia was laughing, readjusting her hat, her gown where their struggle had pulled it awry. "Your husband is the one to ask forgiveness, Mrs. McDermott. His gentility is but skin-deep, as I always suspected! Pray do not think he was attempting to assault me."

He turned his back to both of them and went to stand before the hearth, waiting with curious calm fatality. He could not face either now.

[225]

"I—do not understand——"

"You will, Mrs. McDermott, very shortly. May I sit down? You may believe I gave great consideration to coming here, for it is not exactly enjoyable to me to confess my own sins to another woman——" He could imagine the pretty flush, the downcast eyes. "But I have deep regard and sympathy for you, my dear, and I concluded that it was, in a way, my Christian duty to come. I am going away, you see—to England, tonight. No, of course you did not know. It all arose very suddenly, as I have no doubt gossip will enlighten you." A hand to the eyes there. "But I must not speak of myself. I have—have done grievous wrong, my dear, and it is too late now to mend it, but as my name will be on all tongues in any case, I cannot pay a higher price than I have. And I determined you should learn the truth of it, which all the gossip would not tell you—we women must support each other, you know. He is your husband after all, and"—a smile here—"forewarned is forearmed. You are but a recent bride and perhaps will find a little advice helpful."

"I fear I do not know what you are speaking of." Anne, reserved, remote.

"Oh, I am about to tell you! I—I find it embarrassing to speak of my own defections"—an audible sigh—"but I must. All too often we women are weak-willed where a handsome man is concerned. I—pray forgive me, Mrs. McDermott—I must confess to you that your husband has been my—my lover, in the past—in the recent past. But that is not the extent. I have learned my lesson from him, to what depths he can descend, but I feel it my duty to warn you lest he deceive you also and perhaps bring you to ruin. I hope and pray I shall never set eyes on him again, but you—well, we can but make the best of bad matters."

"I find such moralizing somewhat tiresome, Mrs. Vail. I must ask you to speak more plainly." Sharp. Cold. More mature than he had ever heard her before.

"But of course, my dear. I only try to soften it for you—it will grieve and shock you, I know; that cannot be helped, but you should hear. I—well, to make no long story of it, there is in my possession a note from your husband—a somewhat revealing note. He has pressed me to return it to him, and I meant to do so, but 'twas a small matter, or so I thought, not having the wit to suppose he feared I should use it against him, you see. Yesterday he had the unprecedented effrontery to offer me money for its return— a great deal of money, Mrs. McDermott. I knew him for a faithless husband and had heard him boast how he would coax money from his wealthy wife, but this insult to my own integrity—attempting to bribe me!—seemed the last straw, as perhaps you can appreciate. In short, I decided that you must no longer be kept blind to his true character, and I have come to hand you this letter. Please believe I feel deeply for you, my dear. I realize all too well how impulsive infatuations lead us into——"

"Some women perhaps. May I have the note, please?"

He realized that he was trembling very slightly. He stood motionless, his back to the room, staring at the dead coals, seeing nothing but the contempt in her eyes he heard in her voice. There was nothing to do, nothing to say. This time he was caught. He heard the tiny rustle of paper, and then silence.

And then, unbelievably, he heard her laugh.

"Oh, this is that affair! I quite thought I was about to learn some horrid secret. It is kind of you to exercise such sympathy on me, Mrs. Vail, but I assure you it is misplaced. I was aware that my husband had had a liaison with you before we were married. If you will forgive me, a wife has more reason to worry over openly loose women than the cheating wives of other gentlemen."

"You—knew——"

"Most certainly. And of this as well. My husband and I understand one another, and he told me you were attempting to blackmail him with this letter. That is the real truth, is it not? I

[227]

advised him to send you to me, but he feared you would speak crudely and shock me." Another laugh. "Gentlemen always credit their wives with far more sensitivity and prudery than any woman in fact possesses. Which is fortunate for some wives."

He turned slowly to face them. Anne was still standing, very white but calm, and it might easily be the pallor of controlled anger, the note in her hand, her eyes cool and scornful on the other woman, who had risen.

"So you—will protect him." Celia was unsure now, as incredulous as he. "You did not know. He was too anxious——" She checked herself; Anne laughed.

"Too anxious to recover the letter? I think rather you mistook his anxiety to spare me an unpleasant scene for anxiety over his own position. At all events, you see it is settled between us. And although I appreciate your—womanly sympathy—for me, I cannot precisely welcome the company of a confessed adulteress, nor hearing myself coupled with her only because we are both women. I am sure you have many last arrangements to make for your journey, and I must not take up your time."

Celia stared at her for a moment, compressing her lips, searching for words. At last she said in a low shaking voice, "You will regret it, Anne. I promise you, you will regret allowing him such license."

Anne went to the door and laid a hand on the velvet bell-rope. "You have nothing to say about my marriage, Mrs. Vail. You must forgive me, I had not expected to receive callers and have various duties to perform. I wish you a safe journey to England . . . Elsie, the door for Mrs. Vail."

In what dignity she could achieve Celia allowed herself to be ushered out to the passage. Anne satisfied convention for the maid's sake by accompanying her across the threshold of the room, and halted in the doorway. "Good-by, Mrs. Vail."

He heard the house-door opened. And then Celia: "You will be in my thoughts, Mrs. McDermott. I hope all my wishes for you come true, before long." The door shut. He went back to the hearth, leaning on the mantel, head bent. He heard the door of the room close.

"What a vindictive creature," said Anne thoughtfully. "I do wish I had been wearing a finer gown. I never liked the woman."

He made two efforts to speak before he said, "I thought—I——" and turned to look at her. She met his eyes steadily; she was waiting for him to speak. He said, "It was not true—that it was after our marriage. Before—long before. I—she told me herself she could not be sure—it was mine. But I——"

"I see. Well, that rings true, with a woman like that. I should not expect you to tell me of such a thing." And she was still waiting, to hear it all. She would give Celia no satisfaction, but the amnesty was only public.

He said, "I gave her a thousand pounds for it. She tricked me and kept the note."

"That was rather foolish of you, Dennis. I should not think you would be tricked so easily."

"Nor I." He would not raise a hand to wipe the sweat from his face. "She said I would pay for it—because if you grew to mistrust me—I could not—take money from you. It was not—the thing itself. Not all."

"Yes, she has a mind like that."

He said, "I stole the thousand pounds from you. That blank order. I made it out for one thousand and twenty pounds this morning. And I stole five hundred pounds from you before, part of it for the carriage. I will not do that again." But it was not enough, that half confession. Confession relieving the soul . . . he was finished with all that nonsense, the meaningless proscribed formalities of an antiquated creed, the priest's fatherly admonishings, the mutter of Latin. It was all nonsense, but of course they knew human nature, the churchmen: confession lifting the burden . . . and no man so swift to escape the lessons of his childhood, whether true or false. His mother knotting her shawl, covering the fire: "I will just slip out to confess to Father Hugh while he is nearby. John, you will watch the baby, and Dennis, you will come to keep guard for English while I am with the Father." He said, "I married you to take your money. That was the reason—that was the reason. I made you love me, and wed me, that I might have your money."

She came toward him slowly, up to the hearth. "I think we had best destroy this, had we not? The poker—there is a live coal or two, it will catch." The paper drifted down to the embers; he was clumsy with the poker, but a little tongue of flame licked out at last and the paper flared up. "But that is not true," she said. "No one can create love out of nothing. You could have made me want you, and you could have made me fall in love with you—romanti-cally—and so you did. But you could never make me love you—there is a difference, you know—unless it was there in my heart to love you from the beginning . . . There, it is gone, you need not worry over it any more."

He did not dare touch her. "Anne?"

"And you see, it was—I did. It is very peculiar, when I think of it. Other women have always been in love with you because of your looks and your charm and your manner with them. But I love you in spite of all that. For something other than all that, I do not quite know what it may be." She sighed and looked up at him. "So I can forgive you anything, you see. Doubtless it is foolish, and poor-spirited, and odiously meek of me, but I really cannot help it."

"Anne——!"

"I knew your real reason almost from the beginning. But I do not know—why you have said it to me now. I—think——" She drew in her breath sharply. "I would—like you to tell me, please."

[230]

He could not say it. He had said it so many times to her, in so many ways, and he could not say it now.

"You knew, when I first spoke to her, that I would forgive it. You need not have gone on and told me—all the truth."

"It was the truth," he said at last, "but it is not now. I——" No; he could not; the lie clove to his tongue. The lie. If he said it now it would be the truth, and it must not be, an English, the enemy, and true love only a fairy tale, his father's ghost reproaching him for betrayal; no, it could not be true, he must not let it be true.

He seized hold of her roughly, desperately, and set his mouth on hers to keep the words from being spoken. Any paraphrase of it he would use; he muttered, "It is no longer true, Anne my darling, Anne my dearest, you must believe me. I lied to myself, it was real—it is real, I am not playing a part with you, I am telling you the truth now. The money is nothing. I do not want it, only you, only you, my dear, my dear, for God's sake believe me——"

She took his face in her hands, holding him a little away. "Dennis——" And the words, the damning not-to-be-said words came up in his throat again.

"I——"

"You need not say it," she whispered. "I see it—I know it. It is all right, Dennis, it is all right. I believe you, I know you. I love you so much. We have both been a little foolish. We need never speak of it again." And her arms tightened about him. "Dennis, hold me, I love you." As he kissed her he felt the hot tears on her cheeks and did not know whether they were hers or his own.

3

The clock in the church a square down the street was beginning to strike the hour of nine when he put his hand on the door.

Slade shut it after him and stayed to keep watch. He brushed past the heavy drape into the passage and found Burke in the rear room.

"Did you see the captain?"

"Yesterday morning, in a tavern on Water Street. He has the passage-money and sails on the night-tide. Has Kelleher brought the boys?"

"This afternoon," nodded Burke. "They are abovestairs with my wife. It is a risk. I thought when we made the arrangements it might be best to put it off for a bit. Those special guards——"

He sat down at the table. He was feeling rather tired with today's emotional exhaustion; he was uninclined for this, but it must be done. "I know. I want to get them off on the *Belle,* there is no other ship making direct for Marseilles for several weeks. It will be safe enough, what I have in mind, if I wait until just before she casts off. I want Slade." He went to the door and called the clerk. "I have a small job for you, Slade."

"Yes, sir?"

"Those port-guards. Have you ever met a customs-man?"

"No, Mr. McDermott, I can't say I have."

"Well, you are about to become one. Not an official, only a humble clerk from the dockside warehouse-offices. It is a dark night and they will not pay great attention to your appearance— it will be only for a moment. Now, listen——"

Eighteen

I

It was long past ten of the clock when Quintain put down his pen, yawned and stretched. Commendable devotion to duty, he thought, sitting up in his office this late. But he wanted to have this damned report off his mind. The bare office-room was cold, and he thought longingly of his warm chamber at the hotel, Kitty's arms. Flexing his cramped fingers, he took up the page to read over what he had written thus far. He need not take such pains with it, likely few would read it but himself!

"—And as to the question of a watch on foreign shipping, it is also necessary to consider maritime rulings. It has always been accepted as mandatory that subjects of a given nation, when within the boundaries of another nation, shall conform to the laws of the latter; but the status of a ship in port is less easy to define. It can be argued that shipboard in such a case may be taken as being within the boundaries of its own nation. It has been so argued, and relevant to this present case, there must also be taken into account the fact that the nations and principalities concerned are overwhelmingly Catholic in persuasion, at least one of them traditionally unfriendly to England, and in economic competition with English interests, all of which might lead to official resentment capable of provoking full-scale hostilities. The actual state of——"

He raised his head at the sounds in the passage. Heavy steps, running—a door crashing open down the hall—his own name called excitedly. Lieutenant Richards burst in, almost forgetting to salute in his haste.

"Sentries said you were still here, major—beg pardon to enter so rudely——"

"Yes, what is it?"

"We've got one of your agents trapped, sir—luckiest thing imaginable—down at the docks. I knew you'd want to see the finish —came up to the garrison hell-for-leather for more men, sir; they're holding him with only half a dozen—if you——"

"Good God, do not tell me—how has it happened? Yes, I am with you——" He seized his cloak, thrust a pistol from the drawer through the belt of his tunic.

"If you forgive it, sir, we'd best hurry—I've horses waiting. Dispatched twenty men under Sergeant Coyle and rushed straight in to you—I'll tell you as we go." They were trotting down the passage toward the middle entrance to the old building. "Way it was, those guards watching all foreign ships——"

"What, has Adams not taken them off? I meant——"

"No, sir. Three in port now, at least there were—the Italian has sailed. But some half-hour since, the two watching the *Belle* out of Marseilles"—Richards was speaking in staccato phrases as they hurried—"approached by a man who said he was—customs-clerk from dock-offices, and there was trouble at the next wharf but one—with our guards, who sent him for their help. Thought naturally—caught up to one of these gentry, y' see—hared down to this Italian merchant, found the other guards just as usual.

She'd—already cast off, tide was early. I was there with the men, that's how I came to be in on it. Here, sir——"

Quintain swung up into the saddle. "Go on—we're bound for the docks, you say?"

"Right, sir." Richards raised his voice a trifle as they clattered down the cobbled street, loud in the late silence. "Realized it was a trick, and back they came, all four, and me with them, to the *Belle*. And, damme, if you please we reached the wharf just in time to see a man and two boys boarding her up the plank. Good men, sir—they deserve commendation, acted well—in emergency. I set Corporal King and another at the plank—the rest on—stern and bow decks, watching. We're certain he's still aboard, sir. Found a customs-man busy about 'nother ship—sent him for the two watching the other Frenchman—and it chanced Treherne was there with them. All three were sailing tonight, and we'd hoped—something definite, y' see—last time of trying and all that. We got the two boys, miserable little wretches, and with seven men on the lookout it's sure the man's boxed within the ship somewhere."

"The crew——"

"They made trouble, yes, sir, but we were all armed and all these Frenchies're feared of a pistol. We managed to get 'em herded amidships, sir, lest the man should try to pass himself off as one of the crew, but he's in a long cloak and tricorne, I saw that much, and couldn't very well do so——"

"Good, good. A lucky chance, as you say." Excitement was rising in him. "By God, we'll take one of them at least! A thorough search of the ship——"

"Yes, sir, we didn't dare try it with so few men—he'd slip past, and it's blacker than hell in places. But we've had the plank blocked ever since we saw the man aboard, and it's positive he's still there."

"By God," said Quintain, "we'll take him! How many men—twenty, did you say? They're ahead of us?"

"Yes, sir, by some minutes." They had traversed the center streets of the city, almost deserted at this hour since the theater performance would not end for another hour, and were approaching Water Street. Regardless of the rough paving Quintain spurred to a gallop. Chance! he thought. Had he not said it to Adams? It was the only way they might hope to take these agents. So far chance had not favored them—tonight it evidently would. He drew rein at the street fronting the harbor and let Richards take the lead, down past two wharves and the black swaying hulls of ships. "Rotten boards—holes," said Richards, pulling up and dismounting. "Break the nag's leg, major." He flung out of the saddle without protest, followed the lieutenant out on the wharf.

There were several ships tied up there; the largest was the French merchant, very high fore and aft, looming up in the faint light cast by the sea's reflection of the stars; there was no moon, but it was a clear night. She was tied port-side on to the wharf for loading, and the plank was still down. As he came up with Richards he took it in with one quick comprehensive glance. Six feet of black water stretched under the plank between ship and wharf—the tide was pulling at her. The rail was high, and there were men clearly visible on the high platforms of the decks. At the top of the plank stood others. Coyle and his twenty men had evidently just arrived, and Treherne—standing at the foot of the plank, pistol in hand—had detailed half a dozen of them to herd the ship's crew onto the wharf. The sailors huddled into a group, muttering sullenly, and the wiry little man gesturing wildly at Treherne as a babble of French flooded out of him, that would be the shipmaster.

He hastened to Treherne's side. "Good work, lieutenant—excellent! What has been happening? I have the gist of it from Richards——"

"Lord God, but I'm glad to see you!" acknowledged Treherne frankly. "The little French I ever knew has deserted me. Will you tell this Frenchy we're not going to hang his crew, sir?"

Quintain laughed. "I will, but how does it stand? Have you detailed a search?"

"Just commencing, sir. I thought it best to get the crew apart first so soon as we had enough men to keep guard. It's certain the fellow's still aboard, there's six of us scarce had our eyes off the plank since we knew he was there."

"Excellent!" He turned to the shipmaster and with some difficulty stemmed the excited protests. Monsieur the captain was an honest man, of course; he was accused of nothing, nor were any of his crew, but as an honest man he was—*eh?*—only too happy to co-operate with the port-officials in apprehending escaping criminals. Who could believe he took such aboard knowingly? *Non, non, non!* But of course he would have no means of telling whether would-be passengers were criminals or not—that was clearly understood. It was obviously his part as an honest man to allow the official guard to search his ship for this desperate wretch. To aid justice was a noble act.

"Bastard knows all about it," he remarked to Richards aside, "but he'll be chary of getting himself involved, and it'll be easier all round if we give him the benefit of the doubt and let him sail —after we've taken our man."

"Just so, sir," Richards grinned. The captain wept and tugged at his mustaches.

"Sir——"

"Oh, Daly. I understand you are partly responsible for this coup. Good work. You all acted very sensibly."

"Thank you, sir. If I may make bold, sir——"

"Tell me, you saw this fellow boarding? Can you give any description of him?"

"That's just what I were orf to tell you, sir. I only saw 'is back

[237]

—as 'e goes hup the plank, sir—an' I couldn't look at any man an' say, It was 'im—I just don't rightly know, sir. But 'e's a man I *ort* to know, if you take my meanin'—some chap I've seen afore. I don't know where, sir. I can't connect it up in me mind like— I only 'ad a glimpse."

"He looked familiar?" Quintain turned to him with more attention.

"Well, 'e's somebody I seen afore, or like somebody I seen. Acourse that might mean any of a hundred men, sir, but I just thort I'd mention it. 'E's got on a dark cloak an' an ordinary tricorne, sir, that's all I saw."

By God! thought Quintain. If it was—if it could be! Perhaps he had not been such a fool in his suspicions after all. Well, they would soon know. The fellow could not long conceal himself even in a ship this size, with twenty men hunting him.

"We commandeered the torches from the customs people, sir." Treherne at his elbow.

"Yes—very good." Absently he laid one hand on the pistol in his belt, watching the torches moving about the deck above.

2

McDermott at that moment was lying flat in the bottom of one of the *Belle's* boats fastened against the starboard rail of the ship on the afterdeck. He was thinking about luck: a man had just so much allowed him, and when it ran out, any little mischance would bring him down. In his case, an hour ago, it had been that confounded boy straying from where he'd been told to stay, so that it took just long enough—after Slade had called off the guards—to find him, that the guards were coming up at the double as he went aboard. Even then, if he had known, he might have made a break; but he did not know, and Dubois did not know, until they stepped out of the cabin to find the crew herded at pistol-point and six men guarding the plank. Since then he had dared to move only twice, the first time from the cabin door to a projecting hatchway, the second time to his present position.

Now he lifted his head very cautiously and surveyed the situation. The search of the ship had begun, but the top decks, being so bare of cover, would likely come last. There were three men on this deck, the nearest perhaps ten feet from the boat, his back turned. The nearest torches were amidships, but it was light enough here to distinguish outlines if no more. And—he raised his head another inch—at the foot of the plank stood, besides the crew and the men guarding them, two officers and two men.

One of the officers spoke and laughed and he identified Quintain. He let out a breath. Be damned if he would be taken by that arrogant bastard! But it was going to be close—the closest he had ever known—if he got out of this. Quintain's presence closed one possible door of escape, but it was the narrowest one. He might, if he could dodge about long enough to obtain other garments, pass himself off as one of the crew left on board. It had never been more than barely feasible, and now it was not possible at all.

The guard turned and he let himself down into the boat. Two other doors, and not much time to choose and attempt. He could go overboard, and warn them with the splash, and trust to luck to swim to the nearest water-stairs before they reached it. That would be close indeed, hampered by wet clothing, and he was not a strong swimmer. So it would have to be the sloop.

The sloop, a little coastwise thing scarcely big enough to be called a ship, was tied more or less stern to stern with the *Belle*. She rocked gently on the tide a few feet away and a good fifteen feet down from the *Belle*'s afterdeck; she seemed to be deserted; her deck was piled with what looked like crates. She sat so low in the water that the wharf was above her, but she was moored against a water-stairs some forty feet down from the *Belle*'s plank.

Yes, it was going to be close. But if he had to be taken, he would rather be taken that way than lie and wait for them to find him.

He began to inch himself up out of the boat. He lay full-length, finally, on the supports stretching to the boat from the rail. No indication that he had been heard or seen, though he waited. He turned over on his face and lay along the rail, which began to curve here toward the stern. It was a wide flat rail, but he had to balance carefully. He began to edge his way along it, pulling himself with both hands.

There was a man almost leaning on the rail round the curve of the stern, his back to it, but he could not help sensing movement; that meant he must take off from farther up than he liked, making it a jump of four or five feet—and fifteen down. But it was the only way. He went on crawling along the rail, balancing his prone body with difficulty. He seemed to take eternity to gain a foot. The torches moved, casting weird shadows on the wharf, the lower deck. Someone had brought up more torches—customs people working late in the warehouses—that was what Slade had ostensibly been. Slade had orders to get away immediately; he was back in his attic room over Burke's shop now, likely, asleep.

The rail was curving sharply under him now, to the right round the stern. Below him was the swaying black water, and what looked a terrifying distance over it the deck of the little sloop. It would be a crooked jump, he dared go no farther because of the man near the rail ten feet ahead. He lay and rested a moment. It seemed incredible that no one had seen him; out of the shelter of the boat now, a black shape spread-eagled along the rail. But that was the best chance he had seen—no one would be watching the rail up here. They supposed him most probably below decks—there was too little cover above. But they would, of course, search the decks eventually. He thought about this jump, and wished he could be rid of his cloak. He dared not drop it overboard—it might be recovered, and could be identified by the tailor, a dozen people.

He let his body sag to the left and slipped over the rail. He was quiet, but not quiet enough. The man was leaning on the rail now and felt it move. He jerked around. He saw the dark figure poised in the act of turning on the narrow catwalk outside the rail, and he gave a great hoarse shout.

McDermott had no time to gauge the jump. He launched himself into space, kicking the side of the ship as he left it for greater momentum.

The piled crates on the deck of the sloop were packed with, of all things, live hens. He landed slantingly on one and sent others flying, with a crash to wake the dead, and the flimsy lathe tops split at the impact; a dozen or more agitated hens came fluttering out to add to the confusion of other sounds. The incongruity of it set him laughing even as he gained his feet, with no time to discover if he had broken any bones in the fall. He plunged across the narrow deck for the water-stairs and swung himself over the edge of the wharf as a crowd of men swarmed down the *Belle*'s plank and Quintain's voice rose in a roar of excited orders.

"Get him—after him! Treherne—head him off! Richards——"

He knew the waterfront streets; he could shake them off. They were forty feet behind as he set off down the wharf at a tearing run, exhilaration like wine in his veins. Safe now—he had done it—and then he heard Quintain shouting again, the first ragged splatter of shots. In another hundred feet he would be in the long shadow of the warehouses, and a dozen alleys to choose leading up to a dozen streets—safe——

He was face down on the rough boards, the breath knocked out of him by the blow and fall. Rotten salt flavor in his nostrils, and the numbness just beginning in his side. Get up—they will

[241]

close the distance—running and shouting behind. He got up to his feet, and felt the first bite of pain where the bullet had torn into him. He had lost much of his lead. There was no time to think about the pain; it was not hard to run again, down the last ten yards of the wharf; and he saw he had beaten them in spite of his narrowed lead. There were two horses in the waterfront street, troopmen's horses standing untethered. He flung himself at the nearest one, straddling the saddle somehow, gathering the reins, not troubling for the stirrups—being carried at a startled gallop away from the yelling pursuers.

But he dared not keep the horse too far. It would give him away —they would scatter the pursuit, hopefully if vainly. To have him slip through their fingers like that—God, he would like to have seen Quintain's expression! Six squares up Water Street he dismounted and sent the horse clattering away with a slap on the rump. He went through a narrow alley to the next street. He went at a fast walk up that street and down between two old stone buildings to another, working west across the city, toward the newer residential districts and Sydney Street. When he knew he had outdistanced and outmaneuvered any possible pursuit he stopped and leaned against the wall he was passing, dim triumph rising in his mind. He had got away, they would not take him now. The breath was harsh in his throat. He put a hand to his side and felt the hot wetness of blood seeping. The pain was back like fire there.

But it was not bad—not bad, far below the heart. The thing was to get home before loss of blood weakened him. He sagged against the wall. What was it he had just told himself? Get home —yes. Hurry, but not too much. The blood.

He found a handkerchief in the pocket of his waistcoat and another in his cloak. He wadded them together and tore open his shirt and put them against the place where the blood was coming out. The pain jumped up a little in him. He said aloud, "Anne." Get home—yes. Hurry, get to cover.

He began to walk up that street, not as fast as he had gone before.

Nineteen

I

"Oh, Christ," said Quintain. "One man, and twenty to chase him! Are you all blind or paralyzed?"

They listened to his cursing sullenly, those of them who were not still scattered about a dozen waterfront streets, running, hunting, occasionally blundering into one another.

"Monsieur." The shipmaster was pulling at his arm. Vaguely he realized that the man had been babbling something at him for some time. He turned with a glower.

"Yes, yes, yes, you may cast off—no further interest in you— damn you and every board of your stinking French hulk!"

"Sir." A corporal pounding up, breathless. "Sir, we've got your horse—five, six streets away, running loose. There's blood on the saddle, sir."

Quintain struck his fist into his palm. "By God, I knew I hit him! A snap shot, and in this light—he's on foot, then—a bullet in him somewhere——"

"We'd not find him in this rabbit warren of alleys with a hundred men, save by chance," said Richards savagely. "He's making for cover somewhere, where he can be sure of shelter and protection—by the time——"

"Oh, Jesus God!" said Quintain like a prayer. "If it was—if it could be—the thousandth chance! If I dared risk it——" He hesitated, excitement, frustration, a last caution, obstinacy, the primal hunting urge, all struggling in him—remembering Daly's words. They had wasted time, running the streets. There might be a chance—with a bullet in him—— As he stood there he heard a clock somewhere across the city begin to strike midnight. Like all of what had gone before, there was no evidence to this, none at all. But there might be a last throw of the dice. He took the decision.

"Treherne—Richards! I want six men. You will come with me. The rest dismissed." And he thought, three-quarters of a mile to Sydney Street. We might even make it ahead of him.

2

It was not bad, he did not think it was bad, but to lose even a little blood was weakening. The night was getting darker and darker. He was nearly home now. These last few streets had been long, but here there was a wall to lean on and he got along much faster. He held his cloak wadded up on his side; he must not leave a trail of blood.

The night was getting darker, but his mind was clearer all the while—a great light was growing and growing in his mind. He had realized, a while back there as he stopped to rest, that he was saying her name over in a whisper. Get home—to Anne. To Anne. It was the one important thing. And so it began to come clear in his mind, as if the blood were washing away all his bitterness and confused hatred and the lies he had hidden behind.

He had lied to himself for so long . . . but not any longer. He could not fight it any more. Today had been his last battle over it, and he had lost—but he had won too. She was his, he loved her. What he told her, it was all true. Nothing else mattered but Anne, he knew that now. All his foolish little quibblings about allegiances. Two allegiances could live side by side—and love was stronger than hate, that was a thing he had never known. It was individuals who were important, not races or nationalities—he of all men should know that, who risked his life for freedom of the individual. It did not matter, her race or her birth or aught else except that she was Anne and he loved her. He must get home and tell her so. He had been a long time on the journey, and come a far way to find her, but he was nearly there now.

He would tell her—he would say—— He was all right, it was not much farther, here was the corner; he would see her soon, she would be there. Such a fool, such a fool, running away—but he was safe now, he knew the truth now. Race, allegiance, enmities, they had nought to do with what was between him and her.

He must hurry and tell her what he had discovered.

He saw the house for a long time before he found the steps under his feet. It took a longer time, a painful time, to find his key and open the door. Warm scent of furniture oil, candles. Much darker in the house. He got across the passage to the stair. As he pulled himself up the first tread, faint from across the city he heard a clock begin to chime midnight. The last stroke had died away before he was at the top of the stair. He leaned on the bannister and panted. But it was not bad, not at all—only a little blood lost.

He was at the door, and she was there—Anne—across the room, so far away—at her dressing table, brushing her hair. She was looking at him. He did not hear what she said. He wanted to hurry to her, hold her tight, tell her. He must tell her—what he had not said this afternoon. But he could not hear his own voice either, though he knew he was speaking.

"Anne," he said, "Anne my darling, I love you so much." The door handle was torn from his grasp and he was falling, and then everything went away from him.

3

That great stain of blood . . . she was kneeling beside him, trying to tear open his shirt to find the wound and staunch the blood; she was whimpering his name foolishly. "Dennis, Dennis, Dennis——" He was dying, he was dead, and she did not know how to help him. Help. She began to get to her feet, to find help, and then there was a sound at the door.

"Oh, Kincaid—thank God," she gasped. "He is hurt—— I do not know——"

Kincaid paid no attention to her. He came and looked down at Dennis, and, bending, lifted the limp figure up, across to the bed. He began to strip off cloak and coat; she went to help him. "Is he hurt badly? Oh, God, Dennis—it was like a ghost when he came in. I was——" She must not lose her head, she must think what to do. The sight of the wound turned her giddy; she leaned on the bedpost and said faintly, "We must send for a surgeon. I will wake the maids——"

The man looked at her then. He was rather pale himself, and his jaw moved uneasily. He said, "No need, madam, I'll look to him. It's a clean wound, he'll be right enough—I'll see to it."

"Do not be absurd, he must have proper care—how has he been hurt? Is it from—a sword, or——" She shuddered, touching his face. "He is so cold—we must have someone——"

And he actually put his hand on her arm as she turned. "Madam," he said hoarsely, "don't you go adoing of that. Don't you rouse the house or tell any soul—unless so be you fancy bein' a widow."

She found she was leaning on the arm for support. "What—do you——" and they both turned at a movement from the bed.

His eyes were open, fixed on her. She went to him unsteadily. "My darling, what has happened to you? I was so frightened! Do not try to move now, Dennis; we shall have a surgeon to you as soon as Kincaid can fetch——"

"Anne," he said. He drew a long breath which must have hurt him, and then his eyes moved to Kincaid. "Is it bad, Brian?"

"No, McDermott. The ball went clean through without touching aught vital, so far as I can see. It will not have to be dug out of you. A clean wound, you've lost some blood is all."

"Good—good. Anne—not weeping? I am quite—all right—and I do not want a surgeon, do you hear? Kincaid will look to it. No, you will not rouse the maids either——"

"Dennis, I—I do not understand." She clutched his hand tightly. "What has happened, how were you hurt? I thought you were at your club——"

"Have you any—whisky, Brian? Go and fetch it—wine no use at a time like this." The man went off without a word and she bent over the bed distractedly.

"Dennis, are you in great pain? All that blood—whatever has happened?" But he lay with eyes shut, only returning the pressure of her fingers, until Kincaid came back with a flat bottle.

"Here you are, McDermott." Her first alarm quieted a little, she sensed something between them, an unspoken understanding. She looked from one to the other uncertainly.

"Good." He raised himself and Kincaid pushed between them to support him, hold the bottle as he drank. "Better—in a moment."

"Are they after you?"

"No. I got away safe."

She said with a little gasp, "Dennis, I—what is it?" But half her words were drowned by the sudden loud clamor and knocking below.

"Hello the house! Open up! Open in the King's name!" A clatter of hoofs, men's steps heavy in the street.

Kincaid said something in his own tongue in a frightened voice. She got to her feet, her heart for some reason beginning to pound again.

"Anne," he said. He was propped up against the pillow; his eyes were very bright, his nostrils dilated, his voice suddenly strong. "Anne, listen to me. Listen! You have a choice to make and make at once, do you understand? Those are soldiers down there at our door. They are hunting a criminal. Your friend Quintain is at their head. You can go down and tell them I am lying here with a bullet wound in me, and within a week you will be a widow. Or you can go down and lie to them. And God help me, whichever you do I will still love you."

She stared at him as a fresh outburst of knocking sounded. She felt herself going even paler. Then she bent and kissed him.

As she opened the door and went out to the passage she heard him say, "Get these breeches off me—my dressing gown—give me the bottle again. The stained garments under the mattress—hurry!"

It was a dreadful clamor they were making. She had brought the candle from the bedchamber; she stopped and lighted the eight candles in their standard on the table by the door. In the mirror over it she saw her reflection, and pinched both cheeks hard to bring back her natural color. She caught her dressing gown more firmly about her and heard a stir in the passage behind her as the maids, wakened, came sleepily to investigate the noise. She opened the door.

At once the hall seemed full of big men in uniform, crowding in together. The foremost halted and said in a surprised voice, "Anne!"

"Well, Harry, this is a somewhat odd hour to call." She made her voice cross, sleepy. "Whatever is all this shouting about?"

"I must apologize indeed, but we are after an escaped criminal, and—certain information—places him somewhere in one of the houses on this street. If my men might search——"

"A criminal! I assure you there are none such here. To come knocking us up at midnight and after—— I thought at least a war had been declared, to hear such a noise!"

"You—had retired?" he asked in an odd tone. She wondered quite suddenly if she had got any blood on her dressing gown; she dared not look to see.

"Only just, as you see. What in heaven's name are you doing, out running the streets at such an hour with a patrol of soldiers?"

"I told you—we have been pursuing a wanted man. I have—some reason to believe he is in the immediate neighborhood."

"So you wake the whole street and turn everyone out of bed hunting?" She did not think any other nearby houses were being invaded. A search—they would find—— Was there blood on the carpet there in her chamber? His clothes—Dennis—no time to think.

"Did we not wake—your husband?" he asked. The men were crowded to each side of him, breathing audibly, like a pack of hungry wolves, she thought. "It is not precisely—usual—for a lady to answer her own door—in the middle of the night." He sounded as if he were waiting for something.

"As it chanced," she said coolly, "I had only recalled that I left a somewhat valuable bracelet downstairs, and had come to fetch it lest it prove a temptation to the maids in the morning. Yes, my husband is sleeping—or was when I came down. I daresay your noise has wakened him by now."

His gaze flicked rapidly over her, the two maids standing petrified behind her clutching shawls over their night rails. "I see," he said slowly. "I fear I must ask your permission to search the house. I should like—to be sure."

She tried to think of something to say—some way to stop him. She began to speak, hardly knowing what she said, only to register a protest to stop it until she could make some plan—and then she heard, incredibly, Dennis's voice behind her.

"Search the house? What is all this about?" Mildly indignant, irritated, his usual voice firm of timbre. She saw Quintain's eyes move beyond her; she could not turn. She must not faint now—not now, not here.

"Mr. McDermott," said Quintain, and there was flat resignation in his tone on the name.

"Why, it is Sir Harry. I could not imagine—did you find your bracelet, my dear? I seem to recollect your saying somewhat about coming down for it, before I dropped off."

She turned slowly to face the stair. He was standing on the lowest tread, easily, hands in the pockets of his silk-padded dressing robe; he was examining the crowd of men in the passage with lively interest. "Dear me, are we being invaded?"

"I was just explaining—to your wife," said Quintain, "that we are on the trail of a criminal—and should like to search the house. I ask pardon for such a rude entry, but the matter is somewhat urgent."

"Evidently. I deduce that there must be a substantial reward on the man's head. Have you a warrant for such a search, Sir Harry?"

"No. It arose so suddenly, you understand——"

"Of course, of course. I assure you we are not in the habit of harboring criminals, and I feel tolerably sure some one of us in the house, my wife or myself or one of the servants, would have heard any unlawful entry." Kincaid was coming down the stair behind him. "None of us has been out of the house this evening."

"Most certainly we would," she found her voice. "In any case, why should such a man break into a private house?"

"Perhaps Sir Harry suspects one of our servants of giving clandestine aid to the criminal, my dear."

"That—may be the case," said Quintain. He had continued to stare at his erstwhile host fixedly during that little exchange. The maids began to babble excited protest and she turned to quiet them.

"Of course you have done nothing of the sort, do be still, I never heard such nonsense! If there is a criminal in the house he has broken in of himself, and I cannot believe——"

"But I think, in spite of the lack of warrant, we should allow the men to search. After all, they must have some reason to suspect that their man is nearby—or they would never come knocking us up like this, would they? I would really prefer a search made— just to be sure."

"Thank you," said Quintain noncommittally. "Treherne—Richards—take your men and search the house, quickly. Look for blood stains, remember." The hall wavered before her eyes; she recovered herself with a desperate effort. Dennis stood there so casually, not even leaning on the bannister . . . The men crowding past her, past him, up the stair, down the passage, into the parlor. "You—have been at home all the evening, you say?"

"Yes," she said. "Yes, we have. Do you suspect the man entered earlier tonight?"

Quintain hesitated. "It is not only this house—information placed him——"

"I see. Well, I repeat I should certainly think someone in the house would have heard"—turning to the maids—"none of you heard aught of an unusual disturbance at the rear of the house?"

"Ow, no, sir"—a quavering reply—"not a thing, sir. Ow, is it a murderer, sir? Why for would 'e be coming 'ere, sir? We——"

"I've no idea. Is it a murderer, Sir Harry?"

"No," said Quintain shortly. And all the while the sound of men moving about the house, tramp of feet abovestairs, down this passage.

"I find this quite exciting. If you take him here, do we share in the reward? Well, no matter."

"You have been—together here—all the evening." It was not a question; she answered it, her tone annoyed.

"Good heavens, Harry, this is the outside of enough! To come disturbing us like this and cross-examine us on top of that! Yes, we have been here all the evening, since dining, in the withdrawing room down the passage; we had only just retired." She did not lie habitually; he would not believe her capable of telling a lie, she knew.

He wore a deflated, half-ashamed, half-rueful expression. "I see. I must apologize to you indeed. I—you understand, we have certain duties to perform."

Kincaid spoke from halfway down the stair, in a hoarse voice. "There's nobody here but them as belongs here, sir. I been about upstairs all evening, barrin' a few minutes I come down to fetch up a new bottle an' fill Mr. McDermott's decanter as he sent an' asked for. I'd take my oath there's none hidin' in the house."

"Very likely not, no. I can only apologize again." The men coming down the stair, up the passage.

"Nothing, sir. Everything looking quite usual. No reason to suppose he ever came here, though you sounded almighty hopeful——"

"Yes. You found no blood anywhere?"

"How ghoulish," said Dennis pleasantly. "Is this man supposed wounded?" Quintain did not answer.

"No, sir, not a trace."

[253]

"Well, so that is that. I apologize again. We must—try elsewhere."

"You might well apologize, Harry. Such an upset——"

"I am sorry to disturb you." He looked back at her husband. "Very sorry."

"Not at all, Sir Harry. It is the duty of all good citizens to co-operate with law-officers, is it not? I only regret you have not taken your man."

"Doubtless my—information—was faulty. Very well, lieutenant, we are finished here. I will apologize once more and say good night." But he turned back at the door from following his men. "If I do not see you again, Mr. McDermott—well, no matter. I am to leave for England soon—my commission here is completed. You may be sure you and Anne have my wishes for—continued happiness. But very likely you will be visiting England with her, and I shall have the pleasure of seeing you again."

"That is kind of you." He inclined slightly. "But my business keeps me somewhat occupied."

"Harry, must you stand here making formal conversation at this hour with the door open? We will see you before you leave, but for heaven's sake do not come shouting under our windows again in the middle of the night!"

"It was unpardonably rude—duty—but I will not keep you." He gave Dennis one last long look. "Your—servant, sir. Good night. Servant, Anne." He strode out.

"Now get back to your beds, all of you," said Anne with forced briskness to the maids. "Such a fuss over nothing. Of course it is perfectly safe; the soldiers searched. Did you not hear them say the criminal is not here? It is quite all right——" He was leaning on the bannister now; he looked very white. She heard the men outside in the street, mounting, riding away, a more subdued spatter of hoofbeats on the cobbles. The maids disappeared, still clutching one another and protesting.

"Bolt the door," he said in a whisper.

She had forgotten that. She went to do so hastily. When she turned again he was lying crumpled on the stair and Kincaid was bending over him.

4

He came back slowly, in drowsy comfort. There had been something—but it was over now, everything was all right now. It returned to his consciousness bit by bit, and at the same time he was aware of hands moving about him, doing things to him, and pain, but not bad. He opened his eyes and saw Kincaid's face close above him.

"Brian," he said, "they will never beat us. They cannot keep us down."

"They cannot. This will hurt you now, take a breath for it." Sting of cauterizing liquor in the pain, sharpening it.

"They will never beat us. We will fight free of them—if it takes a thousand years."

"If it takes two thousand," said Kincaid, and pulled the bandage tight with a grunt. "There you are, McDermott. It will heal clean in a week or ten days—two weeks at the outside." He straightened, and there was a doubt and a question in his eyes. McDermott smiled and turned his head.

"Dennis——" She was there in Kincaid's place, but closer; her hands were cold. "Oh, I was never so frightened in my life! Are you truly all right? My darling——"

"Go away, Brian," he said. "Go away—it is all right." He did not watch the man out of the room. "My dear, you have a great deal more courage than I ever suspected."

"Oh"—she buried her head in his shoulder—"I was not brave

at all, I was frightened to death! And you standing there so calm——"

"Anne. What do you suppose I had done, that they came hunting me?"

She lifted her head and looked at him; her mouth quivered on a little smile. "I am not sure I want to know. You will tell me or not, as you think best. But I will tell you this much, Dennis. Women—we are peculiar, you know. No woman in the world has much concern for the laws men make, as to the letter of them. It is only how they affect us. I know you, and I know you would never be concerned in aught that was truly very wrong, no matter what the law might say of it."

"My very dear."

"And something else too"—she was settling the blankets over him gently—"because I love you, and that means—what is it the marriage service says?—forsaking all others—no matter who or what, Dennis—friends, or kin, or race—or the law—or even His Majesty the King . . . Have you much pain, my darling? Will you sleep? Would you like——"

"I would like you—just to stay with me, that is all . . . I love you, Anne." He was very tired, but it was a comfortable, satisfied tiredness. He felt himself drifting toward sleep. He would sleep now. It was over, it was safe. They would not hang him this time. And she was here, and she loved him.

He reached out and grasped a little fold of her dressing gown, to hold her near, before the dark tide of sleep overtook him. Smiling, he slept.